ALSO BY
DARCY COATES

The HAUNTING *of* BLACKWOOD HOUSE

DARCY COATES

Poisoned Pen
PRESS

Published by Poisoned Pen Press, an imprint of Sourcebooks
P.O. Box 4410, Naperville, Illinois 60567-4410
(630) 961-3900
sourcebooks.com

Originally self-published in 2015 by Black Owl Books.

Library of Congress Cataloging-in-Publication Data

Names: Coates, Darcy, author.
Title: Haunting of blackwood house / Darcy Coates.
Description: Naperville, Illinois : Poisoned Pen Press, [2019] | "Originally self-published in 2015 by Black Owl Books"--Title page verso.
Identifiers: LCCN 2019042382 | (trade paperback)
Subjects: GSAFD: Paranormal fiction.
Classification: LCC PR9619.4.C628 H39 2019 | DDC 823/.92--dc23
LC record available at https://lccn.loc.gov/2019042382

Printed and bound in the United States of America.
VP 13 12 11 10

CHAPTER 1
SÉANCE

"YOU'RE GIFTED, MY DEAR. The spirits are clamoring to speak with you. Come."

The woman stretched her hands toward Mara. They were contorted by rheumatism, their skin papery and spotted from age. Mara didn't want to touch them, but her mother stood behind her and nudged her forward with one hand.

Mara turned her head. She didn't dare speak in anything more than a whisper. "I don't want to."

The clink of jewelry echoed in the small room as Mara's mother bent to murmur into her ear. Her mother always dressed elaborately for their séances: strings of pendants from deceased relatives, bangles with skulls and occult words notched into them, and the heavy, powerful perfume she wore on significant occasions. Mara hated the perfume. It permeated whatever room they were in, building up in the atmosphere until it turned her stomach and made her dizzy.

"Be polite." Mara's mother kept her voice low and soft. Her breath tickled Mara's ear. "Miss Horowitz has offered to be your mentor. It's a huge honor. Take her hands."

Mara was struggling to breathe. The dimly lit sitting room, with its mess of antique and arcane objects, unsettled her. The small, round séance table was draped in an off-white crochet cloth. A single candle sat in its center. Animal skulls, ancient books, jars of dead insects, and a slow, ticking metronome filled the shelves. Complex, ragged ink paintings covered every gap in the walls. The curtains were drawn, but they couldn't muffle the roar of the storm outside.

"Take her hands," Mara's mother repeated. Her long fingers squeezed Mara's shoulders. It was offered as a comforting gesture but held a hint of warning.

Mara tried to swallow, but her throat was too tight. She raised her hands. If Miss Horowitz noticed their shaking, she didn't show it. The old spirit medium thrust her own hands forward like a praying mantis snatching its victim out of the air, and the fingers pinched Mara's firmly enough to hurt.

"Now, my dear, concentrate." Miss Horowitz pulled closer to her so that they both leaned over the round table and Mara had nowhere to look except the sagging, blotchy face. The candle sent hard shadows dancing through the skin creases and collected gloom around Miss Horowitz's eyes. "You've inherited incredible talents. I can feel your power swelling inside of you. To unlock it, all you need to do is focus. I will channel, and we will see which spirits answer our call tonight."

Thunder shook the windowpane. Mara flinched at the noise, and Miss Horowitz's hands tightened, sending sparks of pain through the girl's fingers. The jingle of jewelry was warning of her mother's movements, and Mara glanced toward her out of the corner of her eye. Elaine's face glowed in the candlelight as she watched her daughter. "Try, darling," she whispered. There was a deep, hungry need in her voice. "Miss Horowitz says you could be the most powerful medium of your generation. You just need to realize your gift."

Thunder cracked again. Mara couldn't stop shaking as she closed her eyes. Miss Horowitz had said to focus, but she had no idea on what. She didn't want to imagine the spirits her mother said lived around them. She'd seen them enough in her nightmares: skeletal, neither human nor corpse, they were trapped in a twilight space without reprieve as they watched the mortal realm with angry, coal-black eyes…

"They're coming," Miss Horowitz crowed. Mara dared to inch her eyelids open. The older woman was swaying, her head rolling so violently that Mara was afraid her neck might have broken. The medium's bloodshot eyes were turned far back in her head, exposing the whites.

The storm, already severe, seemed to redouble its efforts. The rain's bellow nearly drowned out Miss Horowitz's gurgling, croaking voice. "Speak with us, living ones! What messages do you wish to share with your mortal vessels?"

I don't want to do this. I don't want to see any more. Mara tried to pull away but couldn't free her hands. She turned toward her mother, but Elaine's eyes were focused completely on the spirit medium. Reverent trust filled every feature of her face.

"Come!" Miss Horowitz's voice rose into a wail above the thunder. "Speak!"

The table shook, causing the flame to flicker. Mara smothered a scream. She hadn't been aware of crying, but wet tracks tickled her cheeks.

"Come!"

The shaking intensified. Miss Horowitz's mouth gaped wide to expose heavily worn and irregular teeth in gums that had receded nearly to their roots. She threw her head back and forth, her floating gray hair coming free from its knot to hang about her face in oily strands. A string of saliva dripped over her jaw.

Then Miss Horowitz snapped forward as though an invisible being had hit the back of her head. She gasped. Her eyelids fluttered, and her hands trembled. Then she said, in a voice deep and guttural and wholly not her own, *"Beware the home that craves you, child. Your gift and your curse are the same. Beware the home that craves."*

The last words were expelled as a bellow that matched the thunder's crushing volume. Mara's heart fluttered. Terror had frozen her. She couldn't draw breath. As Miss Horowitz's eyes rolled down to fix on Mara, fear and shock and oxygen deprivation swarmed together to grant her reprieve from the séance. She passed out.

4

CHAPTER 2
CHANGED PLANS

"UGH." MARA DUG HER thumbs into the bridge of her nose. The dream was hanging around her like a bad odor. Worse, her neighbor's television was set far too loud. Its tacky laugh track felt as though it was boring into her brain.

This is a good day, remember? You're going to get your own house today—probably, maybe—and you'll be out of this dump by the end of the month. It's good. We're good.

A child somewhere farther in the apartment complex shrieked, and Mara had to fight the impulse to beat her forehead against the window. Instead, she slumped into the plastic chair. She didn't own much furniture, and most of it—the chairs, the folding table, and the mattress—were arranged in front of the window. The little square of natural light was her relief from the stark gray-plaster walls and threadbare carpet. It also gave her a good view of the avenue's entrance. Neil wasn't due for another ten minutes, but she fervently hoped he would be early. Now that she was so close to escaping the tacky downtown apartment, she couldn't bear to spend another hour inside it.

You're gifted, my dear.

"Get a grip," Mara growled. She chewed at her thumb as she watched a crumpled newspaper sheet blow through the alley. *It's been four years since you moved out. You're in control now. Don't waste another minute thinking about the crazy bat.*

A glitter of silver caught her eye, and Mara exhaled as Neil's large car cruised toward her apartment. She snatched her jacket off the back of the chair, stuffed her keys into its pocket, and left her room at a brisk jog. She had to kick the door on the way out to make it lock properly, and one of her neighbors yelled, "*Oy*—keep it down out there!"

Mara took the stairs two at a time, passing the room with the wailing child and the seemingly incessant rumble of laundry machines. The apartment door's hinges squealed as Mara pushed into the sunlight. The weather forecasts had been predicting a sudden slide into a drizzly, cold autumn, but the day was warm and clear enough to still be deep summer.

Neil's car idled in the street. In sharp contrast to the grimy stacks of budget apartments, the car was large, clean, and obviously cared for.

Neil leaned across the seat to pop open the passenger door for Mara. He looked unashamedly delighted to see her, and Mara's insides gave a little flip. Suddenly, that morning's dream didn't seem so important.

"Good morning." He pressed a warm kiss to her cheek as she settled into the passenger seat. "How'd you sleep?"

Horribly. "Can't complain. You?"

"Great, thanks." Neil waited for Mara to buckle herself in before putting the car in gear and pulling away from the curb. He navigated them out of the narrow lane and then reached behind his seat to pull out two paper bags and a thermos. "I'm guessing you skipped breakfast."

The scent of something hot and good filled Mara's nose, and she grabbed the bags and shook them open. "Sweet mercy. This is the sole reason I'm dating you, you know."

Neil laughed. "There's french fries in that one. And a salad in the other. I thought you might eat some healthy food if I bribed you with something bad."

"Fool's hope," Mara said through a mouthful of chips. "But thanks anyway. *Oh my goodness—you got ginger snaps.*"

"I figured you'd like that."

"You're a saint." Mara snuck a glance at Neil as she ate. Approximately the size of an ox and twice as gentle as a kitten, he needed the oversized SUV just to sit comfortably. His fresh-pressed shirt sat well on his broad shoulders, and she thought he might have actually bothered trying to comb his sandy-brown hair that morning, though it seemed incapable of holding any sort of style. He was trying to smother his grin, and a tint of color around his ears told Mara he was enjoying her reaction to the food.

The car's speedometer hovered a fraction below the legal limit

7

as Neil wove out of the downtown streets and into the wider, prettier suburbs with practiced ease. The house they were viewing was near the outskirts of town. It had been put on the market just the day before and ticked all of Mara's boxes—it was affordable, not a complete dump, and in a good neighborhood. Mara was prepared to buy it that same day if the real building looked as good as the photos.

Neil was coming with her as moral support and to give his opinion of the building. He worked as a carpenter and had offered to keep an eye out for symptoms of termites or shoddy building.

She sometimes wondered how she'd ended up with Neil. In Mara's eyes, he was nearly—not quite, but nearly—perfect. But Neil was religious. And the concept of religion grated against every fiber of Mara's being.

They were mirrors of each other in many ways. They'd both been raised in spiritually focused homes. But Neil had embraced his family's beliefs as he'd become an adult whereas Mara had left home the day she'd turned eighteen.

I suppose our situations aren't quite identical. He never had to sit through all-day séances or listen to a drugged-up medium tell his mother she was Cleopatra reincarnated.

"What's up?" Neil had pulled up to a set of lights and was watching Mara out of the corner of his eye.

She realized she'd been frowning and cleared her face. "Nothing. I'm good."

Neil smiled at her, but he let the silence stretch.

Mara sighed and leaned back in the seat. "I had the dream about the séance again."

"Damn." Neil's hand found hers and squeezed. Mara felt a flutter of pleasure at the sensation of the large fingers wrapped around hers. Neil was steady. Neil was safe. He respected her and her beliefs. That was more than she could have hoped for in a partner.

"It's fine." She squeezed back as Neil rubbed his thumb over the backs of her knuckles. "I'm over it. Today's going to be a good day. This house could be the one. I mean, it probably has a wood lice infestation for the price they're asking, but…"

"Ha!" The light turned green, but Neil let his hand linger on hers for a second before moving it back to the steering wheel. "I'll just be glad to see you out of that apartment, wood lice or no."

Mara wrinkled her nose. "It's not a *bad* apartment."

"Sweetheart, you live next to a meth addict, and the police detained your landlord three times in the last month."

"Yeah, you're right. It's a terrible apartment." Mara leaned against the window to watch the large elms rush past. She didn't want to say it out loud, but she desperately, crushingly hoped that the building they were viewing could be hers. Deadlines were squeezing in all directions, and she needed to find a place to live quickly.

She'd been working as a packer in a warehouse, but the company had recently laid off half of its staff, Mara among them. On the downside, she was jobless. On the upside, when coupled with four years of scrupulous saving, her severance package was enough to pay for a small house. That was all Mara had ever wanted: a place to call her own, where she wouldn't be curtailed by an irate landlord's whims or forced to move if she didn't want to. And the rental agreement for her current apartment was up at the end of that month. If she renewed, she'd be tied to the tiny, shabby building for another three years. She didn't think she could survive it.

Neil had already asked if she'd like to stay in his house, but Mara had shot that idea down before he'd finished speaking. When she'd left her parents' home, she'd promised herself she would never again sleep in a building tainted by spiritualism, astrology, clairvoyance, or religion. And Neil's childhood home stank of religion. A cross on one wall, church music mixed into playlists, religious books stacked among the thrillers—they were all things Neil barely noticed after living around them his entire life, but they made Mara's skin crawl.

Despite that, Neil and his mother, Pam, were genuinely nice people. Neil was a relaxed Christian. Mara knew he attended church and had like-minded friends, but his faith didn't saturate his life.

The topic hadn't even come up until their third date. Mara had nearly walked out of the restaurant when he'd told her he was a Christian. But by that point, she was too attracted to him for an easy break, so she'd cautiously given him a chance. She was glad she had. He'd sympathized with her feelings about growing up in a spiritualist household and understood why she didn't ever want to repeat the experience.

Neil's phone started blasting a bright pop song. He pulled onto the dirt strip beside the road and pressed the speaker button on his cell phone. "Neil here."

"Oh, good; I caught you." The voice on the other end was breathless. Mara recognized it instantly. Jenny, their real-estate agent, seemed to live in a perpetual state of oxygen deprivation. Neil either didn't notice or pretended he didn't, but Mara found it fascinating. She liked to think of their agent as Breathless Jenny. "I'm so sorry about this, honey, but the apartment's gone."

"What?" Mara dropped an uneaten fry back into the bag. "But it was only listed last night!"

"Oh, hello, Mara." Jenny's apologetic voice took on a note of anxiety. "I wish I had better news for you. But it was a really good deal, honey. A couple viewed it this morning and gave us their down payment on the spot. I'm so sorry to disappoint you."

"It's okay," Neil said.

Mara seethed. "It is *not* okay—"

Neil grabbed a cookie out of the bag and pressed it into Mara's mouth to silence her. "It *is* okay, Jenny. Do you have any other places we could see today? We're in the car right now."

Mara glared daggers at Neil as she chewed through the cookie. He gave her a contrite smile in response.

"Well…well…" A sound of rustling paper came through the speaker, and Mara could imagine Breathless Jenny's desk, cluttered and chaotic, just as it had been when they'd first met her. "Ah…I'm sure… No, the Westbrook house is already bought, isn't it…?"

"Take your time," Neil said gently.

"Okay…there's a really nice place in Reddington, but it's a bit outside your budget."

Mara swallowed the cookie. "How much?"

"Well…it's nearly double…"

"Nope." Mara was frustrated almost to the point of tears. The loss of the apartment stung. If she didn't find a home within the next few days, she'd be forced to either renew her lease or find a short-term alternative—and both of those options would leech her savings. She snatched the thermos out of the cup holder to give her hands something to do. Neil had made her chamomile tea. She suspected it was the expensive, organic, loose-leaf stuff his mother kept for special occasions. The thought warmed her slightly but not enough to cut through the disappointment.

Neil pressed a hand over the phone to muffle his voice. "Mara, I could lend you—"

"I'm not looking for handouts," Mara barked. Neil blinked then gave a slow nod and removed his hand from the phone. She squeezed her eyes shut. *Crap, did I hurt him?*

"W-well." Jenny was clearly feeling the pressure. "There are empty plots of land—or, uh—"

She broke off, and the rustling stopped. The silence stretched out for so long that Mara began to worry the call had been disconnected.

"There is one place," Jenny said at last. Her voice held a strange, cautious tone. "It's been on the market for ages. It's a little bigger than you were looking for but under your budget."

"What's wrong with it?" Mara asked automatically. She kept her eyes focused on the thermos lid so that she wouldn't have to see Neil's face. *Why'd I have to snap at him? He was only trying to help.*

"I'm going to be up-front with you, honey. It'll need a bit of work. And…and it doesn't have a very nice history." Mara waited impatiently for Jenny to collect herself. The paper noise was back, but this time, Mara thought their agent might be fanning herself with a stack of loose sheets. "Are you familiar with Robert Kant?"

Neil inhaled sharply, but the name was new to Mara. "No. Should I be?"

"He—uh—he wasn't a good man, honey."

"He was a serial killer in the early 1900s," Neil murmured to Mara before turning back to the phone. "Jenny, are you saying the house is connected to him?"

"I'm afraid so. He spent the last four years of his life living there before he…well…hung himself."

"Shoot," Neil said.

"No, hung," Jenny corrected patiently.

Mara, intrigued, chewed at her thumb. People could be squeamish about living in a building that had once housed a killer, as if the very walls had somehow been tainted. Her parents, especially, had been big on the concepts of spiritual residues and bad energies. But to Mara, a house was nothing more than a collection of bricks and wood. Simply being in proximity to an unpleasant human shouldn't materially reduce the building's worth. And if no one else wanted it…

"Where is it?" she asked.

Jenny sounded surprised. "Well, if it doesn't bother you…it's called Blackwood House, and it's a half-hour drive from town. We could meet there now, if you like…? Let me give you the directions."

Mara snuck a glance at Neil as he typed the address into his navigation system. His face was placid, but a faint tightness around his lips told her he wasn't entirely happy. She returned her gaze to the thermos.

"Okay," Breathless Jenny said. "I'll be there as quick as I can, honey. Have a safe drive, now."

The call ended, and Neil pulled the car back onto the road. Mara struggled to find the best way to phrase her thoughts, but Neil broke the silence first.

"I'm sorry we didn't get the house you wanted. I know you're disappointed, but even if this new place isn't a good fit, we'll figure something out."

Mara finally raised her eyes. Neil's face held none of the distance or hostility she'd been dreading. Instead, he looked anxious. He kept shooting her glances as he did a three-point turn. She felt her throat tighten and muttered, before she lost her courage, "I'm sorry I snapped. You were being really generous, but—"

"I know." His warm smile was back. He took her hand and laced his fingers through hers. "Independence is important to you. I get that. In fact, I kinda like it."

Mara leaned over the seats' divider to rest her head against his shoulder. She could feel his muscles shift when he turned the steering wheel, and he smelled like herbs and sawdust. She never would have expected that combination to smell as good as it did on him. "Love you."

"Love you too." Neil took the opportunity to kiss the top of Mara's head. Then he added, in a breathless tone, "*Honey.*"

Mara broke into uncontrollable laughter. "Oh my gosh. I swear, if she calls me *honey* one more time—"

CHAPTER 3
BLACKWOOD HOUSE

"LANGUAGE," NEIL SAID GENTLY.

"Oh. Excuse me. *Holy crap*. Is that better?"

Neil chuckled. They'd parked in what was supposedly Blackwood House's driveway, but Mara was struggling to believe it was real. Her savings would have been enough for a decent-sized apartment or a one-bedroom house with a tiny yard if she was lucky. But Blackwood was huge. She counted ten windows on its two floors, plus it seemed to have an attic. It was almost large enough to be a modest hotel. *Jenny must have made a mistake. There's no way this is within my budget, no matter how many serial killers you put in it.*

The real estate agent hadn't been exaggerating when she said it would need some work, though. The house looked as though it might not have seen human habitation in decades. The dark-gray wood was sagging in places, and the roof was missing patches of shingles.

The house sat at the end of a very long lane. They hadn't passed any other buildings in the last ten minutes of the drive, which Mara found surprising. It wasn't far enough from the town to be a serious impediment, but the environment made her feel entirely isolated.

The area was heavily wooded with thin, tall trees. Mara glimpsed a tight, curved tree line at the edge of the backyard. The trunks were all a deep slate gray, which she guessed might have been the inspiration for the house's name.

"So," Mara said. "How about we do some exploring?"

"You don't think we should wait for Jenny?"

"Nah." Mara gave Neil a grin. He grinned back and opened his door. Together, they followed the narrow pebble path toward the building's front door. Half-dead weeds grew high on either side and pushed through the small white rocks below their feet. Tiny insects flicked away with every step. Mara was thankful she'd worn her long jeans instead of her shorts.

The building looked increasingly grim as they moved closer. A medley of desiccated, torn cobwebs hung about the awning. Half of the windows had cracked panes, and the other half were entirely broken. Lichen and moss grew across the house's wooden front and clung to the closest trees.

Mara jogged up the stairs to the porch and peered through one of the windows. The room beyond was dim and murky thanks to the dirty glass, but she could see the outline of a large armchair. "I think this place is furnished."

"It can't be in good condition," Neil said, looking through

the window next to her. "But there might be some salvageable stuff."

Mara followed the porch to the door. She expected it to be locked, but to her surprise, the handle turned with a painful screech. The door drifted inward, and Mara had the impression that she'd broken a seal. The air that came through the opening smelled heavy and musty and cold.

The windows had built up too much grime to let much natural sunlight in, making the inside seem washed out. Mara stepped over the threshold and found herself in a large entry room. A staircase ran up the back wall, and archways stood to her left and right, opening into a dining room and sitting room, respectively. There didn't seem to be any light switches.

Mara moved into the sitting room. She'd been right; it was furnished, though the viability of the pieces was dubious. Two moth-eaten, mildewy armchairs sat beside the empty fireplace. A rocking chair rested under the window. Mara nudged it with her foot, and it creaked painfully as it rolled back on its struts. A badly decayed cross-stitch piece hung on one wall, blue-and-pink flowers surrounding the words "Home Is Where the Heart Is." Mara wrinkled her nose. "Ew."

She walked into the dining room and found Neil standing at the table. His lips were set in an unhappy firmness, and she moved forward to see what had disturbed him.

The dining table had five sets of plates laid out, and three serving trays sat in its center. Some of the cutlery was propped on the plates' edges as though the occupants had been interrupted in the middle of a meal. The setting was covered in dust, and there were dark stains—dried sauces or decayed vegetables, Mara thought—next to the shriveled, leathered lumps that were barely identifiable as meat. One of the glasses had shattered, and its shards were scattered across the off-white tablecloth.

"Wow," Mara whispered, leaning closer to inspect the dehydrated food. "It's like their meal was disturbed and they never came back."

Neil made a vaguely unhappy noise in the back of his throat, and when Mara reached forward to poke one of the dried lumps, he grabbed her hand. "Don't *touch* it!"

"Why? I'm pretty sure they're not going to finish it."

"Mara," Neil hissed, trying to choke back his anxious laughter.

"Okay, okay. Let's check out the rest of the place. I can't believe the house's owners just…*left* stuff like this, though. No wonder they can't sell the building."

Neil hadn't released his hold on Mara's hand, and she didn't try to pull free. She liked the way his fingers felt. They were rough and calloused from woodworking and delightfully strong. The juxtaposition between Neil's intimidating physical attributes and his kitten-sweet personality always gave her a thrill.

She led him toward the stairs at the back of the entry room. The wood groaned under their feet, and Mara paused after the fourth step. "This isn't going to collapse, is it?"

Neil bounced on the step experimentally. "It shouldn't. There doesn't seem to be anything wrong with the structure; it's just old wood."

"Good." Mara kept climbing, pausing again at the halfway point to clear a cobweb out of their path. The top of the stairs opened onto a long hallway with multiple doors opening in each direction. Mara tried the first and found a fully decorated bedroom. She scrunched her nose at the sight of a multitude of dead moths littering the floor. "How long since anyone's lived here?"

"It would have to be a while." Neil let go of her hand to open the closet door. Half a dozen moths fluttered out, and he waved them away. "I'd say at least a decade."

Mara went to the window. It overlooked the backyard—or what was left of it. The forest behind the house was gradually taking it over. Weeds grew so high that she thought they would reach her waist. Small trees poked through the lawn, and shrubs clustered around what might have once been a stone bench. The clearing was a decent size, though. *Large enough to hold vegetable gardens and a patio.*

"Any idea how far those woods go?" Mara asked.

"Probably a fair way." Neil sounded distracted, and Mara turned. He stood facing the door. His fingers drifted over a cluster of marks on the wood, then he withdrew his hand as though he'd been burned. He stepped away from the door, his nostrils flaring and a tight scowl on his forehead. "There's blood in these scores."

"Huh?" She nudged him out of the way and bent close to the door. There were long scratches in the wood. The white paint had clearly been cleaned, but tiny flecks of something dark remained in the notches.

She turned back to Neil, who was running his thumbs over his short fingernails. His lips were set in a tight line.

"What? You think someone was locked in this room and tried to claw their way out?"

He didn't answer, so Mara took his hand to stop the anxious motion. "Come on. It's a weird house, and it's making you nervous. These marks were probably made by a dog, and the black flecks are dirt they couldn't scrub out."

"Probably." Neil nudged the door open with his foot, and Mara had a sneaking suspicion he didn't trust her theory. "Did you want to see more of the house?"

"Hell yes." Mara followed the hallway and looked into each room she passed. Some were bare, and others were fully furnished. One had an antique, rusted crib below the window, with a dead-eyed doll propped in its corner.

This is really a magnificent building. Why's it been empty for so long? A killer called it home for four years, but there's got to be more wrong than just that, surely.

Mara turned and found Neil waiting for her in the doorway. "Hey, Neil, what do you know about the guy who lived here?"

"Robert Kant? Not much. In the early 1900s, there was a spate of disappearances—mostly children—in this area that was eventually attributed to Kant. He's a bit of a local legend."

"Jenny said he lived here for the last four years of his life. Do you think he killed anyone in this house?"

Neil's smile looked forced. "Probably. Maybe. I think I heard that one of his intended victims escaped and gave away his location to the police. That *could* have been this house."

"Huh." Mara turned back to the cot.

"Darling, sweetheart, light of my life—why the questions?"

"I just want to know why no one's bought the place. I can imagine it being empty for a few years. But this long? What's wrong with it?" Mara bent to pick the doll up, but a screech of tires interrupted her. She peered through the window and saw Breathless Jenny climbing out of her hot-pink car.

"C'mon," Mara said. "We'd better go meet Jenny before she breaks her neck. I can't believe she's wearing high heels to visit a house like this."

CHAPTER 4
OFFERS

THEY MADE IT TO the front door as Jenny neared the end of the pathway. As Mara had predicted, the plump, middle-aged woman was fighting a losing battle to keep her shoes stable on the white stones. For once, she had an excuse to be breathless when she greeted them. "Oh, there you are, honey. And you, uh, found a way into the house."

"Door was unlocked." Mara extended her hand to shake Jenny's then moved aside so Neil could do the same. She couldn't help but notice that Neil received a far warmer smile.

"Well, that's… It's meant to be locked…well. You got a head start on the inspection. That's good."

Jenny looked as though she would dearly like to sit down but was going to great pains to avoid touching the cobwebbed wood. She tugged on the front of her blouse to fan the fabric as she fixed a plastic smile to her face. "Bit muggy today, huh? All right.

So, this is the Blackwood house. It was built in the late eighteen hundreds by a woodcutter. As you can see, it's held up remarkably well for its age."

A lone shingle, unable to cling to its precarious perch any longer, slid off the edge of the roof and crashed onto the driveway behind them. Jenny pretended not to notice.

"I know you're eager to settle on a house quickly, honey. I'm told the plumbing still works—the last owners redid it—but there's no electricity, I'm afraid. Though you have a magnificent fireplace to keep you warm at night, and of course, it has excellent insulation."

Mara glanced upward at the multiple gaping holes in the roof. It took a great deal of self-control to bite her tongue.

"And I know being *plugged in* is important for you young folks. You'll be happy to know that Blackwood House has excellent compatibility with the Internets."

"Oh my gosh," Mara murmured just loud enough that Neil could hear her. He smothered a smile as he squeezed her hand.

Breathless Jenny had fished her phone out of her pocket to demonstrate and frowned at the lack of service bars. "Ah—that is—it's *usually* compatible. The Internets are probably having some power issues today."

"*Oh my gosh*," Mara repeated. Neil squeezed her hand harder.

Jenny put her phone away with a nervous chuckle. "It was working last time I was here. Though that *was* a while ago. But I'm sure you can find someone to install some extra Internets if you need them."

Mara was speechless. Neil cleared his throat to keep Jenny from noticing the incredulous, enthralled look on Mara's face. "You said the last owners redid the plumbing. How long ago was that?"

"Well, let's see now… I suppose it would be a little over twenty years ago."

Neil whistled. "It's been empty a while."

"Yes, well, honey…" Jenny's eyes darted toward the house, and Mara caught a flicker of anxiety in them. "The…the *deaths*, you know? It's not… That is…" She collected herself and continued in a bright voice. "But it's perfect for a young couple like yourselves. There's plenty of room for a nice big family."

"So, Robert Kant did kill people here," Mara said.

Jenny's smile faltered. "E-excuse me?"

"You said there were deaths here. How many?"

"Oh, well." Jenny fished a crumpled contract out of her pocket and used it to fan herself. "Awfully muggy today, isn't it? And I, uh, believe there were six victims. Plus one who got away."

"Were they all children?" Mara took a half step closer, and Jenny impulsively stepped backward.

"W-well, I'm sure we could look up the d-details for you, if you're really—"

Jenny trailed off, and Mara let the silence extend until it was uncomfortable.

"Not all," Jenny said at last, fanning herself so quickly that the contract flapped uselessly. "The first was the house's original owner. Then… Kant killed three boys and two girls. All under fifteen. The last…intended victim managed to escape and notify police."

"Six victims in four years," Mara mused, glancing back at the house. "And you said Robert Kant was hung?"

Neil took mercy on their sweating Realtor. "He hung himself before the police reached him," he murmured. "Sweetheart, this is a tiny bit morbid. We can look up the details later if you like."

"No, that's okay. Just to clarify, after he killed the house's original owner, Kant moved into the house? And no one knew?"

Jenny looked nauseated, but she nodded.

"Wow. It was a really different time back then, huh?" Mara's brain was buzzing. She crossed her arms as she regarded the building. Six murders, plus the killer's own demise, would explain the house's low price. She'd still have to hire an inspector to check for further issues, but it was no longer impossible to imagine why no one would buy the building.

That's nothing to deter me, though. It's just bricks and wood. Yes, people died here—and yes, children died here—but people have expired in almost every old house in the country. A building's history doesn't damage its future potential as a home.

"How much?" she asked.

Jenny, caught off guard, stopped fanning herself. "Pardon, honey?"

"How much is the house?"

"You—uh, well, the asking price is significantly less than your budget. And the owner is open to negotiations, too."

Mara gestured toward the lawn in front of them. "And what land comes with the property?"

Jenny's mascara was starting to bleed as sweat ran into her eyes, but she managed to maintain a staunch smile. "I can get the exact survey records for you at the office, but it's a bit over four acres. It extends down the driveway and a little into the woods behind the house."

"Great, thanks. Can we have another look around?"

"Absolutely, honey." Jenny jiggled the doorknob, but it wouldn't turn. She blinked at it. "Did you lock the door behind yourself?"

Mara and Neil glanced at each other and shook their heads.

"Oh…how odd. Well, it was supposed to be locked anyway. Hang on a second, honey." Jenny fished a rusted metal key out of her pocket and fit it into the handle. The lock scraped open, and Jenny pushed the door inward then stepped back so Mara and Neil could go ahead of her.

Mara caught a glimpse of Jenny's trembling, manicured fingers. *She really hates this house, huh?* "It really is quite muggy," she said as she passed Jenny. "Would you like to stay outside, where there's a breeze? Neil and I can have a look around ourselves."

This time the smile was genuine. "Oh, sure thing, honey. Take as much time as you like."

The door creaked closed behind them, sealing out the quiet hum of insects and the rustling trees. Mara took a deep breath and swiveled to face Neil. "Well, what do you think?"

His eyebrows rose. "You're actually considering this place?"

"You're not?" She laughed. "This is halfway to a mansion for the price of a condo. Four acres! It's surrounded by trees, too. You're always saying I should be healthier. Trees are healthy."

"You really don't mind the building? The history doesn't bother you?"

"Not at all." Mara shrugged. "You know I'm not superstitious. This is a once-in-a-lifetime chance, Neil. I know it's miles bigger than I actually need, but am I really going to turn it down in favor of some poky two-room apartment?"

Neil shook his head, but a broad smile had grown over his face. "You're remarkable, Mara. Okay, let me have a look around and make sure this place isn't about to collapse on us."

Mara spent the following half hour drifting from room to room as Neil kicked the walls and opened cupboards. Every few minutes, he made a stifled noise of revulsion as his search turned up dead mice and cockroaches.

The more she saw of the building, the more enthralled Mara found herself. It had an almost magnetic charm. Even the flaws—the warping wood, the crooked cupboard doors, and the old-fashioned furniture—added to its appeal. She could feel her pulse jumping as she rubbed her fingers over the dusty banister. *My house. Yes, that feels right, somehow… This is* my *house.*

Neil, coated in dust, came through the dining room entrance. He brushed his hands on his pants. "Okay. The basic structure seems solid. There's some wood rot, but really, it's far better than I would have expected. Can't find any sign of termites, but you'll probably want an expert to check anyway. I haven't looked at the roof. Based on what we saw outside, I'm guessing it would need a fair bit of work. But I can't find any major deal breakers."

Mara's heart thundered. A giddy, foolish smile bubbled up inside of her until she couldn't contain it any longer. "Neil, I think I'm going to buy this house."

"You're going to buy this house?"

"I'm going to buy this house!" She threw herself at Neil. He caught her up and twirled her around as though she weighed nothing. She was breathing too hard to return his kiss properly, and pretty soon they were both laughing.

"Congratulations, sweetheart." Neil gave her a final, firm hug then placed her back on the floor. "It'll need a lot of work to be livable, but we can fix it up over the next few months."

"We?" Mara echoed.

Neil snorted and brushed loose strands of hair off her forehead. "I'm not about to leave you to deal with this mess yourself. Joel won't mind if I cut back my hours a bit, and I can bring tools from work for when we need them."

Mara hesitated. "Are you sure? It's a big job, and I can't pay you—"

"Nepotism makes the world go around, sweetheart. Let me do this for you. If it makes you feel better, you can call it your birthday present." When Mara hesitated, Neil stooped to her level and smiled into her eyes. "Besides, it'll give me an excuse to spend some more time with you. And that's all I really want."

"Fine, fine, all right." Mara pulled Neil close to kiss him. His lips were warm and pliant, and she felt him relax against her as she tangled her hands in his hair. It was a delicious sensation. She pulled back reluctantly. "Thank you."

"Any time." Neil was grinning. "Want to go break the news to our poor Realtor?"

"Hah, yeah. This place really freaks her out. She deserves the commission."

CHAPTER 5
HISTORY

THEY FOUND JENNY PACING up and down the porch, feverishly sucking on a cigarette. She stubbed it out on the banister when Neil cleared his throat. "Well, how'd it go? Not quite what you were looking for?"

Mara couldn't keep the smile off her face. "No, it's great. I'll take it."

Breathless Jenny's eyebrows shot up. She blinked twice before she could fix her smile then laughed nervously. "R-really? You want it?"

Mara shrugged. "Yeah. I want it."

"Oh. Oh, okay! Great! That's fantastic! Let's—uh—should we—"

Despite having spun the most positive sales pitch she could manage, Jenny seemed completely unprepared for her client's interest. She looked from Mara to the house and back again, and her smile slowly fizzled.

It wasn't the expression Mara had expected. She'd thought Breathless Jenny would be delighted to unload a house she clearly disliked. Instead, she looked frightened.

Crap. There's going to be a major flaw in the building after all. I should have known it was too good to be true. What is it? Does it flood? Asbestos? Rabid squirrels in the forest?

"Sweetheart," Jenny said as gently as she could. "I need to warn you—no, *warn* isn't the right word—that is—"

"Yes?" Mara said. Neil shifted closer to rub his hand across her back. She took a deep, slow breath and said, in a kinder tone, "What is it, Jenny?"

Jenny, past having scruples about smoking in front of her clients, fished a new cigarette out of her bag. She lit it, took a quick breath, and said, "I don't want to frighten you, but you should know: there are stories about this house. Previous owners have experienced—well, they *say* they experienced—some strange things here. Of a supernatural nature."

Mara could guess where the conversation was heading. Neil squeezed her shoulder. *Stay calm*, the gesture said.

"Oh, so it's haunted, huh?" Mara managed to keep her voice civil, but her smile was tight. "Okay. No problem. How about we get back to the office and sign some papers? You look like the sort of woman who appreciates a good contract."

Jenny's smile dipped. "I'm only trying to help, honey. You can't be from around these parts, or you'd know this house has a reputation."

"I'm sure it does."

"Blackwood House was with our agency when I started as a Realtor. It was notorious even then. And after what the last family went through—"

"Hey, do you want me to buy this place or not?"

Jenny sucked on her cigarette then blew a long stream of smoke toward the trees. When she spoke, she'd managed to rein her voice back into a bright, friendly cadence. "It's an excellent property. And an absolute bargain for the price. But I'm both morally and legally obligated to inform you of any impediments to a mutually happy transaction."

"Fine, go ahead." Mara crossed her arms. She knew her smile was closer to a grimace, but not even Neil's increasingly firm squeezes could calm her. "*Inform* me. Is it ectoplasm? Blood dripping from the ceilings?"

Breathless Jenny didn't speak for a moment. Their tenuous civility was nearing breaking point, and she seemed to be trying to speak politely. "Footsteps. Doors open by themselves. Smudgy handprints appear on the walls. Strange noises at night."

"Okay, great. Anything else?"

"And some of the tenants said they saw ghostly figures entering and leaving rooms." Jenny released the last sentence in a quick burst, as though she wanted to get the worst over with as quickly as possible. She glanced at Mara, who gave her a stiff shrug.

"Cool. Now will you sell me the damn house?"

Jenny's eyes narrowed. "You think I'm making this up."

"No." Mara shook Neil's hand off. "I think you're regurgitating what you've heard, which is ninety percent fiction and ten percent natural occurrences that have been misconstrued. Look, I *know* ghosts. I grew up in a house that practically *worshipped* them. We had séances every damn weekend. When I was five, my mother told me my dead grandfather stood at the end of my bed and watched me sleep. Do you have any idea how many nightmares that gave me?" Mara knew her voice was rising, but she was unable to control it. "When I was ten, my dad drowned my pet rabbit because a Ouija board told him to. I started getting panic attacks when I was twelve. Any other kid would have been taken to a doctor. Any *normal* kid. But I got to sit in a circle of costume-wearing freaks as they attempted to summon ghosts to heal me."

Jenny took a step back. She wore a look Mara was horribly familiar with. Countless strangers had directed it at Mara's own parents. *This person is crazy*, it said.

Mara squeezed her hands into fists. She was shaking, and patches of black crept in at the edges of her vision. She lowered her voice, but the hoarse, strained tone still permeated it. "I know everything there is to know about ghosts. And I can tell you definitively that there's no such thing. Every single one of the spirit mediums who had dinner with us was a fake. All of those séances were manufactured. Every message from the dead was a series of normal, natural events that got twisted and distorted until it held meaning. You want to know if I'm okay living in a ghost-riddled house? Sure thing! Bring it on! Because there's no such thing!"

"Mara, sweetheart." Neil had bent so that his chin rested on her shoulder and he could whisper into her ear. His hands—those beautiful, strong carpenter's hands—rubbed her arms. "Breathe, darling."

Mara sucked in a lungful of air. She was dizzy, she realized, and her throat felt raw. She closed her eyes until the unsteadiness passed. When she opened them again, she saw Jenny standing on the edge of the deck, her eyes huge as she tapped her cigarette anxiously.

"Damn," Mara breathed. She opened her mouth to apologize, but her tongue wouldn't form the words.

"Jenny." Neil's gentle voice seemed to defuse the tension in the air. "Everything's okay. We'd still like the house. Why don't you head back to the office, make yourself a nice strong cup of coffee, and relax for the afternoon? You can get in touch tomorrow to organize the purchase. Okay?"

Jenny dropped the cigarette and stubbed it out with her heel. She looked pale, but she nodded. "Yes, yes, of course, honey. Let's do that. I—" She glanced at Mara.

"Sorry." Mara's anger was fading, and deep humiliation was taking its place.

Breathless Jenny recovered her Realtor's smile with surprising elasticity. She waved the lingering smoke away as she backed down the stairs. "It's quite okay, honey—nothing to apologize for. This—this is good. You might be just the sort of person this house needs."

"Yeah. Yeah, probably."

"I'll send the official paperwork through this afternoon." Jenny turned and began the laborious walk across the high-heel-hating stone pathway. "You two take care, now."

"Bye," Mara whispered while Neil waved their Realtor off with a bright smile.

Mara held still until Jenny's hot-pink car had disappeared around a bend in the road and the rows of dark, spindly trees blotted out the color. She felt deeply, hotly ashamed of herself. *I've been free for four years. I should be past all of that…*junk. *What's wrong with me?*

She turned to Neil. He stood close to her, one arm around her shoulders to comfort and brace her. She pressed her hand to his chest and felt his heart beating. *Strong. Steady.* "I'm so sorry, Neil. That was awful."

"Shh." His other arm snaked around her waist to envelop her in a warm hug. "C'mere. You're still shaking. Do you want to sit down?"

"I'm fine now." Mara closed her eyes and breathed deeply. *Herbs and sawdust.* "Thanks for fixing everything."

"I'm just sorry the house has such a messed-up history. Do you still want it? It's not too late to back out."

Mara tilted her head to look over Neil's broad shoulder. Blackwood's gray walls—adorned with countless spiders' homes, clusters of moss, and blooming stains—hadn't lost any of its charm. If anything, its appeal was growing with each moment she spent near it. "Yeah. I definitely want it. More than anything."

"All right. Let's get some lunch. You'll feel better after food."

"Sure thing, Mum," Mara said, and Neil grinned as he kissed the top of her head.

CHAPTER 6
STALKERS AND DELUSIONS

"I'VE GOT TO ASK. You hate even the mention of spirits, but you're buying an allegedly haunted house. It doesn't bother you?"

"Heck no." Mara snorted as she dismantled her burger. They were sitting at a back booth of one of the town's cozier cafés. Neil had a steak with extra salad. Mara had ordered a burger with a double serving of fries and had threatened to add pancakes before she was done. "Because it's not haunted."

Amusement hovered in Neil's shining blue eyes as he watched her divide each layer of the burger into its own neat pile. He still wore the tightness around his lips, though, and Mara knew the Realtor's story had, in some slight way, unsettled him. "Even though no one else wants to stay there? Even after what they've experienced?"

"There are three simple explanations." Food compartmentalized, Mara began shoveling it into her mouth. "First, mass delusion. It's more common than you might think. Imagine five people are in a room. One person says, 'Can you smell that?' Another person says, 'Oh yeah; it's like boiled cabbage.' A third person agrees. All of a sudden, even *you* can smell it. The air's perfectly clear, but because everyone is telling you to smell the boiled cabbage, you become convinced you can."

"And there's a mass delusion about Blackwood?"

"Could be. You've already got the perfect setup for a classic haunted-house narrative—a serial killer's home. All you need is for one occupant to say there's a ghost. Suddenly, every other family that lives there can feel presences following them and claim the doors open all on their own. The more people parrot these claims, the more prevalent they become. Of course, you'll probably have a few enablers on the way—people who like the drama so much that they invent stories just for kicks. And their families will follow along like the happy fools they are. If you're *expecting* and *looking for* a ghost, you can bet you're going to find one."

"Okay, mass delusion." Neil nudged his side of salad toward Mara, but she shoved it back. "That's one explanation. What else?"

"There could be a physical catalyst. A gas leak can create highly realistic paranoid hallucinations. And many supposed hauntings have been attributed to EMF emissions, which can make you see and hear things that aren't real and induce a feeling of terror."

"Have something green."

"No. The third option—and, arguably, the most interesting—is a house stalker."

"Pardon?"

"Stalkers don't exclusively focus on people. Sometimes they can obsess over objects—such as houses. It's not common, but it does happen. There may have been a stalker who frightened each new occupant away so that he could have the house all to himself. It's surprisingly easy to manufacture a fake ghost."

"Huh. Imagine trying to talk your house into getting a restraining order. *He's no good for you, honey. He doesn't respect your walls.*"

Mara scowled. "You're not taking this seriously."

"I'm taking this *very* seriously. It's important that your house feels safe at night."

She gave his chest a playful slap.

"Okay," Neil said, grabbing her hand and kissing its back before she could pull it away. "Where does that leave you?"

"It's all ridiculously simple. First, I know ghosts don't exist, so I'm in no danger of succumbing to the mass-delusion effect. I'll get someone to check for gas leaks and EMF emissions. And time should have fixed any danger of house stalkers."

"It's only been twenty years since the house's last occupants."

"Yeah, but remember it's been a long-term problem, since the early 1900s. Even if the stalker started when he was a teenager, he'd be dead by now. Or at least way too old to be a serious threat."

"So, that's it, then? It comes down to boiled cabbage, gas, or stalkers?"

"Exactly. There's nothing wrong with Blackwood that can't be fixed with a few simple tools. And it's mine." Mara laughed. The reality was starting to sink in, and with it came nearly hysterical excitement and anxiety. "I have a house, Neil. All mine."

He beamed at her. "You deserve it. I'm so happy you found a place you like."

"That's the incredible thing. I don't just like it. I *love* it. It's ridiculously big for just one person, though. I'll probably go insane trying to keep it clean. But there's actually room for a garden out back."

"Do you like gardening?"

"I've never done it before. But I'd like to." Mara felt giddy and shoved her half-eaten food to one side.

Neil offered her his hand, and she took it gratefully. The contact helped center and focus her. He rubbed his thumb over her knuckles fondly.

"It probably wouldn't seem too big with another person living there." Mara was breathless, and she didn't dare look at Neil's face. "I mean, you'd fill it up pretty well."

"Yeah?"

"If you wanted."

Neil squeezed her hand. "I can't leave Mum right now—"

"Oh. Oh yeah, of course."

Mara tried to pull her hand back, but Neil tightened his grip. He brought his second hand under her chin to raise her head so that she couldn't avoid his eyes. "But that isn't going to be permanent. And then I'd love to help fill up that house. You know, Jenny was right—it's the perfect size for a family. If that's something you want."

His smile was one of the most beautiful things Mara had ever seen. She was glad she was sitting; she didn't think her legs would hold her up. "Yeah."

"I love you," Neil whispered.

Mara tried to lean forward to kiss him, but the booth's table stopped her short. He laughed and bent toward her, meeting her in the middle, and her heart flipped as his lips grazed over hers. "Mara," he whispered, and his hand caressed her cheek and pulled her closer so that he could kiss her properly.

"All done here?" The waitress's frosty voice cut through Mara's daze, and she and Neil broke their kiss and collapsed back into their seats.

Neil mumbled an apology, but Mara pushed her plates toward the edge of the table. "Actually, can I get some pancakes?"

The waitress didn't answer but turned a simpering smile on Neil. "Anything for you, honey?"

"I'm good, thanks."

"Sure thing." The waitress didn't take her eyes off him as she scooped the plates up.

Mara couldn't fail to notice how much effort the waitress put into sashaying her hips as she returned to the kitchen. "What a jerk."

She was used to Neil attracting attention. He had an easy, comforting aura. His strong jaw, captivating smile, and muscles that stood out even under loose clothes certainly didn't hurt either. Luckily for her, he was almost always oblivious to flirtation.

His eyebrows drew together. "You look worried."

Mara shook her frown off and laughed. "No, just thinking about how lucky I am."

"With the house? Yeah, it's actually sort of surprising Jenny didn't suggest it before today. She'd probably given up trying to sell it."

"That too." Mara tilted her head to one side. "But that wasn't what I was thinking of. How'd I end up with you, Neil? Why'd you ask me out?"

Neil's eyes crinkled as he smiled, and he raised his hand to caress her cheek. "You were sitting under the big elm in the park and reading *Emma*. I couldn't get over how beautiful you looked. It took me at least twenty minutes to get up the courage to ask you out, you know."

Heat rose across Mara's cheeks. She couldn't keep herself from leaning into his touch. "And you've stuck with me ever since. Why? I'm broken. I have enough baggage to fill a freighter plane. I yell at our Realtor. But you—you have all of your crap together—you could have any girl you wanted—"

"I want you." Neil's eyes, sweet and firm, captivated Mara. Perfect conviction laced his every word. "I want you more than I've ever wanted a woman before. When I'm near you, I feel like I'm exactly where I'm supposed to be."

Mara closed her eyes and nuzzled his hand. "Stop being so nice."

"Only when you stop being so lovable."

That made Mara chuckle. "Want to get out of here?"

"I don't mind, but what about your pancakes?"

"Yeah, I'm pretty certain that waitress is going to spit in the batter. Let's go."

CHAPTER 7
RELOCATION

BREATHLESS JENNY TURNED OUT to be a surprisingly staunch ally in Mara's fight to move house. With her rental contract ending with the month, Mara's days were filled with phone calls to arrange inspections, pay taxes, chase up forms that were moving sluggishly, beg for expedition whenever it was possible, and, of course, the eternal search for a new job.

They cut it close. Mara was on the last day of her contract when Jenny dropped off Blackwood House's keys with an anxiously whispered, "Good luck, honey!"

Mara waved to the hot-pink car as it crawled out of her alley then opened her fist to grin at the tarnished, rusty key. *My own home. It may be a dump, but it's* my *dump.*

She fished her cell phone out and left a message on Neil's phone while she climbed the stairs to her apartment. He was at work and likely wouldn't finish until late that afternoon. Mara would have to be patient. She needed his car to move her few possessions.

Mara wiggled the door handle until it opened, and entered her room for the final time. It felt incredible that, after four years, she'd finally have a house of her own. The incessant sacrifices and innumerable cut corners had paid off.

She owned very little that she wanted to take with her besides her wardrobe. Just her phone, toiletries, a collection of gifts from Neil, and a small bag of canned food she'd bought to get her through her first day at Blackwood. She hadn't seen the building since the inspection two weeks previously and didn't want to commit herself to any large purchases until she had a better feel for what she needed.

Mara crossed to the window and sat in the small plastic chair. She tried to immerse herself in an ebook on her phone to pass the time but couldn't stop checking the clock every few minutes. After half an hour of futile half distraction, she put the phone down and leaned on the sill to watch the alley. Her heart skipped a beat at the sight of the silver car parked at the curb below. *Neil. He must have gotten my message and left work early.*

The car wasn't idling, which meant Neil was coming inside. Mara grimaced as she turned around. In the six months they'd been dating, Mara had never invited Neil into her room. She'd seen his house; his family wasn't quite wealthy, but they were very comfortably upper middle class, and their home had been decorated with a great deal of care. Rows of photos hung on the walls and cluttered the lace-coated mantels. The furniture had a quaint, homey vibe, and there were bowls of potpourri in the bathroom. It was the polar opposite of Mara's apartment.

Mara knew Neil wouldn't like her home, and she'd been hoping to avoid an uncomfortable scene by never letting him see it. *Maybe I can head him off on the stairs.* A brisk knock made her cringe. *Damn. Too late now.* Mara crossed to the door, took a breath to brace herself, and pulled it open.

"Hey, I got your message. Ready to—" Neil paused in the entryway as his eyes roved over the one-room home. Mara's mattress—a bed frame would have been too expensive—was propped against one wall. A portable cooker, single pot, plate, and spoon sat opposite. The foldable dining table and plastic chair sat below the window, and a cardboard portable wardrobe held her clothes.

Mara felt color rise in her face. She kept her home clean. Her clothes were arranged neatly and washed often. She'd painted the windowsill with a half bucket of white paint someone had thrown away. But she still knew it was a pathetic living compared to what Neil enjoyed, and mingled embarrassment and injured pride scorched at her insides.

Neil took a step into the room and swore. That startled Mara. She'd never heard anything harsher than fake swears—*cripes, shoot,* and *sugar* were his favorites—leave his lips.

"Mara—" He broke off and pressed one hand to his mouth. His voice was thick. "Have you seriously been living here?"

"Of course I have." Mara crossed her arms defensively.

Neil's eyes scanned the seeping cracks that ran up one wall and the exposed wires clustered in one corner. His mouth turned into a hard line. "I had no idea—you should have said something."

"And what?" She knew an aggressive note was crawling into her voice, but she couldn't fight it.

Neil blinked at her, brows constricted. "You could have stayed with me. I know you don't like Mum's home, but we could have gotten an apartment together—"

"I don't need you white knighting your way into my life and solving my problems," she snapped. "I've been quite comfortable on my own, thank you."

Neil didn't reply, but she could see the hurt in his eyes. Her anger deflated like an eviscerated balloon. *Crap.*

He wasn't judging her, she knew. He was berating himself for not having helped. Neil was a fixer; the desire to solve problems was as central to his personality as Mara's love of french fries was to hers. And seeing a problem he could have fixed, but hadn't, was agony for him. More than that, he worried about her. Even after six months of dating, Mara still wasn't used to having another human altruistically interested in her welfare. It unsettled her almost as much as she liked it.

Mara's pride still stung, but the expression on Neil's face cooled the burn. She stepped close to him and reached up to lace her fingers around the back of his neck. She pulled his head down until their foreheads met, then she smiled into his wide blue eyes. "Hey, I'm sorry I snapped. But I survived three and a half years without you, remember? And I'm proud that I did. I want to make my way through this world on my own two feet."

Neil sighed heavily. His arms wrapped around her lower back and pulled her closer, capturing her. She found she didn't mind at all; his large hands stroked her back, and she shivered at the sensation.

"I know," he said. "And I admire that. But I could've helped if you'd said something." He shuddered. "Did you even have enough to eat? Crap, no wonder you always seemed hungry—"

Mara kissed him, hard, to stun him into silence. When she pulled back she couldn't stop herself from laughing. "Jeez, no, it's not *that* dire. I just hate cooking, and your food is freakishly tasty. Listen. I could have had a nicer apartment if I'd wanted it. But I've been saving instead. I wanted my own place. The more money I spent on useless things like televisions and curtains and…I dunno, white-picket fences or whatever fancy housewives spend their money on…the longer it would have taken to buy a house. I was comfortable. Don't you dare feel sorry for me, Neil. I'm finally getting everything I've wanted, all on my own efforts, and I feel damn good about it."

Neil studied her eyes, testing for honesty, then nodded. "Okay. Let's get you to that new house, then. Do you need help packing?"

"Hang on a second." Mara pecked his lips a final time then ducked out of his grip, picked an empty cardboard box off the foot of her bed, and went to the window ledge. She'd arranged Neil's gifts there to brighten her room, and she swept them into the box in a smooth motion. "Grab the wardrobe, and we're ready to go."

Neil hesitated. "You don't want anything else?"

"Nah. It all sucks. C'mon. I've got a somewhat larger but equally sucky house to move into."

Finally, Neil smiled. It was what Mara had been waiting for, and she felt all of the tension melt away. He picked up the cardboard wardrobe in a fluid motion, braced it against his shoulder, and followed her out of the door. This time, Mara didn't bother kicking it closed.

CHAPTER 8
COMPROMISES

"HOLY CRAP. I DON'T think I could *buy* a boyfriend as good as you are." Mara, nestled in the car's overly large passenger seat, dug through the brown paper bag Neil had given her. She found it impossible to choose just one item. She pulled out both the chocolate and the meat pie and began alternating bites of each.

"There's some muffins Mum baked, too," Neil said, not trying to disguise his delight as he watched Mara out of the corner of his eye. "And there's a really nice apple-and-walnut salad—"

"Dear, sweet Neil. Will you never learn?" Mara found the salad container and smiled at it fondly. "You can eat this later."

She tossed the plastic packet into the backseat then turned as it made a strange thudding noise. "Hey, what's with all the boxes?"

"Just some equipment."

"From work?"

"Mm-hmm."

"Thanks for picking me up so quickly, by the way." Mara returned to the chocolate with gusto. "Did you have to cut your shift very short?"

"Not too badly. Autumn's usually a slow time of year anyway, so Joel doesn't mind me reducing my hours."

Neil was a partner in his carpentry business and had a small crew working under him. Mara had met the other partner, Joel, a few times and thought he was a little too affable for his own good.

"So…" Neil drummed his fingers on the steering wheel.

He was trying to sound casual, but Mara knew him too well. She narrowed her eyes. "What is it?"

"Oh, nothing. I was just thinking…"

"Give it to me straight. I'm a big girl."

Neil chuckled, and the tension dropped from his shoulders. "I can't hide anything from you, can I? All right. I know how important being independent is for you. And I really, really like that. But—"

"But you want to help." Mara took another large bite of the meat pie to hide her smile as Neil exhaled deeply.

"Yeah. We've been together for a while. I want to be able to do things for you once in a while."

Mara dropped the uneaten food back into the bag and folded the top over. "You already do way more than you should. You're constantly buying me food—it's going to make me fat, by the way—and you've already offered to help with the house's repairs. I'd say that's plenty."

"The house is kind of what's bothering me actually." Neil kept his eyes fixed on the road, but Mara could tell he was distracted. The speedometer was hovering slightly over the legal limit.

"Go on."

"It's a mess, Mara. The roof is collapsing, it's full of rotting furniture and dead bugs, and there's no phone reception. If something happened to you—"

"You checked the house out yourself and said it's sound. It's not about to collapse on me."

"I could have made a mistake, though. What if the floor gives out, or you step on a rusty nail, or the boiled-cabbage stalker is still hanging around?"

"*Boiled cabbage*—you're mixing up my metaphors, Neil."

"My point is, it's at least five hours' walk to town, and you don't have a car. If anything goes wrong, you'd be trapped with no way to communicate with the outside world. I'm not asking you to move in with me or anything. Just let me arrange a hotel room for you until the worst of the issues are fixed."

"You've got a better chance of convincing me to eat one of your salads."

Neil sighed heavily. "Mara—"

"I know." She squeezed his arm. "You want to help. And I really, truly appreciate that. But I'm also really, truly excited to live in my new house. The damage isn't anywhere near as bad as you're making it out to be, and I'm confident in my ability to defend myself if I bump into a geriatric stalker. Please, *please* don't be anxious about me."

Neil worried at his lower lip. The car was coasting nearly ten kilometers faster than it should have been. "Would you be open to a compromise?"

"What did you have in mind?"

"Could I stay with you tonight? Just in case."

Mara tilted her head to one side and tried not to grin too broadly. "A sleepover? That's not a compromise at all. You're more than welcome."

The car began to slow down. "Great. I can stay until eight the following morning, but then I'd have to get to my work. Is that all right with you?"

"Absolutely." A thought struck her, and she raised her eyebrows. "Will your mother be okay with it?" She quite liked Neil's mother, Pam, but the older woman held what Mara could only describe as *traditional values*.

"I already ran it past her—she'll be fine by herself for tonight."

"But we'll be all alone. *Together*. It's absolutely scandalous."

Neil grinned. "Let me put it this way. I'm her only child and still unmarried at twenty-six. I think I could take up residence in a bordello and she'd turn a blind eye provided it produced some grandchildren."

Mara had to laugh.

CHAPTER 9
HOME

THEY LEFT THE MAIN road and followed the incline into the country area. Another turn moved them out of the farming land and into a heavily wooded landscape. The road, which had been sealed until then, turned to dirt and narrowed so much that Neil had to pull over to let vehicles driving in the opposite direction pass.

Blackwood's driveway was a long stretch from any other signs of habitation. Mara couldn't help wondering what had prompted the original owner to choose that plot of land. She knew that, if she followed the dirt road farther, it would eventually lead into the next town. But Blackwood House had been built nearly halfway between the two points of civilization and didn't seem to have any close neighbors.

Her driveway was a little over four kilometers long. The path was potholed and rough, but Neil's car managed it without trouble. Partway along, green and autumn-yellowed trees gave way to the spindly, gray-trunked monsters that surrounded Mara's house.

They turned around a final bend and found Blackwood looming ahead of them. Mara dug her fingernails into the car's seat as an almost electric excitement rushed through her. The house looked even better than she remembered. It was hardly going to win the Cozy Home of the Year award, but it had personality, and it suited Mara perfectly.

Neil pulled up in the patchy yard and squeezed her hand. "Ready?"

"Absolutely."

Neil opened the trunk while Mara followed the white-stone path to the front door. She took the bronze key out of her pocket and fit it into the lock. The metal scraped, and when the door opened inward, Mara felt pulled forward like a morsel of food being sucked into a monstrous fish's mouth.

The entry room was exactly how she remembered it. The aged wood groaned around her as she turned on the spot. To her left, the long-unfinished meal still sat on the table. "Home Is Where the Heart Is" hung on the wall in the room to her right.

Home. It was such a warm word. Mara had lived in houses before but never a true home. Blackwood felt innately good— innately right—as if she'd found the one place on earth she actually belonged.

Footsteps behind her announced Neil's arrival. He carefully placed her portable wardrobe into the corner of the room then crossed his arms as he surveyed the entryway. "We should have hired someone to clean the place out a bit."

"I didn't legally own it until this morning," Mara said, shrugging. "Besides, no point in wasting money on something I can do myself."

To call the house a bargain was an absolute understatement. Mara's savings, which she'd expected to almost entirely lose on an apartment, had covered Blackwood and left plenty to spare. Even after she paid for spare wood and tiles to repair the aging building, she'd have enough to last her at least four months, provided she didn't buy too many frivolities. Four months was plenty of time to find a job, and she could spend her spare hours making Blackwood more comfortable.

"What's first, boss?" Neil asked.

Mara twirled then faced the stairwell. "There's no electricity, so we'd better pick a bedroom before night sets in. Somewhere that will get moonlight through its window."

"Good plan. We might find something on the second floor; it's less cluttered than downstairs and should hold its heat better. I'll grab some more stuff while you start exploring."

"Meet you up there."

It wasn't until she was halfway up the stairs that Mara questioned Neil's last phrase. *More stuff? Does he mean my box of trinkets? Or maybe he brought something for dinner. I wouldn't complain if he had; tonight feels like it needs something more special than canned tuna.*

On the second floor, the wide hallway branched to her left and to her right. Mara searched through it and found three empty rooms. The first two had shattered windows, but the third's glass was only cracked. Mara held her hand near the pane and felt a whistle of cold air. *Maybe I can find some cardboard to cover it.*

All of the other bedrooms were furnished, and Mara didn't want to imagine the insects and cockroaches that might be living among the old wardrobes and under the decayed rugs. Her new room wasn't large, but it was at least clear and didn't have many cobwebs lurking around the roof. Floral wallpaper—shabby, peeling, and discolored—coated the wall around the door.

"Mara?" Neil called.

"In here."

He backed into the room, two stacked boxes filling his arms. Mara recognized the cartons from the back of his car and frowned. "I thought you said that was equipment from work."

"Some of it is." He gave her an apologetic smile. "But I brought some extras just in case."

"Just in case of *what*?"

"In case my beloved girl didn't bring anything to sleep on, for instance." Neil dropped the boxes into the corner of the room. "Or anything to cook on." He caught hold of Mara's wrist and tugged her close. "Or to heat herself when it gets cold at night." Kisses peppered her cheeks, forehead, and nose.

Mara, laughing, squirmed against him. "I swear you're like the paranoid mother I never had. I don't need you fussing over me."

"Really, truly?" Neil quirked an eyebrow. "Were you just going to sleep on the floor?"

Mara tried to worm herself free, but Neil's grip was too solid to escape. "Of course not. I was going to take one of the house's mattresses and flip it over."

"Ma-*ra!*"

The abject horror in Neil's voice made her laugh uncontrollably. Neil seized on her moment of vulnerability and pulled her closer, pressing her to his chest and lifting her from the ground. His arms wrapped around her, seeming to engulf her. Mara, breathless and delighted, stopped fighting and allowed herself to be held.

Before meeting Neil, she'd hated feeling vulnerable. To be weak was a source of shame and fear. It made her a target. It *hurt.* But Neil could make her feel entirely powerless in a way she loved. His arms never squeezed too hard, and his words were never harsh. To be vulnerable around him was to be safe. So she draped her arms around his neck and let her body fall limp as he held her and kissed her hair.

"Mara, Mara, Mara…" he murmured. The adoration in his voice was almost too sweet to endure. "I love you. So damn much. Please be safe."

Mara opened her eyes at the final words. There was a pang of fear in them as though some deep, anxious emotion was inches from escaping its restraints. *He seemed so cheerful today. Was it just a cover for this worry?* She raised her hands to run them through his hair, and he pulled her closer in response. "Neil. Shh, it's okay. Everything's going to be fine."

"I know." Neil took a deep breath, kissed her hair a final time, then gently lowered her back to the floor. He looked a little sheepish but still didn't remove his hands from her back. "I know. You're a firecracker. Of course you'll be fine."

Mara pulled him down to kiss her. His lips were hesitant, and she took control, pulling him in deeper. She was hungry for more; her right hand gripped his shirt, and her left slipped underneath it to brush across his chest. He shivered in response, and she spread her fingers to press against the muscles.

A clatter startled them apart. They turned, both breathing heavily, to see that one of Neil's boxes had toppled from its partner and spilled its contents across the floor.

"Huh." Neil, still flushed, squeezed Mara's hand before crossing to the box. "I can't have stacked them properly. We'd better unpack before it gets too late, I guess."

"Yeah." Mara's heart raced, partly from the thrill of the kiss and partly from the startle. She followed Neil and knelt to open the first box. As she sorted through the contents, intrigue grew into incredulity. There were two sleeping bags—he'd clearly planned to stay with her that night—and pillows. Below those were rolled foam mats and a small gas heater. Then a portable stove and a heavy icebox, toiletries, a compact first aid kit, and duct tape. "Where'd you get all of these?"

"What I didn't already own I bought or borrowed." Neil was returning the spilled contents to the box that had overturned. Mara caught sight of multiple flashlights and spare batteries, a radio, an umbrella, gloves, a roll of garbage bags, towels, and spare blankets.

"Do you intend to move in?"

Neil pecked her cheek as she leaned too close. "No, but you do."

"I was going to buy most of this stuff tomorrow," she groused.

"And now you can enjoy it tonight. Hang on; the floor is disgusting. I'm going to see if I can find a broom."

Mara huffed as Neil left, then she turned to explore the icebox. He'd packed meats, breads, fresh and dried fruit, and a bag of lettuce. "Why does he even bother?" Mara muttered, shoving the lettuce aside. She restacked the boxes to clear the floor as much as she could then stood and wiped her hands on her jeans. Neil was right; the floor was beyond gross. She was going to have a fun time cleaning her way through Blackwood's rooms.

It took Neil several minutes to return. When he did, he carried not only a broom and dustpan but also a rucksack from his car. "The old owners left plenty of cleaning supplies—though the mop would probably make the floor worse. But at least you can make use of the buckets and washtubs."

Mara took his rucksack and held it off the ground while Neil swept around her feet. "That's kind of strange, isn't it? It's like they abandoned *everything* when they left. Not just the big furniture, but blankets, clothes…even their dinner on the table. What would make a family leave so quickly and never come back?"

He hesitated midsweep. "Maybe you were right about the gas leak."

"I don't think so. Jenny was able to arrange for the gas and water to be reconnected while the paperwork was still going through. I had an inspector come down a couple of days ago, and he gave it the all-clear for leaks."

"Strange." Neil collected the grime into a tidy pile, and Mara knelt to brush the dust, dead flies, grime, and desiccated plaster into the dustpan. She then carried it to the adjacent room, which had a pane missing in its window, and emptied the dirt into the backyard. When she returned to the bedroom, he had unrolled both sleeping bags and was fastening strips of duct tape over the crack in the window.

Mara approached him from behind and wrapped her arms around his torso. He was so tall that she could barely reach his shoulder blades, but she kissed them and felt the reverberations in his chest as he murmured happily.

"There's still a few hours of sunlight left," Mara said. "I thought we could spend it making a list of the major stuff that needs fixing. That way I can order some supplies tomorrow."

"Sounds good." Neil broke his strip of tape off the roll, and Mara released him reluctantly. He dropped the tape back into his box and dug out a notepad and two pens. "Want to work together or separately?"

"We'll get through it faster if we split up."

Neil ripped a sheet from the pad and passed the rest to Mara. "Let's divide it by floors, then. D'you want the top or ground?"

"I'd love to see more of downstairs while there's still light. Just note the major stuff like missing windows or rotten wood. We can worry about cosmetic issues later."

"On it." Neil headed into the hallway. Mara went the opposite direction and took the stairs down to the ground floor. She started in the dining room and jotted down the broken windows and where one section of the wall was decaying from water damage, then she followed the entryway into the kitchen.

"Cripes," Mara murmured. The room was a mess. Rat and cockroach droppings littered the counters, and pots, plates, and baking pans lay askew. Judging by the dark stains in the dishes, the house's old owners had been saving the washing-up for after dinner.

She'd have to throw the dirty pots out, but the collection in the drawers looked to be high quality. She thought she could use them after giving them a good wash. The same went for many of the plates and the cutlery.

Mara turned from the kitchen. Other than the mess, the room's structure seemed to be sound. She'd have to check if the gas stove still worked, but she could worry about that later.

Past the kitchen was a laundry. An ancient washing machine and dryer sat against one wall. Mara opened the washing machine's lid then dropped it back in place as she gagged. Clothes had been left to mold and decay, and the smell was appalling. *Looks like I'll be using the town's laundromat until I can afford a new machine.*

The laundry had a door leading into the backyard, but it was falling out of its frame. Mara examined it and thought it might only need new hinges and a fresh lock. She noted them in her book.

She retraced her steps to the kitchen and took its other doorway into what she guessed was a recreation room. It had very little furniture—just a tiny boxy television with antennae sticking out, two crumbling lounges, a wooden table and two chairs, and a cupboard. Mara opened the cupboard door and gasped as a rat shot past her and scurried into the kitchen. She made a face as she watched its tail whisk out of sight, then she turned back to examine the small collection of games inside the cupboard. She recognized Monopoly and Battleship, but the others weren't familiar.

A creaking noise reached her, and Mara closed the cupboard doors. She listened to the sound for a moment before identifying the steady, repetitive groans as belonging to the rocking chair in the living room. *Neil must have come down. He can't have finished upstairs that quickly, surely?*

Mara followed the noise, moving through the recreation room's other door and into what she assumed was a library. Solid wooden shelves lined the walls, but they were devoid of books. Past the library was the sitting room. Mara paused in the doorway. The fireplace remained empty and cold as though begging for a handful of wood and a spark. "Home Is Where the Heart Is" hung on the wall beside her. The lounge chairs seemed even more moth-eaten than the day before, if that was possible. And the rocking chair rolled on its struts, back and forward, back and forward as its wood groaned. Mara was alone in the room.

"Neil?" she called.

"Everything okay?" The faint reply came from above her head.

Mara stared at the gently rolling chair for a moment, then

crossed to it and placed her boot under the strut to stop its motion. The creaking was silenced. "Yeah, everything's fine."

She backed away from the chair and returned her pen to the paper, writing "Breeze in the living room; source unknown—possibly the fireplace?"

The room's windows were intact except for a small crack running across one pane. Mara made a note of that then returned to the foyer. There was some decay around the doorway, and several floorboards were rising. She wrote them down then opened the front door to look outside.

The sun was already setting. Mara was used to living in the heart of the town, where trees were a luxury. The dark trees around her house were thin but grew high, and the boughs were smothering the dipping sun and welcoming shadows into Mara's home. *Thank goodness Neil thought to bring flashlights.*

She climbed the stairs and found Neil at the end of the hallway, scribbling notes about a patch in the wall where the wood had been eaten away to leave fist-sized holes. He turned at the sound of Mara's footsteps and smiled. "All done downstairs?"

"I got the worst of it. We'll need to throw a bunch of stuff out, but there's still plenty of furniture that's good to use."

"What a find, huh?" The warmth in Neil's voice was genuine though hints of tightness still lingered around his mouth.

She laced her hand through his as they walked back to their makeshift bedroom. "Ready for some dinner?"

"Absolutely. I hope steaks are okay."

"Never leave me."

CHAPTER 10
NIGHTFALL

MARA SCRIBBLED A LIST of high-priority shopping while Neil set up his portable gas cooker. She would never admit it to his face, but she was becoming increasingly grateful for his planning. While she'd been prepared to slum it on the least damaged of the house's furniture for the first few nights, there was something beautifully comforting about having a clean sleeping bag and fresh pillow, not to mention flashlights and a heater. The air was cooling as night set in properly, and Mara was cocooned in one of Neil's blankets.

"I didn't get time to examine the roof." He dropped two steaks onto the sizzling cooker. "It looks pretty bad from the outside, but thankfully, it's not impeding us right now. All of the ceilings on this floor are fine, which is surprising—I would have expected some water damage at the very least. But it's good news for us. It means we can save the work on the roof until later, after we've patched up the holes on the first two floors."

"How long's the whole job likely to take?"

Neil thought for a moment. "Well—it'll just be you and me working on it, but the house's structure is basically solid. As long as we don't find any larger problems, the bulk of the major repairs should be done within a fortnight, and I'd say we can fix up the small stuff—the repainting and repairing cosmetic flaws—over the next six months."

"Six months isn't too bad."

"Not at all. Of course, we'll need to get electricity run through here, too. That's going to be a large job, and it's not something I can do. I'll ask around my contacts and see if any of them will give us a friend's discount."

The smell of cooking meat permeated the room as Neil flipped the steaks, and Mara inhaled deeply. "You're the best, Neil."

"I am, aren't I?" His mischievous grin made Mara laugh, and he scooted backward to sit next to her. "I can't promise to be here every day, but Joel should be okay with me taking the afternoon off work for the next few weeks. I can swing by around three and stay into the evening."

Mara rested her head against his shoulder. "I'd really like that, but your mother still needs to see you occasionally, too."

He gave a small nod. His mother hadn't been coping well since losing her husband eight months before, and Neil had moved back into his childhood home to look after her. He said Pam often floated about the house aimlessly and skipped meals unless he was there to watch her.

It worried Mara. She'd heard stories about couples dying

within a year of each other—either from grief or because the change in their life was too great to reconcile—and dearly hoped Neil wouldn't have to lose his mother prematurely, too.

It put him in a difficult situation, though. He was an only child, so the responsibility of caring for his mother fell to him alone. He was already juggling his work and home life, and Mara's new house would place additional strain on him. Even just staying with her for the night was a huge sacrifice. As far as Mara knew, he hadn't spent such a long stretch of time away from home since his father had passed.

Neil moved back to the cooker to scoop the steaks off. An idea had been hovering around the back of Mara's mind during the two weeks between buying Blackwood and moving into it. She licked her lips before asking, "How are things at home?"

He didn't look at her, but his voice was cheerful. "Not too bad. The doctor's talking about weaning Mum off the sleeping pills. She still seems lost sometimes, but she hasn't had any more major lapses in memory. She knows what year it is and things like that."

Mara stared at her folded hands. "Tell me if I'm being horribly rude here, but have you thought that your mother might do better in a new environment?"

"Yeah, I have." Neil sighed as he settled next to her and handed her a plate. It was loaded with not just the steak but also potato salad, precooked beans, and a handful of the lettuce Mara had found in the icebox. "I suggested it to her the other week, but it upset her too much to pursue it. She'd probably do better if she were somewhere that didn't constantly remind her of Dad, but at the same time, she's not ready to let him go. And I don't think a simple change of house would be enough. She'd need a new purpose in life, too. Right now, she doesn't have anything to fill her hours."

Mara's mouth was dry. "You know, Blackwood's got plenty of room. Once there aren't any holes in the roof, you and your mother could stay here. I—I dunno—she might like to help with making it a proper home, or something—"

Neil was silent for a very long time. Mara was frightened to look at him. She dreaded seeing signs of reluctance, but when she glanced up, his shining eyes only reflected surprise and deep gratitude. "You'd be okay with that?"

"I think I would." She shrugged awkwardly. "I mean, I'd ask that she didn't bring any of the religious stuff into the house—or, at least, keep it in her room—but, well, I don't think I'd mind living with her if it's *my* home. That makes a difference, y'know?"

"Mara—" Neil's voice was thick. He pressed a warm kiss to her forehead then gave her a broad smile. "Thank you. I don't know if she'll go for it—she probably wouldn't want to move within the next few months at least—but maybe that might just work."

"Yeah?"

"Yeah."

Mara couldn't stifle her grin as she leaned against Neil's shoulder. A hot glow had started in her chest. Unlike an apartment or small house, Blackwood had plenty of room for the three of them without any stepping on toes. Pam was a sweet, gentle woman, and Mara loved Neil more than anyone else in the world. She thought the three of them could be happy together.

She picked the carefully arranged pile of lettuce leaves off her plate and dropped them onto Neil's. He groaned.

CHAPTER 11
FOOTSTEPS IN THE DARK

WHEN MARA PUSHED INTO the bathroom, toothbrush in one hand and flashlight in the other, she was confronted with a bizarre distortion of her face. The large mirror over the sink had been shattered; a tennis-ball-sized impact area marred its surface, and a spiderweb of fractures spread out from it, turning the surface into a freak-house installation. Mara saw two dozen copies of her own brown eyes blinking out of the panes and made a face at them.

The remainder of the bathroom showed its age. The porcelain bathtub had chips and cracks running down its side and would likely need to be replaced. The toilet's lid was missing. A handful of the wall's tiles had fallen loose and lay among the dust and dead insects that gathered in the room's corners.

The water had been reconnected at the same time as the gas, but that didn't mean it would actually come through the pipes.

Twenty years was a long time for anything to sit dormant. Mara turned the sink's tap and listened to the horrific grinding rumble that began below her feet and seemed to travel through the house. The tap shuddered, then deep-red water spewed from it.

Mara gasped and took a step back. She knew it was only rust, but the liquid was such a vivid color that it was easy to imagine it as blood. She watched in fascination as the stream painted the sink scarlet before gradually lightening and eventually clearing. She let it run for a few minutes more before scooping up a handful to taste it.

The water was surprisingly cold. It tasted as though it was saturated with minerals, but it wasn't an unpleasant flavor, so Mara propped her flashlight upright on the sink to illuminate the room, dunked her toothbrush under the water's flow, and began brushing.

A sound echoed above her head. Mara turned the tap off and looked toward the ceiling. There was silence for a second, then the groaning noise repeated, moving toward the back of the bathroom. *Feet straining aged wood. Neil must have gone to check the roof after all.*

Mara turned the tap back on and resumed brushing. The footsteps continued through the attic until they'd almost faded from hearing and then returned, pacing above her head. A sprinkle of dust, disturbed from the ceiling, fell into the sink.

Motion in the spiderweb mirror made Mara jolt, and she swiveled to face the bathroom's doorway. Neil stood in the opening. His face was pale and eyes wide. He spoke in a whisper. "Do you hear that?"

Mara turned the tap off again and dropped the toothbrush into the sink. She stared at the ceiling and listened to the footsteps reach the end of the house, turn, and resume pacing.

"Damn it." Her mouth was dry. Half of her wanted to believe it was the wood flexing as the air cooled, but there was no mistaking the steady tempo of the creaks. There was a person in her attic.

Neil crept closer and felt for her hand in the dim light. His blue eyes, normally so bright and optimistic, were filled with fear as they followed the creaks.

Mara scowled and snatched her flashlight off the counter. "Stay here; I'll check it out."

"Are you insane?" he hissed, tightening his grip on her hand so that she couldn't leave. "Haven't you watched any horror movies? The moment we split up, we're *both* getting murdered by the boiled-cabbage stalker."

Mara squinted at her partner. "You're really fixated on that metaphor, aren't you? Okay, you can come with me if you want."

"*Or*, consider this." Neil seemed to be trying to keep his voice light, but the sheen of sweat over his forehead betrayed him. "We could get in my car and leave right now and *not* die horrifically."

"No one's going to die horrifically. Ten to one, it's a homeless guy who thought this was an abandoned building he could sleep in, or a kid here on a dare. You can stay downstairs if you want, but I'm going to have a talk with them."

"I am *not* letting you go up there alone."

"Then come with me. I don't get why this is such a big deal for you."

The creaking fell silent then, and both Neil and Mara raised their eyes to the spot, not far above their heads, where the intruder rested.

"Please," Neil began, still keeping his voice to a whisper.

"Nope." Mara pulled toward the bathroom door, and Neil, unwilling to release her hand, followed. "At least let's bring a knife."

"Yeah, that would be smart. But don't charge in there waving it like a madman. I want to *de*-escalate this situation, okay?"

Neil retrieved the small paring knife he'd used to prepare dinner and wiped it clean on his jeans. He looked as though he wished he'd brought a butcher knife instead. Mara waited in the hallway and kept an eye on the staircase at the end of the passage in case the intruder tried to come down, but the footsteps didn't resume.

"Ready?" she asked as Neil joined her.

The house was pitch-black. Neil had picked up his own flashlight, and their two beams brought small patches of the dark-wood walls into relief. "This is crazy," was all he said before leading her to the stairs. He evidently didn't want her entering the attic first.

The stairs started at the end of the hallway and rose up the side of the wall. They were narrow and rickety, and it was impossible for Mara and Neil to keep them quiet as they climbed toward the hatch that opened into the attic.

"It's bolted on this side with a padlock," Neil whispered. "Whoever's up there can't get down to us."

"Can you break it?"

A sigh. "Probably. It looks rusty."

Neil used the back of his flashlight to beat at the lock. On the third strike, it came free and clattered to the floor below them. With a final pleading look at Mara, which she refused to acknowledge, Neil took a fortifying breath and pushed the trapdoor up.

The metal hinges wailed as the hatch flipped over. Neil climbed an extra stair, so that his head and shoulders were in the attic, and swiveled. After a moment's pause, he continued climbing. Mara followed.

The attic stretched the length of the house. At the roof's peak, the ceiling was high enough that Mara could have stretched her arm up and still not touched it.

Streams of cold moonlight fell through the holes in the ceiling and painted strange mottles of light over the attic's contents. More than a hundred boxes were stacked around the room. White cloths covered large, hulking shapes like shrouds, and the floor was coated in dry leaves. Mara panned her flashlight across the space but couldn't see any movement. "Hello?"

When no reply came, she nudged Neil and indicated that they should start searching. Neil swallowed thickly, shifted the knife in his fist, and moved toward the closest stack of boxes.

"We know you're here," Mara said as she began moving along the other side of the house, parallel to Neil. "We could hear you walking. I'm not angry, but I want you to leave. This is private property."

The only sounds she could make out were the crunches of their boots on the dried leaves and their shallow breathing. Neil stopped beside the first shrouded shape and whisked its cloth off. Underneath was a full-length mirror.

"If you make yourself known, we'll let you leave peacefully." She reached a shape on her side of the room and pulled the fabric away to expose a wardrobe. She opened the door, but the inside was empty. "We won't press criminal charges."

Neil's beam of light shook faintly as he directed it into each dark crevice and hiding spot he passed. The deep shadows were playing tricks on Mara's eyes, so she searched slowly and methodically as they continued along the length of the building and pulled the cloths off each piece of furniture. By the time they reached the opposite wall and faced each other, Mara was shivering from the frigid air.

"Did we miss them?" Neil mouthed.

Mara frowned and shook her head. They'd both been thorough, she knew. Every gap a person could hide in and every cupboard had been searched. She paced back along the attic until she reached the largest hole in the roof. While the others were no bigger than her head, this gap was easily wide enough for a person to climb through. Mara pushed her torso through it, ignoring the faintly panicked noises Neil was making, and shined her flashlight across the roof. It was empty. She then directed her beam to the front lawn and scanned over the shrubs and trees clustering about the driveway.

"My best guess," Mara said, pulling back inside, "is they got out through this hole and climbed down the side of the building. Which means they wanted to avoid being caught and will move on pretty quickly."

"Okay." Neil looked relieved. He turned his light across the attic a final time. "Okay, cool. I really hate this, Mara."

"Hah! Yeah, I know." She turned away from the hole. "C'mon. It'd be smart to search the house before we go to sleep, but I'm pretty sure we won't be disturbed tonight."

They wove toward the open trapdoor, picking their way around the boxes and discarded furniture. Mara paused beside one large cardboard carton and nudged the lid open with her shoe. Inside was a stack of VHS tapes. "Do you think this is all from the last owners?"

"I don't know how long they lived here, but some of this stuff looks…well, ancient." Neil waved his flashlight toward a tarnished, scuffed grandfather clock. "Some of the boxes look like they'd be twenty years old, but others are almost falling apart. Maybe a series of owners left their unwanted possessions here."

Mara reached the exit and began climbing down the narrow stairs. Neil followed and pulled the trapdoor back in place behind them. Once they were on the second floor, she stretched. "Okay, ready to search this place? Just in case?"

"I wouldn't sleep otherwise."

"Sure. We'll cover more ground if we split up—" Neil frowned, and Mara chuckled as she gave him a playful shove. "That was a joke. Calm down."

They moved through the upper floor quickly. Mara stood

in the hallway, watching both the staircase up and the staircase down, while Neil went into the rooms one by one and ensured they were empty. Then they moved to the ground floor, where they repeated the motions; she guarded the stairs at the back of the foyer and the front door while he cycled through the downstairs rooms. By the time he appeared in the dining room entrance and shrugged, Mara was completely sure they were alone. She kept her smile bright and her trembling hands discreetly hidden as she went to him. "See? No one got murdered."

"Yeah." Neil sighed. He seemed to be relaxing. "Hey, did you know you have a basement?"

Mara raised her eyebrows. "I have a basement?"

"You do. I thought it was a cupboard at first, but there's a door that opens onto a stairwell."

"Damn, this is the house that just keeps on giving. Where is it?"

Neil followed her as she darted into the kitchen. "It's in what I'm assuming is the recreation room. I didn't search it, though—the dust was thick enough to show no one had been down there."

"Well, let's check it out now." Mara hurried through the kitchen and into the recreation room and quickly located a narrow door hidden behind the couch, which blended into the room so well that she had completely overlooked it during her exploration earlier that evening. She pulled the door open and coughed as disturbed dust billowed out.

Neil followed, a pained look scrunching his face. "Hey, do you think we could maybe save going down the creepy stairs for later? Sometime when it's not, you know, midnight?"

"No." Mara angled her flashlight's beam at the stone steps and walls. It was a narrow stairwell—it would have to be traveled single file—but unlike the rest of the house, it was free of spiderwebs. The air that came from inside was almost arctic cold. "I've never lived in a house with a basement before. I want to see what it's like."

Neil grimaced.

"C'mon. We can turn it into a fun game—What's Scarier, the Basement or the Attic?"

Neil's grimace intensified.

"You don't have to come if you don't want to." Mara began descending the stairs. She hadn't taken three paces before Neil's footsteps began following hers.

The stairs continued deep below the house. When the floor finally leveled out, Mara was shivering and her breaths plumed in the frigid air. She turned in a circle and panned her light across the room.

It was a disappointment. Instead of extending the length of the house as she'd hoped, the basement was no larger than the bedroom they were camping in. It was completely bare save for a thick layer of dust and stains on one of the walls.

"A pipe must've burst," Mara muttered as she ran her fingers over the dark-red blot that ran down the stones. "We'll have to get that looked at."

"Is it just me, or is this room way colder than it should be?" Neil had his arms crossed over his chest and drew shallow breaths. "It's underground, so it really should be insulated against temperature fluctuations."

"The stones probably trap the cold." Mara scanned the room a final time and sighed. "Well, it's not very exciting, but at least now I can say I have a basement. Ready to go someplace warmer?"

"Please."

CHAPTER 12
GHOSTS

MARA LAY IN HER sleeping bag and held her hands toward the gas heater as she listened to Neil brush his teeth. Their exploration of the house had eaten up a lot of time, and Mara's phone said it was nearly midnight. And its battery was low. Without electricity, it would be dead by morning.

She'd been watching her phone's status throughout the evening. Two-thirds of the time, it displayed no signal; for the other third, either one or two bars appeared. That was better than she'd anticipated. Contact with the outside world would be limited but not quite nonexistent.

Neil turned the tap off, and his footsteps shuffled down the hallway. He appeared in the doorway and paused there, smiling at Mara.

"What?" she asked.

"You look really cute." He came into the room, closing the door behind himself. "I like seeing your hair down."

"Really? I'd wear it like this more except I'm innately lazy and ponytails are way less maintenance. Isn't that a nice thought? Slight convenience is more important to me than your happiness."

Neil laughed as he got into the sleeping bag behind her. "Would you believe I like that? You're an individual. You're strong." His hand found her neck and began stroking the hair away from it. "I do love you, Mara."

"It's definitely reciprocated." Her heart missed a beat as his fingers stroked the skin below her jaw.

The heater's glow warmed Mara's exposed skin, and the sleeping bag was unexpectedly comfortable with the exercise mats underneath it. She was feeling drowsy when Neil spoke.

"Can I ask you something personal?"

"What about?"

Neil didn't answer immediately. When the silence stretched to uncomfortable levels, Mara rolled over to face him. He was worrying his lip, and she pressed her palm to his cheek to encourage him. "It's okay. Go ahead."

"You don't talk about your childhood much."

Oh. Mara withdrew her hand. "There's not much to say. My parents were crazy. I'm not. I got out of there, and now my life is starting properly." Neil continued to stroke her hair. She wished he wouldn't. She didn't want to taint such a nice sensation with unpleasant thoughts.

"I know they were spiritualists," Neil said. "I tried to do some research about it, but I'm sure I only grazed the surface. It was a belief that started in the eighteen hundreds, wasn't it?"

"Yeah." She closed her eyes. "*Come and have a séance at Mrs. Smith's this Saturday. Say hello to your departed husband and watch the table levitate.* For a lot of people, it was a fun novelty."

Neil stayed quiet, but Mara knew he was curious. She took a deep breath and continued. "Of course, among all of the gentry who made a parlor sport out of it, there were a few who really, truly believed—same as with any wacky theory. And some of those core believers had children, and their children had children…and eventually I was born."

"There aren't many spiritualists left, are there?"

Mara shrugged awkwardly. She wished they could change the subject; it was setting up a dull ache in the center of her chest. "When I was growing up, it seemed like the entire world believed. But that was only because my parents filled the house with their equally deluded buddies. Almost every day, we had friends come around to talk about their experiences or plan a meeting or discuss messages from the dead. It was an echo chamber. Anyone with dissenting views was either cut out of our lives, or they cut us out of theirs. I wasn't invited to play with the other kids on our street. They'd have birthday parties, and I'd watch them from my window, but I never got to go—"

"Mara, Mara, I'm sorry. Shh." Neil's fingers, quick and anxious, brushed over her forehead.

She realized she'd been scrunching her face and forced herself to relax. "I'm okay."

Neil took her hand and kissed the fingers. "We don't have to talk about it if it upsets you. I'm sorry."

"It's fine. That part of my life is over." Mara's mouth formed the mantra she'd repeated to herself every morning for the previous four years. "It can't touch me now."

She rolled onto her back, inhaled deeply, and held the breath as she stared at the ceiling. The gray wood was mottled from water stains, and Mara let her eyes pick out shapes among them. "To answer your question—there are hardly any spiritualists left. The practice was pretty thoroughly debunked even while it was becoming the latest trend in Victorian England. The mediums were nothing more than stage magicians who claimed to have a direct line of contact with the dead. They used sleight of hand, bells attached to their shoes, incognito assistants, and other tricks to fool their audiences. They'd move pencils or small wads of paper, snuff out candles, create tapping noises, and ring bells, and the more elaborate acts could involve levitating tables or the appearance of ghostly figures—all through completely natural means."

"How were the ghostly figures done?"

Mara snorted. "An assistant, dressed in a white gown and wearing powder, would step out from behind a curtain and startle the crowd before hiding again in the pandemonium. Most séances were done in dark rooms lit only by a couple of candles, so it was easy to fool the unwary."

"I hope this doesn't make you hate me, but that sounds like a lot of fun."

Mara turned back to Neil. Despite the ache in her chest, she couldn't keep herself from returning his grin. "I'm sure a lot of people enjoyed it just for what it was—parlor tricks. The problem comes when people continue to believe it despite evidence to the contrary." Her smile faded. "It boggles my mind sometimes. My parents weren't stupid. My dad had a degree in biology, and my mother worked for an emergency helpline through most of my childhood. It's not like they were societal outcasts or anything. But they really, genuinely believed ghosts were talking to them. Even after decades of being immersed in a culture entirely maintained by charlatans and the charlatans' dupes, they couldn't realize how fooled they'd been."

"Were the tricks that convincing?"

"*I* saw through them. It all came crumbling down when I was eleven and a bell fell out of a medium's pocket. I'd believed blindly up until then, but as soon as the seed of doubt was planted, I couldn't stop seeing the deceit. From then on, I didn't witness a single supernatural event that couldn't be easily explained. Getting access to the internet helped me figure out some of the smarter tricks."

Neil wove his arm around Mara and pulled her closer. She grinned and leaned against his shoulder.

"You really like this house, huh?" he asked.

"I love it."

"Good. I'm glad."

Mara peeked, one eye open. "You don't like it, though, do you?"

Neil hesitated a split second too long for Mara to believe him when he said, "It's a very nice house."

"Uh-huh. You hate it."

"No, no. I don't *hate* it. I just…sort of…*mistrust* it."

"Because it's creepy?"

"Sweetheart, I've watched horror movies that were more comforting than this place."

Mara chuckled. She nuzzled closer to him. "You can always cuddle me if you get too scared."

"Hmm. I might have to take you up on that offer."

CHAPTER 13
NOISES IN THE NIGHT

SHE WAS IN THE master bedroom, facing the window that over-looked the back garden. A violent red sunset tainted the air.

This is a dream, Mara realized. *And not a pleasant one. I should wake up.*

There was a scraping, scratching noise behind her. She turned, but the motion was slow, as though she were moving through syrup. The furniture was no longer decayed and tattered but plush and expensive looking. Pillows had been thrown about the room, and chairs were overturned. Brushes, jewelry, and a basin of water had been pushed off the bureau. The four-poster bed was in disarray and had two of its curtains pulled down.

The sound came from a woman at the door. She wore a long, silky nightdress, and her pale hair cascaded around her shoulders. Mara thought she would have been beautiful except for her hollowed cheeks and the manic, haunted madness in her eyes.

The woman stared at Mara for a moment, breathing heavily, then returned to clawing at the door. She brought her fingers down the surface repeatedly and rapidly, scoring the wood and staining it red from where her fingernails had broken off. She chanted something between gasping breaths. Mara, captivated and horrified at the same time, waded through the thick air to hear.

"Run, run, run," the woman repeated, speaking the mantra as though she no longer knew what the words meant. She looked over her shoulder at Mara, and a frantic, insane terror distorted her face. "*The axman is coming.*"

Mara gasped and started upright. The cold night air bit at her as she blinked at the room.

Neil's arm was draped over her waist. A square of moonlight from the window blanketed his sleeping form, and Mara watched his chest rise and fall in a steady rhythm as her heart rate slowed.

It's just a dream. Probably brought on by all that excitement before bed. She rubbed at her eyes, exhaled, and lay back down. Her heart still jumped as the dream's influence faded. The building felt far less welcoming in deep night than it had earlier, almost as though its very nature had changed during the hours Mara had slept. She'd found it easy to be brave when Neil was with her and she could ricochet off of his cautious nature. But with Neil asleep, her bravado was sapped away by the darkness and unnerving stillness.

Somewhere deep in the house, a low, slow groan began. Mara clenched her teeth as the hairs on her arms rose. *It's just the rocking chair being nudged by a breeze. Nothing to worry about.*

The noise seemed to permeate the building and soak through Mara's self. She stared at the ceiling while she waited for it to stop. The stains across the wood became a makeshift Rorschach test. Earlier that evening, Mara had seen a motley collection of figures and faces. In the middle of the night, though, they looked like bloodstains blooming outward from where a dozen souls had lost their lives.

A door slammed. Mara gasped and clutched Neil's arm. He stirred, his eyebrows contracting for a second, then relaxed back into sleep.

Just a breeze. This house has more holes than a woodpecker's tree. Of course stuff's going to move when it gets windy.

Mara looked toward the window. She could see boughs silhouetted against the dark sky. They were eerily still.

The steady creaking sound was boring into her mind. Mara crossed her arms and balled her hands into fists so that she wouldn't feel her fingers trembling. *Just block it out, and go back to sleep.*

A second noise joined the rocking chair: a child began sobbing. The plaintive cries echoed as they bounced through the house, and Mara suddenly found it difficult to draw breath.

There's an explanation for this. There's got to be. The wind whistling through a hole somewhere, probably. It's only frightening you because it's nighttime.

The sobs broke into a hiccup, then resumed, blending with the chair's groans in a terrible, chaotic symphony. Mara squeezed her eyes closed and pressed her hands over her ears. The sound wouldn't abate. She could feel her blood rushing through her veins, moving far faster than it should have for someone who'd been lying still. Every moan and every wail keyed Mara's nerves up tighter and tighter until she finally snapped and launched into action.

She shuffled out of the sleeping bag, moving carefully so that she wouldn't wake Neil. The building already disturbed him; he'd do better without being exposed to the nocturnal noises, too. He murmured something as Mara crawled out from under his arm, but he didn't wake.

She took her jacket off the top of the nearby box and pulled her arms through the sleeves then wrapped it tightly around her torso as she slipped her feet into her sneakers. The air was bitingly cold. Mara took the flashlight but waited until she was outside the room to turn it on, to keep from disturbing Neil.

The light bounced off the wooden walls and half-open doors. Mara moved carefully, trying to keep her footsteps light. As she passed the master-bedroom door, it slammed closed. She felt the rush of air from its motion and bit the inside of her cheek to keep from crying out. *Just the wind. Just the wind. Just the wind—*

As if on cue, the door slowly and laboriously drew open again, its quiet groan nearly drowned out by the rocking chair and the wailing cries. *I'll have to buy a new lock for this thing.* Mara pulled the door back and stepped into the room to find something heavy to keep it from slamming shut again. A squat footstool sat beside an armchair. Mara put the flashlight between her teeth so she could drag the stool to the open doorway.

The door slammed, and shock made her bite into the flashlight's handle. She spat the flashlight into her hand and turned back to the door. The scores that marred its surface—so much like fingernail marks—stood out clearly in her circle of light. *Run, run, run. The axman is coming.*

Mara exhaled shakily. She moved to open the door again, and in the second before she touched the handle, a horrible idea wormed its way into her mind. *What if the door's locked? What if you're trapped in this room, just like the golden-haired woman, doomed to scrabble and scream for mercy as the shadows drown you?*

"Shut up," Mara whispered, and her voice broke. The handle's cold metal almost felt as though it had an electric charge as she turned the knob. The door opened without complaint. Mara released the lungful of air she hadn't even realized she'd been holding.

She pushed the door fully open then dragged the footstool in front of it to keep it that way. Then she returned to the hallway and listened.

The downstairs noises hadn't abated. If anything, they'd grown louder. She couldn't detect any stirring in her bedroom, though—Neil seemed to still be asleep.

She took the stairs quickly, keeping to their edges to minimize creaking. Once on the ground floor, she turned to the living room.

The rocking chair rolled wildly, bouncing from one end of its struts to the other, the motion almost violent enough to overturn it. Mara cautiously approached the chair and held her hand in front of the window to test for a breeze, but she couldn't feel one.

The wailing continued, seeming to fill the room with its mournful weight. *It really does sound like a child crying. No wonder all of the previous owners panicked.* Mara rotated as she tried to detect where the sound came from. She found it easily: the fireplace.

Of course. The chimney's probably half-blocked and makes the wind whistle as it travels through. And I'll bet it's hitting the chair at just the right angle to set it rocking, too. Mara moved toward the fireplace, hand held outward to feel for the wind. The wailing noise abruptly fell silent.

With the wind abated, the rocking chair began to slow its motions. Mara stayed for a moment, waiting for the sounds to resume, but they didn't. The rocking chair settled into stillness. Quiet returned to Blackwood's walls.

Mara turned to leave and then stopped. *I don't want to be woken again tonight.* She grabbed the chair by its back and dragged it away from the window to resettle it below the "Home Is Where the Heart Is" cross-stitch on the opposite wall. *That should do it.*

She turned back to the foyer and jumped as a distant voice startled her.

"Mara?"

Neil had woken. Mara felt a pang of guilt at the anxious tone in his voice. "I'm here; everything's okay."

She took the stairs two at a time. He met her in the hallway, his hair even messier than normal, and pulled her into a hug. "You're all right?"

Mara laughed. "Of course I am. It's not like the house is going to eat me."

"Ha, yeah, of course." Neil didn't sound reassured. Mara let him keep his arm around her as they returned to the bedroom. She hoped he wouldn't feel her trembling.

CHAPTER 14
MESSAGES

MARA EMERGED FROM SLEEP gradually. She was warm, comfortable, and tired, but a slice of sunlight fell over her face and chased tiredness away. She stretched and felt Neil's heavy arm around her waist.

"Neil?" His warm weight was comfortable, and she toyed with the idea of letting him rest for longer, but she had a feeling they'd already overslept. She tried to worm her way out of the sleeping bag, but the motion disturbed Neil, who tightened his grip and mumbled something about it still being night. "It's morning," Mara said, trying—and failing—to smother her smile. "And you're being clingy."

"Mm-hmm." He pulled her still closer.

"You brought this on yourself," Mara said, reaching behind him and pinching his backside through the sleeping bag.

He started awake and blinked. "Wh—huh?"

"Good morning." She pecked his lips before he could figure out what had happened. "Time to get up."

"Uh." Neil pressed his forehead against hers. "Go back to sleep, Mara. It's too early."

"Sun's already high."

Neil twisted to look behind himself and groaned at the light coming through the window. "Cripes. I'm going to be late for work."

Mara watched him clamber out of the sleeping bag and shake himself awake. He stretched, his muscles straining against his shirt, then turned his smile on her. "Want some bacon and eggs for breakfast?"

"I don't want to make you late," she said then caught herself. "Wait—did you seriously bring bacon?"

"Another half hour won't kill me, and yes." He offered Mara his hand and pulled her to her feet. "Go get changed while I start cooking."

Mara swapped her pajamas for jeans and an old T-shirt in the bathroom. She'd planned to start cleaning that morning and had chosen clothes that she didn't mind ruining. She wasn't brave enough to try running water into the bathtub, so she washed her face and arms in the sink and attempted to control her hair in the cracked mirror. By the time she returned to the bedroom, the smell of bacon saturated the air.

Neil had changed into his work clothes while she was gone and was digging the bag of lettuce out of the icebox. Mara settled, cross-legged, on the sleeping bag beside him. "You're tenacious, but I won't relent, not even for bacon."

He took a handful of the lettuce leaves for himself then dropped the bag back into the icebox with a wry smile. "All right, I'll let you win this time. I called Joel and told him to expect me by nine thirty, and I'd like to check on Mum before then, but I still have a few minutes before I need to leave. Is there anything you'd like me to help with?"

Mara accepted a plate of eggs, bacon, and untoasted bread. "I should be right for this morning. I thought I'd start with clearing some of the junk. I'll throw out that art display on the dining table so we can have an actual surface to eat off of tonight."

"Sounds good. I left gloves, bags, and face masks in the box there."

She grimaced around a piece of bacon. "Face masks?"

"For mold. Don't worry about patching holes—I'll come by after work and start the reconstructive stuff then." Neil was wolfing his food down. "Does your phone get reception here?"

"Most of the time." Mara avoided mentioning that the battery was dead. Neil was a fixer, and the fewer problems she gave him, the less he would feel compelled to do. He was already juggling work, his mother, and Mara's house; she didn't want him wasting his time on recharging her phone, too.

"Great. Call me if there's any trouble. I don't mind leaving work early if you want help or even if you need me to pick you up—"

He's still worried about the house. "I'm sure I'll be fine. There's plenty to do, so I can guarantee I won't be bored."

"Hmm." Neil frowned as he swallowed the last of his sandwich.

"Where'd you go last night, by the way? I woke up, and you weren't there."

"Too excited to sleep," Mara lied. "Went exploring. Now get out of here before your tardiness reaches unforgivable levels."

"I'll clean up first—"

"Don't bother; I can take care of it." Mara plucked his jacket from where he'd draped it on a box and shook it out. "Say hi to your mum for me."

"Will do. Call me if you need me. And Mara?"

"Yeah?"

"Love you." Neil kissed her, and her heart gave a delightful flip. She kissed him back, pushed his jacket into his hands, and shoved him toward the door. She then went to one of the rooms on the other side of the house and watched through the window as he got into his car and sped down the driveway.

She sighed and leaned against the windowpane then jerked back with a grimace. It was filthy. *Well, it's not like I'm going to get cleaner as the day progresses. Better start now.*

Mara returned to the bedroom, turned off the gas heater, and disassembled the cooled cooker. She washed the cooking plate and cutlery in the bathroom then laid them on top of a box to dry. The plastic plates went into a garbage bag. She then tore a spare bag off the roll, found the gloves Neil had told her about, and went downstairs.

She found the dining table's abandoned settings fascinating and almost wished she could leave them as they were. Rather than throwing the plates out one at a time, she picked up the starchy, crunchy tablecloth's edge and wrapped the whole setting up in a bundle before shoving it into a bag. She tied the bag off and dropped it into the foyer.

The tablecloth had protected the table from most of time's aggression, and the surface looked almost new after a quick wash. Mara then worked her way through the eight wooden chairs, taking frequent trips into the kitchen to rinse the dust off the cloth. When she finished, she had a dinner table not even Neil could be squeamish about.

"What next?" Mara muttered then sighed and turned toward the kitchen. It was the natural choice but also the dirtiest room in the building. She grudgingly put on one of the face masks, collected a new bag and stack of cloths, and spent the next four hours throwing out anything too dirty to salvage and cleaning everything else.

"Cripes." Mara leaned her back against the still-wet tile wall and flexed her shoulders as she surveyed her work. She liked to think of herself as decently hardened against gross things, but the kitchen had been a graveyard for cockroaches and mice in various stages of decomposition. She hoped the critters had only congregated there because of the plentiful spilled food and weren't indicative of what she could expect in other rooms.

There were two cooking options in the kitchen: a gas stove, which Mara suspected had been installed by the house's last owners or not long before them, and an ancient wood oven. Mara had tried the stove and was delighted to find it still worked. The oven was halfway to falling apart but still looked like it would be functional provided the vent wasn't blocked.

Mara reached into her pocket to check the time on her phone then remembered she'd left it, dead, upstairs. She looked through the window and guessed it might be early afternoon. *Neil said he'd come around three. What else can I get done before then?*

She was trying to work through the house in the most logical order, which meant recreational and spare rooms would be left for last. *We've now got somewhere to eat and somewhere to cook, so I guess next on our list are the bathroom and bedroom.*

Mara returned upstairs and cleaned out the sink and the toilet as well as she could. She didn't bother cleaning the mirror or the bathtub as they both needed to be removed. Next was the bedroom.

Their temporary beds needed a quick kick back into place, after which Mara packed away the cooker and gave the floor another sweep. She was about to leave when the tattered wallpaper caught her attention. *I wonder if it would be hard to pull off? The wood underneath should still be intact, right?*

Neil's knife sat with the cutlery that was drying on top of the box. Mara took it and approached the wall beside the door. She carefully scored the paper and tried pulling it back. To her delight, the glue had deteriorated over the years, and the paper came away more easily than she'd expected. She caught sight of wood underneath and began tugging harder. The paper pulled free in long shreds. Mara stepped back to throw a wad aside and caught sight of the paint underneath.

She hoped it was paint, at least. A dark brown *something* had stained words onto the wood. Mara could make out

"R HOUSE THIS" and fragments of other letters. Frowning, she continued tearing the paper away until the wall was clear. She wished she hadn't.

**THIS IS OUR HOUSE THIS IS OUR HOUSE
THIS IS OUR HOUSE THIS IS OUR HOUSE
THIS IS OUR HOUSE THIS IS OUR HOUSE**

CHAPTER 15
CHOPPED

THE WORDS REPEATED ACROSS the wood in a variety of sizes and levels of legibility. Mara scowled as she scanned them. "It's *my* house now," she muttered then kicked the pile of wallpaper scraps to one side. The words were faintly scuffed, making Mara think someone had tried to scrub them off before covering them with the tacky wallpaper. "Damn it; I'm going to need a different bedroom now."

The faint rumble of an engine drew her attention, and Mara crossed to the other side of the house to watch Neil's car pull up the driveway. She didn't know what time it was, but she suspected he'd come earlier than he'd promised.

She hurried downstairs and was just in time to open the door for Neil so he could back through it. His arms were filled with new boxes.

"Hello, beautiful." He set the boxes down and kissed her cheek. "Looks like you've been busy."

A clump of garbage bags filled one corner of the foyer, and Mara nodded at them with almost maternal pride. "Got the kitchen clean, and at least one of the ovens is functional. How'd work go?"

"One of our employees—we still don't know which one—finished a wall before the wiring was put in. We're going to have to tear it down and start over. Can't complain otherwise."

"I dunno; that sounds like something I'd get fantastic complaining mileage out of." Mara tweaked open the lid of one of the boxes and saw a jumble of tools. "You came prepared."

"And I can guarantee that the only tool I'll really need is the one I forgot to bring." Neil knelt and pulled a handful of objects out of the box. "I bought you a few things, too. Here."

Mara held out her hands. Into them, Neil dropped a compact USB flashlight, a canister of pepper spray, and a Taser. "You bought me a bug zapper?" she asked, raising the last object up to see it more clearly.

"Just in case." Neil's hand wrapped around hers. There was a flicker of worry in his eyes, but he quickly covered it with a smile. "I can't stay here every night, as much as I would like to. So I want to make sure you're safe."

"Worrier," Mara said fondly. She squeezed his hand and pocketed the equipment.

"I got you something else, too." Neil's smile widened into a more relaxed expression as he turned toward the door. "Come and have a look."

Mara stood on the porch and crossed her arms as Neil opened

the back of his car and began working a two-seater couch out. "What on earth…?" Mara muttered. "How did you even fit that in there?"

"I played a lot of Tetris as a child." Neil freed the chair from the car and flipped it over his shoulder with a grunt.

Mara shook her head as he carried the couch past her. "Hold up. I never agreed to this. Did you buy it? How much did it cost?"

"A friend was throwing it out. I thought you might like it. It'll give you somewhere to sit." Neil crouched slightly as he wormed the chair through the front door. "Where do you want it? In the sitting room?"

"A friend was throwing it out, huh?" Mara narrowed her eyes as she followed Neil. "I guess he was sick of looking at his brand-new couch."

Neil lowered the chair in front of the sitting room's fireplace. "You're not accusing me of *lying*, are you?"

"No." Mara pursed her lips. "But you've stoically refused to look me in the eye since you first announced this."

"Hah." Neil finally turned toward her. His sheepish grin was all the answer she needed.

"Take it back." Mara fought to keep her irritation from creeping into her voice. "I don't need charity."

"Mara—"

"No. I'm sorry you had to go to all of the trouble of bringing it here, but I can buy my own furniture, thank you very much."

Neil sighed and gave an exaggerated shrug. "Well, what a pain. I guess if you don't want it I'll take it to the dump."

"Don't play dumb. Just return it to whichever store you bought it from."

"My friend was throwing it out anyway. And I don't know of anyone else who needs a couch, so—"

"Ugh." Mara pinched the bridge of her nose. Neil was determined to be stubborn; she could tell he was fully prepared to carry through with his threat and throw the chair out. *It would be good to have somewhere comfortable to sit. And it's a nice pattern, too...* "Fine, leave it. But don't think I'm happy about this."

"Love you too." Neil pecked her cheek before she could bat him away. Mara failed to contain her grin.

"Now, is there anything I can help you with, or would you like me to start patching holes?"

"Holes, please. I'm going to clear out one of the upstairs bedrooms." Mara felt an unpleasant lurch as she remembered the writing on the upstairs wall. *He's going to find out about it one way or another; he'll cope better if he hears it from me.* "I got the wallpaper out of our room, and there's a bunch of graffiti underneath it."

"What sort of graffiti?" Neil had fished a pair of gloves out of his back pocket and was pulling them on.

"Eh...mostly gibberish."

He glanced at her, and his eyes narrowed. "What aren't you telling me?"

"Nothing important." Mara beamed at him, but that only deepened Neil's frown. He abandoned the box and climbed the stairs. She sighed and followed close behind.

"Oh," Neil said as he read the message. "Who wrote this?"

Mara threaded her arm through his. "My guess is a vandal. This place was notorious for being haunted, yeah? I'll bet some kid came in during one of its vacant phases and painted that message over the wall to enhance the atmosphere. The next owners obviously didn't appreciate it, but they couldn't afford to remove the wood, so they put wallpaper over it instead."

Neil squeezed her hand. "Move to a different room. One with bare walls."

"Will do, boss."

Mara searched through the upstairs while Neil began work below. The remaining empty rooms all had broken windows, so she eventually settled on a furnished room with intact panes. It would be a lot of work to clear the furniture out, but she decided she'd eventually need to do that either way.

Her new room also faced the backyard. It must have had a blue theme, but the bedspread and curtains were all badly faded. Mara bundled the loose cloths into a bag then worked the mattress off its frame. She'd dragged it halfway down the stairs before Neil noticed and ran to help her. "Don't put your back out," he said, pulling the mattress out of her hands.

"My back's fine, but thank you."

Neil threw the mattress onto the porch where they wouldn't trip over it, then Mara followed him into the dining room and whistled at the sight of the enlarged hole in the wall.

"It's not as bad as it looks." Neil took up the crowbar and began working another damaged plank free. "I'll have this one done before I go home tonight. It won't match the other wood, I'm afraid—there's no way to fake the *super-old* aesthetic you've got going on—but you can stain it a similar shade."

"I'll be happy as long as it looks more like the *before* photo of the Titanic rather than the *after*."

Neil snorted and turned back to his work. Mara squeezed his shoulder on the way past and returned upstairs.

Deciding what furnishings should stay and what should go was difficult. Once the organic, decayed items—the rugs, curtains, and mattress—were gone, Mara examined the wooden bed frame, wardrobe, and bureau. To her surprise, the latter two were empty and solid. The bed, on the other hand, had suffered from its burden. The mattress had become wet at some point and rotted through several of the slats. She kicked at one of them, and it snapped. *This is definitely older than twenty years, and it was probably a cheap bed when it was bought, too.*

It wouldn't fit through the doorway whole. Mara tried to pry it apart, but the wood had fused together. Grumbling, she returned downstairs.

Neil had worked quickly. The damaged part of the wall had been removed, exposing the support beams, and he'd moved on to measuring cut marks on the fresh wood he'd bought.

"I'll pay for that," Mara said, nodding toward the wood. "Just give me the receipt."

"Don't worry; I got it."

"Neil." She narrowed her eyes and put a hint of threat into her voice. "I'll accept your help, and I'll even take your couch, but only as long as you're not out of pocket at the end of this. Give me the damn receipt."

"Okay, okay. Stubborn thing." Neil double-checked a measurement then sat back on his haunches. "I'll get it for you later. Did you need any help upstairs?"

"Huh? Oh, yeah—did you happen to pack an ax in one of those boxes?"

Neil's eyebrows rose. "I didn't, but I found a cupboard full of tools in the laundry last night. You might have some luck there. What do you need an ax for?"

"I want to dismantle a bed, and an ax seems like the easiest way to do it."

Neil jumped to his feet and hurried after Mara as she wove through the kitchen. "Whoa, what? I'm sure there's an easier way to pull a bed frame apart—"

She wrenched the cupboard doors open and caught sight of a large ax sitting in the corner. "No, this'll do nicely." She flicked the cobwebs off it and hefted it to head height.

Neil made a faint noise of alarm and nudged the ax so that the blade wasn't pointed at Mara's face. "You'll lose a limb with that thing."

"Naw, lumber jacking runs in my blood. Apparently, some of my great-grandparents were woodcutters."

"That's not a reassuring resume."

"You need to worry less." Mara tried to lower the ax and use its blunt head to nudge Neil's chest, but the shifting center of gravity threw her off balance. Neil had to step backward to avoid being bludgeoned. "Keep patching the walls. I'll have the bed sorted before you're done."

"Jeez," Neil muttered. "Let me do it at least."

Mara clutched the ax close to her body and ducked out of the laundry. "Not a chance!" She raced up the stairs, ignoring Neil's pleas for her to slow down, and skidded down the hallway and into the bedroom. The bed waited under the window. Mara approached it, raised the ax above her head, and let gravity swing the heavy metal toward the wood. The blade hit the brace near the headboard and became lodged. Mara strained to pull it free then tried wiggling the handle, but the ax wouldn't budge. She turned to find Neil standing behind her, arms crossed, and gave him the sweetest smile she could muster. "I don't suppose you'd be kind enough to free it for me?"

"Mara." Neil seemed to be fighting to keep a smile off his face. "I have a moral obligation to prevent you from decapitating yourself. Yesterday you promised you'd compromise sometimes. So let's compromise. We can butcher the bed if you like, but let me do it."

Mara gave the ax a final tug then sighed. "All right, okay. Have at it, Mr. White Knight."

Neil's calloused fingers brushed a strand of hair away from Mara's face as he passed her, and the simple gesture was enough to fill her chest with a bubbly, giddy feeling. She settled back against the wall and watched him pull the ax free with one hand.

Why was I arguing again? A grin grew as she watched Neil swing the ax in a smooth, practiced motion. His muscles bulged under his shirt, and there was something deliciously attractive about the way he stood, legs braced and head high, that Mara found irresistible. *This is* way *more fun.*

Neil made quick work of the bed. He seemed to have an innate sense of where the fragile sections were and attacked them efficiently. Within a minute, Mara was left with a headboard and bed end, and a mess of splintered braces and slats.

"Don't touch the wood," Neil said as he leaned the ax against the wall. "It's full of splinters. I'll cart it downstairs."

"Or…" She stepped closer and examined the slats. "It's dry. I have a fireplace now. Why don't we have a fire?"

Neil considered the idea, as though testing it for Mara-killing-potential, then nodded. "That could be nice. If you can wait until tomorrow, I'll bring some hot chocolate and marshmallows."

"Heck yes." Blackwood House was proving to be a series of firsts for Mara. *First proper home. First basement. First cozy fire.* She kicked at one of the broken planks, and a flicker of white caught her attention.

"*What did I just say about not touching the wood?*" Neil moaned as Mara plucked the square of paper out from the kindling. It was a small black-and-white photo. She held it up to the window's light and choked.

The photo showed a middle-aged man with a heavy brow, bushy white moustache, and sideburns. The cut of his coat, and the picture's blurry, faded quality suggested it had been taken either in the late nineteenth or early twentieth century.

"What the hell?" Mara muttered.

Neil peered over her shoulder. "Ha, he looks like he'd be fun at a party."

"That's my great-great-grandfather."

CHAPTER 16
VICTOR BARLOW

NEIL WAS SILENT FOR a moment then cleared his throat apologetically. "Sorry. I'm sure he was a very nice man."

"Nope." Mara dropped the picture and shook out her hands, as though simply touching the paper would taint her. "He was a famous spiritualist. The first in our family, if you want to listen to my parents. Where the hell did it come from?"

"Probably wedged into a crack in the bed frame. It must have come loose when I cut it up."

"But…but…why's it in my house?" A horrible, panicky feeling was building in Mara's chest. Her throat felt too tight to draw breath, as though a pair of cold hands had wrapped around it and were slowly squeezing. *I'm suffocating.* Mara clawed at her neck, trying to pry away the invisible influence, as she staggered back from the slip of paper that rested on the floor.

Neil was at her side in a flash. His hands, large and warm and firm, fixed over hers and pulled them away from her throat before she could mar the skin. He dipped his head to whisper in her ear. "Shh. Calm down. Everything's going to be all right. Relax."

"Okay," Mara gasped. "I'm okay."

"Come here." Neil pulled her against his chest and rubbed her back.

Mara fisted her hands in his shirt and buried her face against him as she waited for the rushing, whistling noise to fade. The tightness in her throat abated, and she sucked in ragged breaths. "This is my house." She was shocked at how broken her voice sounded. "I bought it so that it would be a space free from my past. So what's *he* doing in it?"

"You said he was famous." Neil's hands continued to move over her back in a firm, reassuring motion. "And Blackwood was supposed to be haunted. What if one of the owners hired him to talk to the spirits?"

"And…what? He left his photo as a parting present?" Mara laughed but was bordering on hysteria. "I bet he was the sort of jerk who would do something like that."

"Shh, Mara. Can you walk? Let's go downstairs."

Mara let Neil lead her to the ground floor and settle her into one of the dining room chairs. She stared at the hole in the wall while he moved into the kitchen to wash a glass from the cupboards and fill it with water. Through the intact panes, she could see little squares of the weedy grass that surrounded her house. They twitched in the light breeze.

Neil slid into the seat at her side and nudged the glass against her hand. "Here. You'll feel better if you drink something." His hand brushed across her back again, but Mara hardly noticed.

As the shock faded, it was replaced by anger. She felt violated. Her home—her *sanctuary*—had been tainted by a hackneyed spirit medium, one of her own family, the very people she'd been determined to never again cross paths with again. *How dare he enter my house?*

"Did you want to paint any of the rooms? The natural wood look is really nice, but one of my buddies has some leftover off-white cans if you want them."

Mara blinked at Neil, confused by the sudden change in subject, then chuckled drily. "It's okay. I'm fine now. You don't need to try to distract me."

Neil sighed. His fingers lingered on her back, tracing patterns through her shirt. "Jeez, Mara, I'm sorry about this. It sucks, huh?"

"It absolutely sucks." She gulped the water then set the glass aside as the hot anger cooled into decisiveness. "But you know what? I don't care. Just like with the murders. What happened in this building a hundred years ago has no effect on its ability to be a good home today. I don't care if Victor built the damn place. He doesn't own it anymore."

"Was that his name?"

"Victor Barlow, yeah. He was my great-great-grandfather. My parents had a photo of him in the living room. Ugly fellow, isn't he? But they thought he was the best thing since chai lattes. I think he was twisted. Apparently he had a bunch of—and this is in very sarcastic quotes, mind—'groundbreaking spiritual theories.' Which means he was especially efficient at hoodwinking the public out of their money." Mara gave Neil a grim smile. "Sorry to drag you into all of my stupid history."

"I'm just glad you're not hyperventilating anymore." Neil dipped his head to nuzzle Mara's neck. "Want me to get rid of the photo for you?"

"That would be awesome. Thanks." She nudged back. "For everything."

"Any time, sweetheart."

Mara turned back to the hole in the wall. The weeds outside were becoming more shadowed as afternoon merged with evening. "Want to have an early dinner?"

"That sounds good. I brought fresh food. Would you like to start preparing it while I clear the bedroom out?"

"Yeah. We should probably make use of the remaining daylight, huh?"

She found it surprisingly easy to put Victor Barlow out of her mind as she fiddled with the kitchen's dated stovetop. The excited, happy glow from the afternoon had been dampened but not entirely extinguished. By the time Neil reappeared to help her assemble the burgers, Mara almost felt like herself again.

They propped a flashlight upright in the center of the dinner table so that its light diffused over the ceiling, then set the table with freshly washed crockery. While they ate, Neil kept her entertained with a myriad of recent news, gossip, and stories about his neighbor's cat. He was lively and happy, and Mara could almost believe he'd forgotten about her breakdown until he pushed his plate to one side and said, with impeccable casualness, "Is it okay with you if I stay tonight?"

"Huh?" Mara narrowed her eyes over her bun. "What about your mother?"

"She'll be fine. And I didn't get that wall's hole patched after all. I thought I could fix it up tomorrow morning before work."

Mara put her hamburger back on the plate, wiped her hand clean, then leaned across the table to stroke Neil's cheek fondly. "That's really sweet. But I'll be okay. Your mum needs you more."

His eyes fluttered closed as he leaned into her touch. "I'd rather you weren't alone tonight. Especially after—"

"I'm a big girl. This afternoon was nothing." Mara smiled and found it was a genuine expression. "Go home and get some rest."

Neil wet his lips and tried a final time. "Come with me?"

"Nope. Relatives aside, this house is still way cooler than yours. And don't forget—you promised me a fire tomorrow night."

"With hot chocolate. I remember."

Mara moved closer to press a kiss to Neil's mouth. He met her halfway, and his hand curled around the back of her neck to hold her close. She savored the moment then drew back reluctantly. "Now get out of here, you beautiful man. I'll see you tomorrow."

The warm, comfortable glow Neil had lent her lasted until his car's engine faded from her hearing. She stood on the porch for several long minutes after his vehicle's silver roof dipped behind the trees. Then she shuddered and zipped her jacket up.

After four years of running from your family, they've come back to snap at your heels.

"No." Mara ground her teeth as she re-entered the house. "They're not here. They haven't been for decades."

But they were. And not just any cousin or quirky uncle, either, but him. *What did your parents call him? 'The greatest spiritualist of the century,' wasn't it? 'An inspiration.' They were hoping you'd follow in his steps.*

"Neil's right. He was probably just here for a one-night séance or something. Maybe he dropped the photo while he was staying in the spare bedroom. Or it might not have been him at all but someone who admired him."

He's tainted the house, though.

"This is *my* house now!" Mara's voice rose until her words echoed through the empty building. "Mine! You can't touch me here!"

A sprinkle of dust fell from the ceiling and drifted past her shoulder. A low, drawn-out groan came from her right, and Mara swiveled toward the living room.

The rocking chair, sitting below the window, rolled on its struts.

"Shut up!" Mara crossed to it in five long paces. She kicked the chair, but that only made the movements quicken. *What's it doing here? Why did Neil move it back?*

Mara closed her eyes, took a deep breath, then grabbed the chair's back and dragged it across the room. She pressed it against the wall so that it couldn't move no matter how strong the wind was, then let her breath whistle out through pursed lips, slumped, and turned back to the stairs.

She went straight to the spare bedroom, and a small part of the happy glow returned. Neil had not just removed the splintered bed but had also shifted the bureau and wardrobe into a corner, swept the floor, and arranged the sleeping bag and heater in the room's center. *He cares way too much.*

Mara stretched. Aches radiated from strained muscles, and her limbs felt heavy from the day's exercise. *Better make it an early night.*

She brushed her teeth in the fractured mirror, turned the heater on, then crawled into bed fully clothed. The dreams started as soon as she closed her eyes.

CHAPTER 17
INTRUDER

THE NIGHTMARE WAS FRENETIC and disjointed. She saw the ax, its tip darkened by long-dried blood, arcing through the air. Children's voices laughed and chattered and screamed in the background. Their garbled noise was interspersed with the whistle and dull thud of the ax as it dismembered its victims.

Mara gasped and sat upright. Sweat drenched her and stuck her shirt to her back. The room was pitch-black and quiet, but she sensed she wasn't alone. "Neil?"

A creak echoed from somewhere deeper in the house. Mara's mouth went dry. She fumbled for the flashlight she'd left beside her head, turned it on, and swung the light across her room. Everything looked the way she remembered it. No shadowy figures watched her from the corners, and the walls stayed free of scribbled messages.

The creak came again, this time nearer. Mara shuffled out

of her sleeping bag and stood, shivering despite the heater. She raised her eyes toward the ceiling as the sound came closer, and watched as a small trickle of dust fell from where the boards were strained.

There's someone in the attic.

Mara was painfully aware of how loud her breathing was, but she couldn't stifle the noise. She felt wholly different than the night before, when she'd brazenly stormed the attic, Neil at her side. *Because I was safe then. I had Neil. And Neil would never let anyone hurt me.*

She was ashamed of how panicked she felt. She turned toward her phone on the bureau, but it was, of course, still dead. *No car. No phone. And now I have company for the second night in a row.*

The footsteps reached the other end of the house, turned, and retraced their path. Mara shrank backward as they passed over her, barely four feet above her head, and continued along the building.

Then the footsteps were joined by the rocking chair's groans. Mara mouthed a swear word. All rationality seemed to have drained from her. Thoughts of the footsteps belonging to a harmless squatter or teenager had dissipated. *A sane, reasonable person wouldn't return to an occupied house after being kicked out.*

A door slammed. As if in response, the rocking chair's creaking sped up. Mara backed toward the window, desperate for more light than her small flashlight provided, but thick clouds covered the moon and left the outside world in nearly perfect darkness.

The footsteps stopped above Mara's head. She turned her

flashlight toward the ceiling as her stressed, panicked mind tried to guess where in the attic the intruder might be standing. *I'm in the room next to the bathroom, which is halfway along the house. So this would be almost exactly under…*

Motion caused Mara to swivel toward the window.

…almost exactly under the hole.

It had happened too fast for her to be sure, but Mara thought she'd glimpsed a tumble of limbs and hair plunging down the side of the house.

The rocking chair's tempo was frantic. Mara stood rooted to the spot, not daring to breathe, her heart beating itself bruised against her rib cage. Then, with a gasping, shaking breath, she stepped closer to the window, leaned forward so that her forehead pressed against the icy glass, and pointed her flashlight toward the ground.

It was a bad angle. The light illuminated a circle of the long, weedy brown grass but not much more. Mara raised the flashlight higher and stood on her toes to see a few inches closer to the building.

A patch of the grass at the edge of her light seemed to be bent as though something large and heavy had landed on its base and pushed the tips outward. She couldn't see what that object was, though.

Mara swore again and lurched away from the window. Cold sweat trickled down her back. The rocking chair's rhythm finally seemed to be slowing; each creak was longer and more deliberate.

You have to go down there and check.

Mara felt rooted to the floor.

If someone fell from the attic, they'd either be dead or close to it. They could be suffering; you can't just leave them there.

She shook her head and clenched her fists. Tears burned at her eyes, but she took a choked gulp of air and blinked them back.

You have *to check.*

The door slammed. Mara jolted as though she'd been electrocuted, then she burst out of her room, flashlight beam waving erratically. She took the stairs two at a time to the foyer and paused there, panting and swinging the light back and forth. To her left, the rocking chair creaked a final time then fell still.

"Come on, come on, come on," Mara panted, willing herself to open the front door. The house seemed deliberately silent as though holding its breath in anticipation of her choice. She stretched her hand toward the doorknob and touched the cold metal.

The feeling that she wasn't alone persisted. It was so strong that it sent prickles across her skin. She was convinced that there was someone standing behind her, breathing just a fraction too quietly for her to detect. She didn't dare turn around to check.

Stop being such a damn coward. Someone could be bleeding out on your lawn. Mara twisted the handle. The unseen figure felt closer, as though it were stretching a hand toward her, its fingers a centimeter from the back of her neck. Mara lurched onto the porch and slammed the door behind her. The feeling of having company vanished.

"Crap," Mara muttered as she flicked her flashlight over the yard. Heavy rain clouds had built across the moon so that she was only able to see what was in her small circle of light. The tall, sickly trees played tricks on her eyes as their shadows leaped erratically.

She followed the porch as far as she could then slid over its edge. The weedy grass grew halfway up her thighs. She was still wearing her jeans from the day before, but they were thin, and the sensation of the plants scraping against her legs made Mara's heart leap into her throat.

She followed the wall and rounded a corner to reach the back of the house. Then she stopped, one hand pressed against the worn wood, the other pointing her flashlight toward the grass that clustered close to the building. Now that she was still, she became aware of the animal noises that surrounded her. Crickets and bats competed with each other to be heard, their calls rubbing Mara's nerves raw. The trees shifted in the light breeze and scraped their branches together.

"Come on. Keep moving." Mara took a step forward then stopped again. *What if they're already dead? What if their head burst on impact and scattered brain pulp and skull fragments across*—"Keep moving," Mara repeated then staggered down the back of the house and toward the dark patch where the grass had been indented.

She didn't allow herself to stop until she was right beside the area. Then she bent over, hands on her knees, to gulp in dry, shaky breaths. She felt as though she might throw up.

There was a definite indent in the grass. Something heavy had crushed the stalks. But whatever—or whoever—had been there was gone.

Mara felt relief, but not enough to overcome her fear. She stepped away from the patch of grass and focused her light on Blackwood House's face. She could see her room immediately above her.

Mara moved farther back, pressing deeper into the yard until the weeds and shrubs became too dense to move among them easily, and pointed her flashlight higher. Above her room was the roof's hole, dark and gaping. Mara traced the path from the hole, over her window, and to the patch of ground. It was a perfect line.

Someone did fall, then. But they're no longer here. Did the grass pad their landing enough for them to walk away? It's a two-story drop. They should have broken bones at the very least. Even if they were able to walk or crawl somewhere to hide, they wouldn't be well enough for the walk back to town, especially in the dark. What does that mean? Would they hide in the forest? Or go back into the house?

Mara panned her light across the building a final time. A splash of color in the master-bedroom window caught her notice. It slid out of sight before Mara could train her flashlight on it, but she could have sworn she'd glimpsed sunken cheeks and crazed eyes set in a pale face.

CHAPTER 18
SHADOWS

MARA STAYED IN BLACKWOOD'S backyard, mouth open and mind blank, for a long time. She kept her light directed at the window, but there was no further motion.

Did I imagine it? The glass might have caught and reflected the light of the flashlight. I'm so keyed up it would be easy to think I saw a face.

Mara swallowed heavily and began skirting the building, continuing in the same direction as before. As she walked, she kept flicking her flashlight's beam between the land ahead of her, the woods surrounding her home, and the windows of the house, but she saw no signs of life.

The air inside Blackwood was a few degrees warmer than outside. Mara closed the door behind her with a relieved sigh. She held still and listened to the building. There were no footsteps. The rocking chair stayed quiet. She could make out a bat's screech coming from the woods, but the house was almost perfectly silent.

I have to search it. Damn, but I wish I had Neil with me. Mara edged her way through the dining room and into the kitchen. She'd cleaned all of the surfaces the day before, but the cutlery and plates still needed sorting and washing. She opened a drawer, cringed at the sight of five dead cockroaches among the implements, and fished out a long, serrated knife.

With just one person, it was impossible to search the rooms and watch the exits at the same time. Instead, Mara moved slowly and stealthily, pausing often to listen. If another person tried to sneak through the house, she knew she would hear them. The building was too old to move more than a few paces without straining the wood.

She started upstairs, beginning with the master bedroom, where she'd thought she'd seen the face, and working her way down the hallway. She searched in closets, under beds, and behind curtains—any place that was large enough to hide a human. Her new bedroom was the most welcoming out of all of them; the heater had left it warm, and the light she'd left on was comforting. Mara wished she could huddle in the room, close her eyes, and pretend the remainder of the house didn't exist. She left it reluctantly.

The graffitied room made her pause again. She reread the message—*this is our house*—and turned away with a grimace. Once she reached the far end of the hallway, Mara turned around and surveyed the row of closed rooms.

She'd been careful to shut each door behind her, banking on the idea that they were likely to creak when opened. As long as she listened carefully, she should hear anyone who tried to get in…or out.

Mara then turned to the rickety stairs behind her. She tried to suppress the shudder, but it wormed its way out of her. The attic would need to be searched. The thought made her nauseated.

The steps groaned under her feet as she climbed them. Mara placed the knife on the top step and gripped the flashlight between her teeth to raise the trapdoor. Once she'd pushed it past vertical, gravity took over and brought it down against a chair with a heavy *whump*.

She climbed the final steps and shined her flashlight over the long room. The white cloths still lay in pools on the ground where she and Neil had dropped them. A few new leaves had come through the roof's gaps to rest on top of them, but otherwise, the attic looked unchanged from the night before. Mara looped through the room, moving far more cautiously than she had the first time, as she searched through the multitude of nooks and crannies.

Warm air from the heater in the room below had risen through the floor and taken the chill off the attic, and Mara was sticky with anxious sweat by the time she'd gone through the room twice. She wove around an old ironing board to reach the hole in the roof and pushed her head outside to see the ground below.

That's a horrible fall. I wouldn't like to bet on surviving it.

Mara's skin prickled. The sensation of not being alone had returned, but it was stronger this time. She could almost hear it—the tall, gaunt figure pacing the attic floor, hands out-stretched, preparing to push her through the hole and send her tumbling to her death.

Don't let your imagination run away with you.

A floorboard behind Mara creaked. She skidded around, bumping into a chest of drawers, a muffled cry choking in her throat. Her reflection, wide-eyed and blanched white, stared out of a full-length mirror.

Mara pressed a shaking hand to her heart. She felt as though she could collapse. "Get in control," she muttered, trying to steady her hands. "Get downstairs. *Search* downstairs. Then lock yourself in your room and wait for morning."

She crossed to the trapdoor and half climbed, half tumbled down the steps, pulling the hatch closed after her. She wished she hadn't asked Neil to break the lock. After a moment of thought, she brought the knife to her shirt's hem and carefully sliced off a long, thin strip. She then threaded the fabric through the remaining bolts and tied it off. It wouldn't be strong enough to stop the door from being opened, but it would serve as an easy way to check whether anyone had come that way.

The hallway doors had all remained closed. Mara passed them to reach the stairs leading to the ground floor and paused on the landing to listen. Silence.

"Okay." She crept down the stairs, keeping to the edges to avoid loose boards. "One more floor to check. This'll be fine. We're fine. It's all good."

She'd nearly reached the ground floor when the wailing started again. It began as a low and faint cry but gradually built as Mara crossed the foyer and paused in the living-room entryway.

Nothing to panic about. Mara stared at the fireplace, where the noise echoed from, and willed herself not to imagine a child crying. *Just the wind.*

The rocking chair was propped against the wall, exactly where she'd left it. That disturbed Mara. She'd been certain she'd heard its groans shortly after waking up. *What happened, then? Did someone move it away from the wall then push it back? Or was I hearing something else… A door, maybe, dragging on its hinges?*

There was nowhere for a person to hide in the living room, so Mara moved past it and into the bare-walled library, then into the recreation room, and hurried through the kitchen, laundry, and dining room. The wind's wails muffled her own footsteps, but she also knew they would mask any movement made by an intruder, so she searched the rooms quickly. She re-entered the foyer, panting from the exertion, and finally lowered the knife to her side. *I'm alone. I think. I hope.*

She scanned the room a final time as she backed toward the stairs. Something large and pliant got in the way of her legs, and Mara tumbled over it. The knife skidded out of her hand and hit the wall as she landed on her back. She grunted, sat up, and pointed the flashlight toward her feet. One of the garbage bags had tripped her.

Lightning flashed. Mara glanced up, startled, as a square of bright illumination appeared over the wall beside the stairs. And in that square…

Mara screamed. She skittered backward, only stopping when her shoulders hit the wall, and stared in horror at the shadow of twitching, kicking legs suspended high above the floor.

Breathless Jenny's words echoed in her mind. *The killer hung himself.*

The light, which streamed through the window set high in the foyer wall, only lasted for a second. The figure bled into the darkness as it faded.

Gasping almost at the point of choking, Mara clutched her flashlight in both hands and directed it toward the banister.

The space below was empty.

Mara's mouth couldn't even form the words she wanted to use. The flashlight's beam moved shakily as she turned it from the banister to the wall and back again. There was no hanging body. "Impossible..."

She fumbled behind herself for the knife. Her fingers fixed on the sharp end, and the dull blade cut into her. She hissed but didn't dare let it go. Instead, she brought the knife to her chest and clutched it close.

A low drone in the distance joined the fireplace's wails. Mara couldn't think what it was.

I have to get out of here. Neil was right: there's something wrong *with this house.*

Using the wall, she pulled herself to her feet then staggered to the door. The droning became louder when she wrenched it open. *Rain*, she realized even as her legs carried her across the porch and to the steps, which she followed to the white-stone walkway. A large, hard raindrop hit her face. She stopped walking and let her arms slump to her sides.

It'll take all night and half of the morning if I try to walk to town. I could strike out through the woods and try to find another house, but I'm more likely to become lost.

The rain intensified, quickly wetting Mara's skin and soaking into her clothes. Her teeth were chattering. She turned, slowly and reluctantly, to look back at Blackwood. *How long until morning? How long until Neil arrives?*

Lightning flared, bathing the area. Mara darted her eyes over the windows and open door, but they were all empty. The heavy, menacing feeling had abated. The building no longer seemed like a threat; once again, it was nothing more than a house.

"*Uhhhh.*" Mara pressed the backs of her hands against her eyes. *What other options do I have?* Reluctantly, she climbed the porch steps and re-entered the house. When she closed the door, she noticed the wailing had ceased.

She was shivering and craved the warmth and relative security of her room, but her throat felt raw. She went into the kitchen, found the glass Neil had given her that afternoon, and filled it with fresh water. As she drank, she faced the archway leading into the dining room. When lightning flashed, she caught a glimpse of weeds through the hole Neil hadn't finished patching.

Something creaked to her left, and Mara swiveled toward it. *Was that a floorboard? No... It sounded more like...*

She placed her glass back on the counter and slunk forward,

nerves jumping as she edged into the recreation room. The base-ment door inched open.

Mara licked her lips and panned the light across the furniture and walls. There was no movement except for the door, which slowly ground to a halt. *It's just the wind. Remember, this house is holier than a priest's convention. Plenty of breezes and gusts to disturb things. That's all.*

She circled the door and trained her light on the stairwell. It was empty, but she couldn't see all the way down. Gritting her teeth, Mara moved to the door then past it, onto the first step, and crouched so that her flashlight could light the entire tunnel.

The door slammed closed behind her. Mara jolted, and the flashlight tumbled from her hands. She clutched at it as it fell, but missed, and its light went out as it hit the corner of a step. Mara braced herself against the cold stone wall as she listened to the flashlight bounce down the stairwell and finally skitter across the floor.

"Crap." Her voice escaped as a squeak. Mara swiveled to the door behind her and turned the handle. It ground in its setting then squealed and broke off in her hands. "*Crap!*" She tried to fit the handle back into the hole, but something wasn't lining up, and she couldn't see what she was doing wrong without any light.

Mara slumped to her knees. The darkness felt overwhelming, bordering on smothering, and the stairwell was narrow enough to make claustrophobic chills crawl over her arms.

Find the flashlight. See if it will turn back on.

She began creeping down the stairs, using all four hands and feet and taking each step carefully. The stairs were steep, and she had to rely on touch to ensure she wasn't about to tumble to her death. The downward climb seemed to last forever, and the air grew colder the lower she moved. She was trembling uncontrollably by the time she found herself on level ground.

Mara inched forward on her knees, hands outstretched in search of the flashlight. Her fingers brushed over a jumble of uneven stones but couldn't find the metal she desperately needed. It was becoming hard to breathe. Her heart pounded painfully, and she knew she was hyperventilating, but she couldn't stop herself. All she wanted was the safety of a sliver of light. Her fumbling search became more and more erratic as she moved farther into the basement. Her chest felt as if it might explode.

Then a door slammed, and Mara found she wasn't able to breathe at all.

CHAPTER 19
KINDLING

MARA WAS WALKING ALONG the upstairs hallway toward the stairs that led to the ground floor. Strangely, her feet didn't make any noise on the normally creaky floorboards. *Another dream, huh?*

She reached the landing and looked into the foyer. It was filled with unfamiliar furnishings; a coatrack sat by the door, next to a shelf for shoes. The building looked far newer than what Mara was used to. The wood was young and bright, and there were no rotten patches. Despite the freshness of the building, most surfaces were coated in dust. The single jacket hanging on the coatrack looked as if it hadn't been touched in years.

Mara turned and saw she wasn't alone. Robert Kant stood beside her as he tied his rope to the railing. The knowledge of his identity was instinctual, but Mara knew she was right. Robert's face was long, thin, and grizzled. Stubble ran the length of his chin and neck, and a fresh cut on his forehead allowed a trickle of blood to build onto his hooked nose. *Did the final victim cause that when she escaped?*

He looked like a killer, Mara thought. There was something cold and dead in his deeply sunken eyes that suggested his humanity had been worn away decades before. His fingers were long and knobbly but deft as he checked the rope's knot. He then raised the noose at the other end of the rope and slipped it around his neck.

Why'd he do it? Mara wondered as Robert flipped his long legs over the edge of the banister. *The police won't reach him for hours. He could have fled and never been caught.*

Robert sat on the banister with his legs dangling over the other side. He stared at the foyer for a second then tipped forward. Mara flinched as the rope went taut.

She moved out of the dream sluggishly. Something felt wrong about her body as though she were no longer in control of it. She tried to move her hand but couldn't tell if she had succeeded. Darkness surrounded her. *Maybe I've gone blind.* Far above her, thumping noises were interspersed with a voice. Mara felt her heart flip unpleasantly. *Where am I?*

She was cold; she knew that much—so thoroughly, crushingly cold that it hurt to draw breath. There was something hard pressing against her cheek and arm. *Stones. That's right. I'm in the basement, aren't I? How long have I been here?*

The sounds drew closer, and Mara realized they were footsteps—not the slow, ponderous, creaking footsteps from the attic but quick and heavy paces. A voice yelled, "Mara!"

Neil. The thought of him was like hot courage injected into her chest. Mara shifted, found that her hands did work after all, and pushed herself into a sitting position. "Here," she tried to call, but the word escaped her as a croak.

"Mara, answer me!" He was frantic. The pure fear in his voice hurt, and she could hear doors being thrown open as he searched for her.

She swallowed, coughed, and tried again. "I'm here!"

The footsteps paused then resumed, racing closer. Mara tried to stand, but her legs still wouldn't obey her.

"Mara?"

The basement door was wrenched open, and a rectangle of light lit up her world. *Oh good; I'm not blind after all.* Mara caught the silver shine of her flashlight barely a foot away. She raised her eyes and saw that she'd come to rest against the section of wall beside the red stain.

Feet clattered down the steps, then Neil was kneeling in front of her, his warm hands rubbing her arms and cheeks. "Mara—oh, Mara—what happened? Are you hurt?"

"Nah." Mara grinned at the frightened blue eyes. She'd never been so happy to see another human. "Wind blew the door closed behind me, and the handle fell off. Thanks for letting me out. Is it already afternoon?"

"No, it's morning. Jeez, you're freezing. And wet. How'd you get wet? Never mind—come here—" Neil's arms encircled her. He pulled her to his body then lifted her slowly and carefully. "Is that okay? I'm not hurting you?"

"Hmm." Mara closed her eyes and leaned her head against his chest. He was deliciously warm. She wanted him to never let go.

"Okay, hang on; let me get you out of here."

Mara kept her eyes closed and felt the gentle rock as Neil climbed the stairs. She couldn't stop a smile at how ridiculously precious he was being. He cradled her as though she were made of glass. "Did you say it's morning? What're you doing here so early?"

"I read something that worried me, so I skipped work to visit you. But I couldn't find you anywhere, and you didn't answer when I called. You scared me half to death, sweetheart."

"Hmm?" Mara opened her eyes to look at Neil's face. His normally sunny eyes were dark, and he'd tightened his lips into a thin line. "What'd you read?"

He hesitated then shook his head. "I'll tell you later. We need to get you warm first." They'd reached the top of the stairs. Neil turned toward the kitchen. "We'll get you in the car and put the heater on."

Mara frowned. "No, I don't want to leave. Not yet. I've got some thinking to do."

"Mara—"

"I don't want to leave."

Neil held his breath for a moment then released it. "Fine. Okay. Hang on." They passed through the foyer and into the living room. Neil, moving slowly and with infinite care, lowered her onto the couch he'd purchased the day before. "Is that okay? Are you comfortable?"

"Oh my gosh; it'll be fine. I'm not about to shatter if you bump me."

Neil knelt beside her and scanned her face. He cupped her cheek in one hand and caressed her skin with his thumb. "Cripes, Mara, your lips are blue, and you feel like ice. Are you hurt anywhere?"

"No, I'm good. Just let me sit for a bit."

"You might have hypothermia." Neil took her hand and stroked it. "We need to get you to a hospital."

"Hah!" Mara batted his hand away. "No, I don't have hypothermia, and I don't need a hospital. Stop worrying. You'll give yourself an aneurism."

"Nnnh." Neil frowned then stood. "Stubborn thing. Stay here; I'll be back in a moment."

Mara listened to him move through the building. He filled a kettle and put it on the stove then darted upstairs and returned with blankets, the portable heater, and an armful of clothes. He set up the heater at her feet then cleared his throat. "Your clothes are wet. You'll need to change."

"Hmm? Sure." Mara pulled her shirt over her head. She couldn't stop a wicked grin from forming as Neil turned red and pointedly stared at the ceiling. "Underwear, too?"

"Th-that should be fine." He held out the spare clothes, still keeping his eyes averted, then ducked out of the room as soon as Mara took the bundle.

As she shimmied out of her wet jeans and into the new pants, she tried to sort through her memories of the night before. They were jumbled and cluttered and confusing. One thread wove through the whole experience, though: she'd been terrified.

That's ridiculous. I'm supposed to be the strong one. I kill the really big spiders Neil is squeamish of. I suggest searching the attic. I broke a would-be mugger's nose last year then kneed him in the privates for good measure. So why'd I fall apart in the dark?

She remembered standing in the rain, seriously considering walking to town. She remembered vowing that she would jump into Neil's car and ask him to take her away as soon as she next saw him. She remembered shaking so badly that she hadn't been able to hold the flashlight properly.

Let's approach this in our favorite way: with a large helping of rationality. What are we certain of? What are the possibilities?

There was one thing she knew above all else: ghosts didn't exist. Which meant every experience from the night before would have to have come from some physical cause.

First, I heard the footsteps. That was weird. Then I thought I saw someone fall past the window. That was weirder. I can't think of any explanation except that someone was in my attic.

Neil entered the room with a steaming cup of tea then made a faint choking noise and turned away. Mara realized she'd become distracted and hadn't put the sweater on. "Sorry." She shimmied into it. "I'm decent now."

Neil, still red and unable to repress a shocked smile, handed her the cup. "Drink that." He left the room again.

So, someone was in the attic. Or possibly multiple someones. When I checked the backyard, it was clear a heavy object had fallen there.

But I can't imagine a person would be in a fit state to walk away from an accident like that. Unless they had an accomplice to carry them...

A clatter made her turn. Neil was carrying an armful of the bed's broken frame to the fireplace. He stacked some of the smaller fragments in the grate, poked two fire starters under them, and lit the arrangement. He was gone again in a flash.

Next, I thought I saw a face in the window. But I already have a possible explanation for that: the flashlight's reflection. It was such a brief glimpse that I can't know for sure either way. I searched the house, and it was empty to the best of my knowledge.

Mara sipped at the drink. It was chamomile tea; Neil had brought his favorite brand to share with her.

The wailing sound was just the fireplace. I'd thought I'd also heard the rocking chair creaking even though it was against the wall. But it could have just as easily been the basement door swinging. I saw it being blown open with my own eyes. As for being trapped in the basement... Well, that was just a combination of bad luck and terrible timing.

Mara had been so engrossed in her thoughts that she hadn't noticed Neil's return until he pushed a bag of marshmallows into her hands. "Eat those; you need to get your blood sugar up."

"Oh, nice! You got the nongeneric brand." Mara pulled the bag open and began picking out the pink balls.

Neil had brought extra blankets, which he wrapped around her shoulders and legs before turning to tend to the fire. Mara pushed a handful of the marshmallows into her mouth and chewed as she thought.

In that lightning flash, I'm certain I saw twitching legs. The shadows fell in such a way that they would need to be cast by something hanging from the banister, but there was nothing there when I looked more closely. So what was that?

It took her a minute to come up with the answer, and when she did, she almost slapped herself for not thinking of it before. *The light came through the foyer window. And outside of that window is a whole bunch of trees. I saw the shadows of branches being tugged about by the wind, and my overexcited mind interpreted them as twitching legs.*

"How are you feeling?" Neil took her hand and squeezed it. "You're still cold."

"No, no; I'm defrosting nicely. Come and sit with me a moment. I want to leech off your body heat."

Neil finally seemed to be relaxing. He took the seat beside Mara and wrapped his arm around her shoulders. She leaned against him, rejoicing in the sawdust-and-herbs scent, and shook the bag of marshmallows toward him. He took one.

"That's a nice fire you made," Mara said, smiling at the crackling flames. The small pieces of wood were halfway to being consumed, and the fire was beginning to catch on the larger slats. "Thanks."

"Shh. Drink the rest of your tea. I'll make you some more when you're finished."

Mara laughed. "You're like the micromanaging aunt I never had."

Neil kissed the top of her head. He still seemed uneasy, but

Mara couldn't remember ever being so at peace before. Her experience was completely explainable. There were no evil presences lurking in her home—just natural causes, coincidences, and the strong possibility of an intruder... And intruders were only human. They could be dealt with.

The fire and portable heater were taking the chill off her. Mara had no idea how long she'd been in the basement, but it couldn't have been more than a few hours—her clothes were still wet from the rain. That meant she'd woken no earlier than three in the morning. *Just goes to show how crazed a mind can become in the middle of the night. And Blackwood isn't exactly the coziest house I've ever seen. No wonder so many of its occupants thought there were supernatural presences.*

"Mara." Neil kissed her again. "Are you feeling well enough to tell me what happened last night? It was obviously something big."

"Not really. I heard some noises and let them freak me out. Nothing bad happened." She was starting to feel sleepy and nuzzled closer to Neil. He hugged her tightly, but she thought it stemmed more from anxiety than contentedness.

"Did something wake you?"

"Um." *He won't like it, but I need to tell him about the footsteps.* "I thought I heard someone in the attic again."

Neil's arms tightened further. "I found a knife on the kitchen counter."

"Yeah, that's mine. It was just a precaution."

"And the bloody handprints on the wall?"

Mara pulled back and frowned. "What?"

"Didn't you see them? They're in the recreation room."

Mara wormed herself out of his arms and hopped through the library.

Neil jogged after her, calling, "Slow down; you're not wearing shoes. Watch out for nails!"

Now…how do I explain this? Mara faced the recreation room wall opposite the basement door. Bright-red handprints were smeared across the wood. *Is this from the intruder? I should have seen them when I investigated the open basement door, though, surely?*

Neil caught up with her and tried to wrap a blanket about her shoulders. "Come on; we can talk about this later. You need to rest."

An idea struck Mara, and she raised her hand. She'd cut herself when she'd grabbed the knife the night before, and blood was smeared over the fingers and the top half of the palm, though most of it had rubbed off when she'd scrabbled over the basement's floor. *Did I touch the walls last night? I can't remember. The marks look close to the right size…*

"You said you weren't hurt!" Neil's anxious tone had returned with a vengeance. He swept Mara into his arms and, ignoring her protests, carried her back to the fire. "Sit still while I get the first aid kit. Can you remember when you last had a tetanus shot?"

"It's just a nick!" Mara called after Neil's retreating footsteps. "It doesn't even hurt! Jeez."

CHAPTER 20
SURVEILLANCE

MARA SCOWLED AT THE flames flickering in the fireplace. *How'd blood get on the walls? I don't remember touching them, but then, I was panicked, so I very well could have. Poor Neil. They must have freaked him out pretty badly. No wonder he's fussing.*

Neil returned with the kit. She patiently let him clean, disinfect, and bandage the cut even though she thought a couple of Band-Aids would do the job just as well.

"There." Neil tied the bandage off with a relieved sigh. "Are you hurt anywhere else?"

"No, I'm good now." Mara brushed her fingers over the dressing and smiled. "Thanks."

Neil settled down beside her, and Mara retrieved the bag of marshmallows from where she'd dropped it. They watched the flames for several minutes, both absorbed in their thoughts. Neil was the first to break the silence. "I'm concerned about the footsteps you heard last night."

"I am, too." Mara dug through the bag for a pink marshmallow. "I've been thinking about it. There are a couple of nonscary explanations. One, I could have been imagining it. I'd only just woken up, after all. Two, it could be a delusion brought on by some unknown cause. I had the house tested for gas leaks before moving in, but the results could have been wrong. Or there might be mind-addling mold. Or I could just be going crazy. I've heard that if you're worried that you might be crazy, you're fine, so I discounted insanity. But then, does discounting insanity mean I could be insane after all? I sort of got stuck in an infinite loop with that one."

Neil laughed and ran his fingers through her hair. "Okay, other than that."

"Right. Otherwise, the floorboards could be shifting in a very particular way to make it sound like there are footsteps. I can't see that being the answer, though. It would be too much of a coincidence. The final option is, unfortunately, the most likely: that there was someone in my attic for two nights in a row."

Neil continued to play with her hair, but a frown had settled over his eyes. "That's what I'm worried about."

"But that leaves us with a tough pair of questions: *who* and *why*? If the house *did* have a stalker, I can't believe he's still in action today."

"Maybe he passed the job on to someone else."

"It's possible, I suppose, but a heck of a coincidence that two people would obsess over the same building. And it still leaves us with the *why*. If they wanted to rob or attack me, they've had plenty of opportunities. More disturbingly, we've searched for them—multiple times—without finding any evidence of occupation, let alone an actual person."

"And you're a long way from any other properties," Neil said. "They can't be staying here; otherwise, we would have found signs. They can't be driving to the house each night, or you'd hear the car. And it's a hell of a commute if they're walking or biking."

"Maybe they have a house in the woods."

Neil shook his head. "That makes no sense, either. There are no other pathways into this area, which means a squatter wouldn't be able to get to town without using your driveway. And it looked like it hadn't been traveled in years when we came to view the house."

"Hmm." Mara chewed at her thumb. "This is a tough one. Maybe they parachute in and teleport out?"

Neil chuckled. "Well, we can't discount it."

"Regardless of the *hows*, I'd like to stop it from happening again. We can start with buying a new padlock for that attic door."

"I can do one better: surveillance equipment."

Mara's eyebrows shot up. "Come again?"

"I wanted to surprise you with it, but I guess now's as good a time as any. A friend is getting rid of his generator and offered it to me. I can use it to get some basic power hooked up for you. Nothing flashy—not lights in every room or anything—but it would be enough to run a couple of bulbs and some security cameras. You can borrow my laptop for the next few nights, connect it to the cameras, and see into the attic twenty-four, seven."

"Neil." Mara clasped his face between her hands and stared into his bright-blue eyes. "You're brilliant."

The eyes crinkled into a smile. "You like it?"

"C'mere." Mara flipped over to straddle his lap. In the same motion, she pulled his head down to kiss him. He moaned and kissed back. His hands circled her waist, cautious and careful at first then eager as he held her close. Mara felt herself turn to liquid under his touch. His lips felt too good; she tangled her fingers in his hair as his tongue played across her mouth. His hands roved over her back, feeling her through the sweater, then pressed her tight to him. She arched into him—then froze as an upstairs door slammed. The simple sound brought a stab of the same terror she'd felt the night before, like a primal Pavlovian response.

Neil pulled back. "Was that—"

"Just the wind." Mara let her hands rest on his chest, which rose and fell rapidly.

Neil's hands stayed on her back, but his eyes flickered over the room. The tension had returned to his arms. Mara gave him a final, gentle, lingering kiss on his cheek then slipped off his lap. "Guess we need to focus on the task at hand. There's only so many hours in a day."

"Yeah, and we'll have to move quickly to get everything set up for tonight." Neil shifted forward to throw more wood on the fire, and Mara tilted her head to one side as she admired his back.

"Hey, that reminds me: Why'd you come in this morning? You said you read something."

Neil shot her a glance then turned back to the fire. "That's right. But you've had a horrible night. I don't want to throw this on you as well, so let's talk about it later. It's not even important, really—"

"Oh, come on; I'm curious now. Tell me."

Neil settled into the chair beside her but kept his eyes on his hands. "Yesterday, when you found that photo of your grandfather—"

"He's really more like my great-great-grandfather." Mara intertwined her hand with Neil's. "But yeah, I remember."

"Do you also remember saying you wouldn't care even if he'd built Blackwood?" He gave her a tight smile.

Mara gaped at him. "You don't mean—no, you're joking—you've got to be joking. You can't possibly be saying—"

"I did some research last night. Victor Barlow built Blackwood House."

"What the—" Mara flopped back in the chair and stared at the walls surrounding her. *My house. My home. Built by* him?

"It's one heck of a coincidence," Neil said quickly, seemingly trying to move Mara past the shock. "Apparently, he bought this plot of land from the government in the late eighteen hundreds. You might already know, but he was a woodcutter before he became a spiritualist. He built Blackwood over five years or thereabouts."

"Cripes," Mara whispered. She tightened her grip on Neil's hand. "Tell me everything. How long did he stay here?"

"Eight years altogether. Three years after the building's completion. He, uh…" Neil cleared his throat. "Robert Kant, the serial killer, murdered him."

Mara took a moment to let that fact sink in then bared her teeth in a dark, bitter smile. "Good."

"Is it?" Neil looked worried again.

"It's a fitting end for him, huh? If he'd been any good at his job, his precious spiritual friends could have warned him about what was coming. But they didn't, and he paid the price. How'd Robert kill him?"

"Uh…" The worried look was intensifying. "He stabbed him in the basement."

"Nice, nice. Did Victor die quickly? Or did he, like, bleed out over a few hours, or…?"

"Mara, sweetheart, precious lamb, darling kitten. Do you really need to know *that*?"

She pouted. "I can see you're not as excited by this news as I am."

"I doubt even Hannibal Lecter could rival your delight, but regardless, it's way too morbid for me. Did you think that maybe that stain in the basement isn't from a burst pipe, but blood?"

"Ooh, yeah—sweet!"

"No, Mara, it's awful!"

"Let's go check it out again. Victor's last moments, immortalized on my own basement wall!"

"Mara, no! Bad Mara! Down, girl!" Neil clutched Mara about her waist and tugged her back against him when she tried to rise.

Mara laughed and let herself go limp in his arms. He smiled and pulled her closer so that she sat in his lap and could lean against his shoulder.

"Okay, all right; I'll leave it be. Sorry for weirding you out."

"Sorry about your house's history."

"Eh." Mara patted Neil's chest. "Honestly, I'm sticking to my guns. What happened a century ago is no longer important. Victor built this house. Victor died in this house. I didn't know either of those facts when I bought it, and it didn't bother me then, so I won't let it bother me now." She closed her eyes as Neil brushed stray hair out of her face. "Blackwood has nothing to do with Victor anymore. This is *my* house."

The words escaped her before she realized how closely they echoed the red-stained message in the upstairs bedroom. She shivered, and Neil pulled her closer with a gentle cooing noise. "You're still cold. I shouldn't have excited you like that. Just rest for a minute, my darling."

"Pfft." Mara grinned at Neil. He felt good and warm and cradled her gently, and his heartbeat was steady in her ear. "I don't need coddling. But I'll allow it. Just this once." She closed her eyes and enjoyed the touch of his fingers along her jaw and neck. "Love you, Neil."

"Love you too, Mara."

CHAPTER 21
GHOST STORIES

MARA CROSSED HER ARMS and scowled. "These prices are ridiculous. Can't we just get a webcam?"

"If we're going to do this, we may as well do it properly. I'll cover them."

She turned on Neil, ignoring how uncomfortable she was making the pimply sales assistant who hovered behind them. "No. No more handouts, Neil. Don't think I didn't notice how modern and clean that generator is. Your 'friend' wasn't really throwing it out, was he? Or was it the same friend who didn't want his brand-new couch?"

Neil raised his hands to pacify her. "It's fine. I'm the one who wants to install the cameras. Let me take care of it—"

"I'm not looking for a sugar daddy. I'll pay for them."

"We'll call it your birthday present."

"Ah, ah!" She jabbed Neil's chest. "No! You said working on the house would be my birthday present!"

"Okay, make it your Christmas present, then."

"It's *September.*"

"I like to shop early." Neil shrugged blithely as Mara narrowed her eyes.

"September is way too early for Christmas shopping. Isn't that right, Barry?"

Barry, the sales assistant, blinked at her. "Uh, uh…"

"C'mon, Barry; back me up here."

Barry's eyes darted to the muscled, six-foot-four Neil. He swallowed. "I dunno…"

Poor Barry. He has no idea that Neil is the safe one. Mara turned back to the row of surveillance cameras with a huff. "Well, regardless, these prices are stupid. It's *my* house; I'm getting a webcam, and I'll punch anyone who disagrees with me."

"Uh, sure; webcams are over here…"

Neil went outside to make a call while Mara picked out and paid for a cheap webcam. The checkout lines were long, and it was nearly ten minutes later when she pushed out of the store and saw Neil ending his call. He smiled brightly as she approached.

"Ready to go home?" Mara asked.

"Actually, I was hoping we could visit someone first." Neil opened Mara's door despite her objections then rounded the car to get in the driver's seat. "And before I tell you who, I want to remind you that you promised to occasionally compromise."

Mara squinted at him as she buckled up. "What're you planning?"

"I called Jenny. I didn't tell her much, but I think she guessed we were having problems with the house. She said she didn't want to see the building go back on the market, so she bent a few rules for us…"

"Okay, that's promising. I like bending rules." Mara could imagine Jenny, already sweet on Neil, being more than happy to cut through red tape.

"She gave me the contact details for the last occupants. Well, their *daughter*, Chris, specifically."

"Wow, seriously? It's been twenty years. Wouldn't the details be out of date by now?"

"They were, but the people at the number I called were able to give me the daughter's cell phone number. So I called her, and she agreed to meet us."

"Seriously? You managed all of that? I was in that store for no more than ten minutes. You'd make a killing working in a call center."

Neil beamed at her. "You're okay with it, then?"

"Hm." Mara pursed her lips. "I guess there's no reason *not* to meet. But I reserve the right to yell at her if she tries to say there was a ghost."

"She was only eight when they moved into the house, so she might not remember much, but I'm hoping she can tell us about the building, whether she heard anyone walking through the attic and things like that."

"That's clever thinking. We might pick up some clues from her. At the very least, she can tell us why they left their dinner on the table."

"There. Just because I'm not allowed to be your sugar daddy doesn't mean I can't be useful."

Neil took them out of town. The houses were gradually replaced by trees, which occasionally parted to give them a view overlooking a lake.

"Where're we meeting her?" Mara asked.

"She gave me directions to a café that overlooks the water. Apparently, it's a popular stopping place for families that travel through the area. Shouldn't be far now—"

They rounded a bend in the road. Ahead was a large shack-like structure with a dozen picnic tables arranged haphazardly on one side and a grassy parking lot on the other. Mara thought it looked precariously close to the cliff's edge, as though a solid gust of wind could send it tumbling into the lake.

Neil parked, and they rounded the building to the eating area. It was empty save for two families, an elderly couple, and—at the table closest to the overlook—a lone woman. She waved to them.

"Chris?" Neil asked as he shook her hand. "Thanks for meeting us. This is my girlfriend, Mara."

Mara shook the woman's hand as well. Chris looked younger than twenty-eight and had a pale, pinched sort of face, but her smile seemed genuine. "No problem. Sorry for dragging you out here instead of inviting you home. My pop's going into Alzheimer's, and I don't want to remind him about Blackwood if I can avoid it."

"I'm sorry to hear about your father," Neil said at the same time as Mara asked, "Why not?"

Chris blinked at Mara then laughed delightedly. "Wanna dive right in, huh? Okay. Let's." They slid into their seats—Chris on one side of the table and Mara and Neil on the other—and leaned close together as though it were a discussion that couldn't survive eavesdroppers. "Before I share my side, I want to know—how long have you been in Blackwood?" Chris asked.

"Uh…" Mara counted the days and was surprised at how few there were. She felt as though she'd already been staying there a month. "Today's the third day."

"Wow. And it's already bad enough to call me?" Chris propped her sharp chin on her laced fingers as her eyes darted between them. "My family made it a solid two weeks before running."

"Why?" Neil's troubled expression had returned. "What happened?"

"A whole buncha stuff. My parents—bless 'em—tried to shield me from most of it, but I still saw plenty. At first there were footsteps and slamming doors in the night. No one thought much of it at first. There were five of us: my mum, my pop, and my two younger brothers—though James was only a baby at the time—and we all thought it was one of the others making the noise. Then there was that infernal rocking chair that wouldn't stay quiet. Dad eventually threw it out."

Neil frowned. "We have a rocking chair, but I can't say it's been loud."

That's right; he hasn't heard it yet. Mara opened her mouth to say something but decided to let Chris continue her story instead.

"Mum says she felt cold spots and sometimes even presences.

But she only told me that years after we moved, so I don't know how accurate it is. What else? Sometimes the tap water would run red."

"Rust," Mara said, and Chris shrugged.

"Could be. My younger brother said he heard crying at night. I remember my parents arguing a bunch, but I'm not sure about what. Mum was convinced our house was haunted, and she tried to call local priests, but none of them wanted anything to do with it. One thing that really freaked us out was the master-bedroom door. It had scratches over the wood. Dad sanded them off on our second day in the house, but on the tenth, the marks were back."

"Seriously?" Neil's face looked calm, but he'd clasped his hands on the table, and his knuckles bulged white from the tension. "We've seen that door. You're saying the marks...reappeared?"

"Are you sure we're talking about the same door? Because Pop destroyed it. When the marks came back on the tenth day, he pulled the door off its hinges, took it out to the backyard, and chopped it into little slivers. I remember being really scared. My pop was a meek, nerdy accountant—he never even yelled at me when I misbehaved. And there he was, down to his undershirt and pajama bottoms, dragging this huge ax toward the door with a look of such intense...ugh, what's the word? Hatred? Malice? My mum locked the door and didn't let him back in until he calmed down, which was hours later."

Neil was chewing at his lip, so Mara wrapped her arm through his to calm him. "Well, we've got a door in the master bedroom with scores across it. You don't know how they could have gotten there?"

Chris shook her head. "Sorry."

"Might've been a vandal after you left. What else happened?"

"Well, with everything going on, Mum wanted to move. But my pop had spent a lot on the place and insisted we could stick it out. Things just got worse, though—we were getting hardly any sleep and yelling at each other during the day. James, who was just a baby, cried incessantly. Then my other brother, Paul, started acting odd and saying things that didn't make sense. He told me children came to visit him in the middle of the night. He called them the red children."

"Bad dreams?" Mara asked.

"Guess they might've been. Mum says I started sleepwalking, though of course I don't remember it. She also says things were moved around the house. There was a bunch of junk in the attic which we mostly threw out that turned up again after a few days, and no one's sure who brought it back in."

Mara was engrossed. She leaned even closer to Chris, despite the tension in Neil's arm. "What made you leave? There was a whole dinner spread over the table."

"Ha!" Chris slapped the bench, startling Neil. "Really? No one threw it out? Sorry about that. The last day was pretty crazy. Mum and Pop had been arguing a bunch, and James seemed even more unsettled than ever. So Mum cooked up this huge meal. I think she was trying to reunite us as a family or something. But we'd barely started eating when Paul excused himself. He said he needed to get something from his bedroom. But he didn't come back and didn't answer when Pop called him. Mum got really worried and went to look for him. She was barely out of the dining room when she started screaming her head off."

For every inch Mara drew nearer, Neil seemed to shrivel back an equal distance.

"We all ran out, of course, and saw Paul at the top of the stairs. He was standing on the banister. Not *beside*, mind, but *on*. He was a plump six-year-old; it's a miracle the wood didn't break. Anyway, he'd somehow found a length of rope and had one end tied to the banister and the other around his neck."

Chris flicked a speck of dirt off the table. "I've never seen Pop run so fast. He got to the top of the stairs in what seemed like less than a second and pulled Paul back just as he started to teeter forward. Good thing, too; the fall probably would have broken his neck. Mum was still screaming. The baby was crying. I saw Pop staring at Paul with this look of absolute despair. Paul's eyes were blank. It was like the person inside had been sucked out and left nothing but a human husk. He didn't seem to know where he was or what he was doing."

Neil made a faint, anxious sound in his throat.

"Pop looked from Paul to us and back again then said, 'We're going.' That was it. Mum took James, Paul, and me and bundled us into the car. Dad grabbed an armful of our clothes and our more important memorabilia. We stayed in a hotel room until we could rent an apartment. Then we sold Blackwood for a pittance and never went back—not even to collect our furniture."

"Wow," Mara breathed.

Chris shrugged and pulled a cigarette pack out of her pocket. She offered the box to Mara and Neil, both of whom declined, then lit one and took a deep drag. "My parents don't like talking about it if they can help it, but I've caught snatches over the years. My pop said the house made him incredibly, irrationally angry—like he was always half a moment away from snapping. Mum says she never felt safe there. Once we were away from the building, Paul seemed to lose most of his memories of it, and James finally started sleeping through the night again."

"Do you have any idea what could have caused that?" Neil's voice was raspy, and Mara squeezed his arm in an effort to comfort him.

"I did some research afterward, but I didn't come up with any convincing theories. I'm glad we got out, though, considering its history."

"You didn't know about the murders when you moved in?" Mara asked.

"I didn't—I was just a kid, remember—and Mum and Pop had only been told about the first ones. That murderer. Rob, uh—"

"Robert Kant." Neil's mouth was in a firm line. "What do you mean by *first ones*?"

"Well, he was just the beginning, wasn't he?" Chris glanced between her companions and swore. "No one told you about the others? There've been a whole bunch of violent deaths in Blackwood. Some suicides. Some murders. If deaths could stain a place, consider Blackwood saturated."

"The house is nearly a hundred and fifty years old," Mara said, speaking carefully. "It's a rural property that, for most of its history, would have been a long way from any hospitals. Of course you can expect a certain number of deaths to occur in it."

"How many were there?" Neil asked, and Mara shot him a glare.

Chris shrugged. "I didn't look into it very thoroughly. It was starting to weird me out, plus my research options were limited before the internet. But I was able to confirm eight deaths in addition to Robert's murders."

"Jeez," Neil said.

"There's nothing wrong with the house." Mara was starting to feel attacked, as though the criticisms leveled at Blackwood applied to her personally. "I'm sorry you didn't have a pleasant two weeks there, Chris, but everything you've told me is explainable. *Of course* you were all on edge after a fortnight of disturbed sleep and a crying baby. And Paul—you said he was only six, right? Kids often do stupid, bizarre things. If you're trying to imply he was possessed or—"

"I never said he was," Chris said.

Neil leaned close. "Mara, calm down."

"Okay." Mara inhaled deeply and tried to force her voice back to its previous subdued volume. "Sorry. But I really do think your experiences were a combination of bad luck, a stressful situation, and group hysteria. No offense."

"None taken." Chris exhaled a plume of smoke and gave Mara a searching look. "I get the impression you don't believe in ghosts."

"I'd put more stock in the Tooth Fairy being real."

"I never believed in them when I was a kid," Chris said, turning to gaze over the drop-off to the blue lake below. "And truthfully, I have no clue what I believe now. But, for those two weeks I was inside Blackwood, every shred of my being knew that ghosts were real. I wouldn't return there for all the money in the world."

CHAPTER 22
DUSK

"FOR THOSE TWO WEEKS, I knew ghosts were real," Mara mimicked around a mouthful of the burger Neil had bought her before leaving the eatery. "Could she even hear herself?"

"Hmm." Neil kept his eyes on the road. The hardness hadn't faded from around his mouth.

"Clearly, *something* weird was happening to them, but it wasn't supernatural. They were strung out and stressed and went into it with preconceived notions of the house being *tainted* by previous deaths. I mean, how ridiculous is that?"

Neil glanced at her out of the corner of his eye. "Did you know about them?"

"The other deaths? No. And I don't want to. As Chris so elegantly showed us, becoming obsessed with a supposedly grisly history can only build up ideas about what your own experience should be like."

"Hmm."

Mara watched Neil's face. Her rants weren't producing the usual smiles and chuckles. She pulled a fry out of the bag and held it toward him. "Here."

He opened his mouth, and Mara slipped it inside. She was relieved to see his face soften as he chewed it.

"Don't let Chris worry you, okay?" She took a fry for herself and turned her attention back to the road. "It's been twenty years since she was in Blackwood. People naturally embellish stories over time—plus, a lot of it came secondhand from her parents."

"What about the scratches on the door? And the rocking chair she says they threw out?"

A wicked grin spread over Mara's face. "Well, I guess Blackwood could be home to ghosts who also happen to be interior decorators. *No, darling, we simply* must *have a rocking chair by the fire; otherwise, the house's feng shui will be* completely *thrown off! Oh, and look how precious these bloody handprints are when coupled with the sinister wall writing! We simply* have *to add more!*"

Neil finally laughed though he shook his head at the same time. "C'mon, Mara; don't joke about stuff like that."

"What? You can't seriously think Chris is right."

"I…" He hesitated. "I want to keep an open mind."

Mara felt hot frustration bloom in her chest but squashed it. *Calm down. He's anxious. Let him process this at his own pace.*

"Anyway," Neil continued quickly, "we'll get your surveillance equipment set up. At the very least, that should be a solution for the footsteps if they happen again."

It was midafternoon by the time they arrived back at Blackwood. While Neil installed the webcam and generator, Mara moved through the house to reassure herself that the nighttime visitor hadn't returned during her absence. The strip of shirt was still tied around the attic trapdoor's lock, and the rooms seemed untouched. She stopped to examine the prints on the walls of the recreation room and pressed her hand over one to measure the size. It didn't match exactly—her hand seemed slightly larger— but the marks were smudged and overlapping, making it hard to get an accurate comparison.

"Come and have a look," Neil called from her bedroom. Mara jogged up the stairs and found he'd set up their makeshift surveillance center on top of the bureau.

"Sweet." She bent to look at the setup. The laptop connected to a series of extension cords that ran out the window and down the side of the building to the generator Neil had installed in the backyard. A USB cord snaked out of the room, down the hallway, and up the stairs to the attic. The laptop showed a hazy, low-contrast image of the attic.

"It's bad quality right now because the lighting is inconsistent," Neil said, indicating the shafts of light coming through the holes. "Its night vision isn't great, either, but it'll be good enough to see anyone who's up there."

"I'm not expecting them to be back tonight," Mara said, thinking about the indent in the grass. "But better safe than sorry."

"Right. Now, if there's nothing else I can help you with, I'll go and fix that hole I abandoned yesterday."

Mara pecked Neil's cheek and watched him leave. She then took one final look at the laptop screen, on which the cluttered furniture and decaying boxes seemed to blend into each other, before turning to follow Neil downstairs.

She'd been procrastinating because she knew it would be a slow, labor-intensive task, but it was time to clear out the kitchen drawers and clean what she could. As she plucked dead insects off the cutlery, she marveled at how different it felt to know the person who had owned them. She'd had no scruples about adopting the furniture before, but the more intimate knowledge of the family that had purchased, used, and enjoyed the knives she was polishing made her feel vaguely squeamish. *Relax. It's no different from secondhand. And you've owned a lot of secondhand stuff over the last few years.*

She could hear Neil whistling between the whine of the circular saw and the drill. It was a comforting sort of noise and made her feel less alone. The daylight gradually turned to gray tones as the sun dipped behind the trees. The light was affecting Mara's eyes, so she set aside the still-to-be-cleaned plates and shelved the washed ones in the freshly scrubbed cupboard. Neil appeared in the doorway.

"Well, your dining room is officially whole," he said as Mara wrapped her arms around him and rested her head on his chest. "And I got partway through the rotten patch in the foyer, too. I can finish it off tomorrow."

"Heading home now? Say hi to your mum for me."

"Don't worry; I'm coming back. I'll have dinner with Mum and make sure she's settled then spend the night with you."

Mara frowned. *The talk with Chris really unsettled him. But this is my house, and they're my house's quirks. I can't rely on Neil; I've got to figure this stuff out for myself.* "As much as I appreciate the offer, I'm pretty well set up here. I'll call you if there's any sign of trouble, okay?"

"Mara—"

"No, come on. I've got to draw a line somewhere. You already skipped work today because of me. I don't want to suck up any more of your time."

"Well, *thank goodness* I skipped work, or my girl would be doing an impression of a Popsicle by now."

"It wasn't that bad," Mara grumbled. "And I'm putting my foot down. My house, my rules. I'll see you tomorrow, *after* you're finished at work, okay?"

Neil sighed and dipped his head to rest it against Mara's. "Is there anything I can say to change your mind? Anything at all?"

"Nope."

"All right, fine. See you tomorrow, beautiful." He kissed her softly, his hand lingering on the back of her neck, then left to collect his equipment.

The anxious prickles started to develop not long after Neil closed the door. Mara rubbed them off her arms as she moved to the dining room window to watch his car disappear around the bend. *That was the right choice. You can't become too dependent on him…or let him become too dependent on you. It's your house, after all.*

"My house," Mara repeated as she turned back to the building. "My *home.*"

A door slammed.

Mara glared at the ceiling then snatched Neil's flashlight off the dining room table. "Not tonight." She began circling through the building and checking its problem areas. "Tonight's going to be peaceful and enjoyable." She wedged the rocking chair even more firmly into its corner and made sure that the basement door was shut. Then she jogged up the stairs to work her way through the second-floor rooms.

As she stood on the landing, the master-bedroom door drew open with a tenebrous moan almost as though it were inviting her inside. Mara glowered at it then slipped into the room.

The twilight filtering through the window was strong enough to show the scratches without Mara's flashlight. She approached the door and ran her fingers down the markings. *Probably made with a knife by the same hooligan who thought it would be funny to graffiti my room.*

The door, nudged by a breeze Mara couldn't feel, ground forward. She knocked it back to the wall, pressed the footstool against it to hold it in place, then returned to the hallway. She checked that all of the other doors were secure in their latches and retied the length of cloth around the attic's trapdoor. She made the knot tight so there'd be no way to undo it without snapping it, then returned to her bedroom.

As twilight slipped into night, the webcam's image became grainier, and Mara had more difficulty discerning where one piece of furniture ended and another began. *Maybe Neil was right. Maybe I should have splurged on a more expensive model.*

She pulled her alarm clock out of her box of possessions and checked the time. It was a little before six. The last two days, the footsteps hadn't started until after eleven. *I had hardly any sleep last night. I should catch a few hours while I can. I'll get some dinner when I wake up.*

Mara set the alarm for ten thirty then slid into her sleeping bag and closed her eyes. She was drifting in the place between sleep and wakefulness when she thought she heard the faint, slow groan of the master-bedroom door gliding closed.

CHAPTER 23
COLD COMFORT

THE RED-HAIRED WOMAN CRADLED her child tenderly as she rocked him. She was middle-aged and plump with a sweet, matronly face. Mara imagined she would be the sort of woman who might spend the afternoon cooking treats for her family then have friends around for tea and to go over the latest gossip in delighted whispers.

The rocking chair's struts creaked as the woman bounced her feet against the floor. She was murmuring a lullaby to the child. Mara didn't recognize the tune, and she thought the words might be in a different language. The woman's hair was such a vivid red that it suggested she could have come from Ireland or a Nordic country.

That wasn't the only red on her. Blood drenched the front of her dress. It was smeared over her hands and up to her elbows in the same way that Mara imagined flour might get all over her from an afternoon of baking. Drops had sprayed across one half of her face and dribbled down to her chin.

Mara turned and saw the husband lying face down in front of the fire. The blue rug under him was turning purple from the blood that drained from his wounds. An ax sat embedded between his shoulder blades.

"Hush, my darling, hush. It's all right now." The woman, cooing to her son, shifted him in her arms. The child's head lolled backward. Mara saw its eyes, wide and empty in death, before his mother curled her hand through his hair and pressed him back against herself. "Hush, sweet one." The woman closed her eyes, tilted her head toward the ceiling, and kicked against the floor. The rocking chair's struts groaned as it rolled.

Mara jolted awake, gasping and shivering. She clutched at the sleeping bag behind her, half hoping that she might find Neil there, and was crushed that it was empty.

She pressed her hands over her face and tried to slow her breathing. A creak—almost like a leftover phantom from her dream—reverberated from the ground floor. Mara's heart jumped. *Damn it!*

Mara crept out of the sleeping bag and turned her flashlight on. The alarm clock said the time was a little after ten, and patches of moonlight, filtered through the trees, painted strange designs on the floor. She went to the laptop and shook the mouse to bring it out of hibernation. The webcam still showed the attic. Its night vision had turned on though it didn't help much: she could make out the walls and one big cabinet, but the rest of the screen was a jumble of indistinct shapes. She watched it for a moment, but there was no movement. The creaking downstairs repeated.

What's causing it? The rocking chair can't be moving, and I checked that the basement door was closed. What else? Is there a person downstairs?

Mara moved out of her room. She turned her flashlight on the trapdoor at the end of the hallway and was relieved that the barely visible strip of white cloth was still intact.

The creak was so subtle that it almost felt like a part of the house, as though the building itself were breathing around her. It seemed to have a different timbre to the familiar rocking-chair sounds.

Mara crept down the stairs, her flashlight's beam flickering over the walls and furniture without finding any signs of movement. She stopped when she reached the foyer and waited for the noise to guide her on which direction to take. The house was quiet for a moment, then the creak repeated behind her. It felt close. Mara turned toward the dining room and edged inside. Her light shimmered on the polished-wood table and Neil's spare tool chest, which he'd left propped neatly against one wall. *I shouldn't have sent him away. I could really do with company right now.*

No, don't be stupid. You're letting the darkness get to you again. There's nothing to be frightened of; it's just an old house making the sort of noises an old house makes. The sound could even be wood flexing in the cooling air—

Again, the creak came from behind Mara. She twisted to face

the foyer, and her light glanced over a dark shape hanging below the stairs.

Mara's body moved against her will. She stumbled backward, half choking in her attempt to draw breath and scream at the same time. Her light jittered over the ceiling and walls for a beat before she could redirect it toward the space below the staircase.

It was empty. Mara crept forward, her heart a frantic, pounding tempo in her ears, to skim the light over the foyer.

I imagined it. My flashlight must have caught a patch of shadow. There's no one here, and certainly no one hung from the stairs.

A faint rumble made her turn toward the door. A vehicle was coming up the driveway. Mara pressed a shaking hand over her mouth to muffle her breathing. *It's the intruder; he's come back.*

She turned her flashlight off, crossed to the front door, and opened it a crack. Moonlight made the white pebble path glow through the weeds. The rumble gradually grew closer until a car came around the bend. Mara recognized the silver SUV and slumped against the wall, breathing freely. *Neil. Thank goodness. There's something about night in this place that makes my imagination go wild.*

Neil's car ground to a halt and powered down. Mara watched him carefully as he got out of the car. His face was set in hard angles, and a frown was fixed over his eyes. It suddenly struck her as odd that he would come back so late in the evening. She turned her flashlight on and hurried out to meet him halfway. "Neil!"

He moved to her with long, quick paces, reaching out for her as he did. "Thank mercy—are you okay? Has anything happened?"

The questions startled her. She took his hand and found his fingers were cold. "I'm fine. Is something wrong? Did anything—". An idea came to her, accompanied by a fresh wave of fear. "Oh my goodness—Pam—has something happened to your mother—"

"No, no, nothing like that." Neil pulled her closer and leaned his head against hers, kissing her hair tenderly. His voice was strained. "You need to get out of this house, Mara."

She blinked. "What? Why?"

"I spent this evening researching. I'm sorry; I know you didn't want to know about its history, but I couldn't—" He shook his head again, as though the memories were hurting him. "It's really bad, Mara. You can't stay here."

Mara's worry was being swallowed by irritation. She took a step back from Neil. "What are you talking about? It's a good house. There's nothing wrong with it."

He let her move away but didn't drop her hand. "There's something horribly, fundamentally wrong with Blackwood. Please—come and stay with me. Or I'll buy you a place of your own if you want. But you have to get out of here. *Tonight.*"

The irritation had become fully formed anger. "I like it here. I'm not moving. And if you think for a single second I would live in a house you'd bought me—"

Neil dropped her hand. His voice had taken on a sharp edge. "Why not? What's wrong with that? No, don't make that face—I want to know. Why won't you let me buy you things? Why won't you let me help? It makes me feel like crap to be rejected all the time."

Mara couldn't have erased her glare even if she'd wanted to. "Yeah, I bet you'd love that, huh? To have me reliant on you. Living in *your* house. Spending *your* money. Trapped—"

"Trapped! Seriously? Is that what you think I'm trying to do?"

"Oh, maybe not intentionally, but that's what would happen. *My house, my rules.* Do you know how many times I heard that from my parents? I'm not about to put myself in that sort of situation again. I don't want to *owe* anyone. As soon as you owe people, they have power over you. They can *hurt* you."

Neil made a faint choking noise. "I would never hurt you, Mara. *Never.* Don't you know that?"

"Oh yeah?" She waved her arm toward the building behind her. "What's happening right now? You're trying to dictate my life! You want to take Blackwood away from me. My home! Imagine what would have happened if I'd let you give me a loan like you wanted to. 'Well, Mara, this house is technically mine, so now I'm selling it.' But look at this: *I* own Blackwood. *I* get to decide whether I stay or not. No one else. Just me. *And I'm staying.*"

Neil sucked in a breath. She'd never seen him as angry as he was then. His face was blanched white, and his hands, clenched at his sides, shook.

Mara was suddenly, sickeningly aware of how vulnerable she was. The nearest town was hours away if she had to walk. She didn't have the means to contact the outside world. And there were no neighbors to hear her scream. *If he wanted to, he could kill me. It wouldn't take much; he's strong enough that one or two solid punches would do it.*

Then Neil closed his eyes and relaxed his hands. When he spoke, his voice was low and careful. "I never meant to hurt you, Mara. But I'm starting to understand I might have unintentionally. All I want—the only thing I've ever wanted—is to make sure you're safe and healthy and happy." He sighed, and the motion seemed to deflate him a little. "I come from a family where gifts are signs of love. I didn't realize they might have a different meaning to you…that they could make you feel at a disadvantage."

Instead of speaking, Mara wrapped her arms across her chest. The anger had drained from Neil's eyes. In its place were anxiety and regret, and the emotions cut through her own fury more effectively than any apology he could offer.

"You're strong—far stronger than I am." He kept his eyes fixed on the ground between them. "And insanely smart, and capable. I agree—I have no right to decide any part of your life. I was trying to keep you safe. But you're capable of making your own decisions."

Mara held her hands out to Neil and was gratified to see the unhappy expression dissolve. He stretched his arms wide, and Mara dropped the flashlight and snuggled into the hug. His arms enveloped her, and his breath was hot on the top of her head as he kissed her hair. He was shaking.

"I'm sorry I yelled," she mumbled. "And sorry for saying those things about you. I know you didn't want to hurt me."

"I love you, Mara," he whispered. "So damn much."

She couldn't reply but squeezed him tighter. He rocked her as he stroked her back. "I'm not going to try to insist on anything else. Of course it's your choice whether you stay or not. But would you let me tell you about what I found?"

"Ha. If it made you race down here in such a panic, it's bound to be interesting. Sure."

"Want to look it over in my car? It's heated."

"There's also a heater in my room."

Neil hesitated. Mara could feel him raising his head to glance at Blackwood, and his hands held her a little tighter. Then he nodded. "Sure."

CHAPTER 24
HISTORY

NEIL WENT TO HIS car and retrieved a stack of papers from the passenger seat before they returned to Blackwood. Mara couldn't stop herself from glancing at the space under the stairwell as they passed, but it was, of course, empty.

Mara led Neil to the bedroom. He started the heater while she settled cross-legged on the sleeping bag and waited for him to join her. His face was still pale, and a haunted look lingered in his eyes. He smiled when he caught her watching him then sat opposite her and unfolded his papers.

"How do you want it?" he asked. "Piece by piece or in one big lump?"

"Give me the lump first."

"Right." Neil clasped his hands under his chin. "With the exception of Chris's, every single family to live in Blackwood experienced some sort of violent death. In most cases, the entire family died."

Mara raised her eyebrows, but Neil's face was serious. She cleared her throat. "Okay. I can see how that would make you worried. Want to tell me about them?"

Neil began spreading pages out. Many were handwritten, but some were printed. "Chris's story this afternoon worried me, so I started researching as soon as I got home. What I found was really, really awful. I called Jenny to ask why she hadn't told us—because there are laws about disclosing things like these to prospective house buyers—but her excuse was that you'd signed a form saying you were okay with the house's history." Neil shook his head. "Of course, you only signed the form based on the Robert Kant business."

"To be fair, I did kind of scream at her that I didn't care about the building's past."

"Even so—she should have told you. I think she was a little too eager to sell the house."

Mara shuffled closer. "Okay. What'd you dig up?"

"Jenny gave me a list of all of Blackwood's previous owners. There were eight in all." Neil sorted through the papers and pulled out a handwritten list. "The first, of course, was your great-great-grandfather, Victor Barlow. He'd not long built the house when Robert Kant, traveling cross-country, murdered him. Yesterday, I told you Kant stabbed him, but it turns out he actually used an ax—his signature weapon."

Images and voices flashed through Mara's mind. The dream of the red-haired woman, cradling her dead child while her husband lay with an ax imbedded in his back. *Run, run, run. The axman is coming.*

"I couldn't find an accurate account of what happened to Victor's body, but it seems Robert buried him somewhere on the property. Robert then took up residence in Blackwood without anyone knowing. Over the next four years, he lured five children back to the house, where he butchered them with the same ax he'd used on Victor."

Sweat stood out on Neil's forehead. Mara sensed how difficult the discussion was for him and scooted around to sit at his side. She leaned against his arm. "Take your time."

"Thanks," he murmured. He took a deep breath then continued. "Robert's last target, a girl, managed to escape. She ran back to town and alerted the police. By the time they arrived to arrest Robert, he'd hung himself from the banister in the foyer."

A chill traveled up Mara's spine. She hoped Neil wouldn't feel it. "It's weird he didn't try to run away. He would have had a great head start."

"True. Maybe he couldn't live with himself anymore."

"What happened afterward?"

"The house was cleaned, of course. Some people talked about demolishing it, but it was a sturdy, new building and was eventually bought by a large family. They lived there for a total of twelve years. During that time, all six children died. Two drowned, one cracked his head on a post, one was splashed with boiling water in the kitchen and died from a resulting infection, one cut her chest open on their gardening equipment, and the youngest climbed into the chimney and suffocated."

Mara closed her eyes.

"The parents, grief-stricken, apparently killed themselves in a suicide pact. Their bodies weren't found until a full month later. Again, there was talk of destroying Blackwood, but it was sold to a young couple instead. Their story is less clear, but it seems the wife went insane, and her husband locked her in their room to keep her from harming herself. There are records of doctors visiting her and trying to cure her. The couple lived in the house for a little less than two years before the husband also succumbed to insanity, possibly induced by the isolation and stress of caring for his wife. He killed her. Just like Robert, he used an ax. A doctor, on a routine visit, found the husband sitting beside his wife's body in the master bedroom." Neil cleared his throat. "She'd apparently tried to claw her way out of the locked door and left deep scores in the wood."

"You're joking," Mara said.

"I wish I was. The house was meant to have been cleaned—again—and the door removed."

Mara shook her head. "That lends credence to my theory: someone was obsessed with the house's history and replicated some of its more noteworthy attractions."

Neil moved on without agreeing. "The husband was taken to an insane asylum. After that, the house was empty for a while. It was next bought by a couple with a young child. That was shortly after World War II. They lived here for a year. The wife killed her husband with, believe it or not, an ax. She then smothered her child. They found her dead in the rocking chair, holding her baby. No one's really sure what killed her; she wasn't injured in any way and had no poison in her system. The main theory is either a heart attack or an aneurism."

Mara fixed her eyes on the floor. Her head buzzed. *I dreamed that. How did I know? How could I have possibly known?*

"Again, it had a long period of being empty. A new, large family took it in the sixties. Much like Blackwood's first family, the five children began dying one by one, a few months apart. One became tangled in cords and was strangled. Another fell into the water tank and drowned. A third was, apparently, bludgeoned to death by his sibling. That very same sibling then had a seizure and passed in the middle of the night. The family, reduced to the husband, wife, and one remaining child, fled the house. I can't find any records of where they ended up or what happened to them."

The heater felt far too cold for what Mara needed. She pressed closer to Neil, and he tightened his arm in response. "Are you okay?"

"Fine," she grunted. "Keep going."

"There's not much left. Blackwood's reputation of being a haunted house was thoroughly cemented, and no one wanted to touch it. It was ultimately bought in the eighties by a man who was strongly interested in the paranormal. He, his wife, and their two children took up residence. Police records indicate he had diaries filled with notes about his supernatural experiences in the house. He wrote about dark impulses coming over him. He believed the house demanded violence to sate its appetite, and he was frightened that his hand might be turned against his family. He began trying to find a buyer for Blackwood. Too late, though."

"He killed his family," Mara breathed.

"Not quite. He and his family were found dead from ax wounds. The children had been killed in their beds and the parents downstairs. It was clearly murder, but no suspect was ever identified. It's still listed as an unsolved crime."

Neil, having shuffled through his notes, placed them to one side. "The final family was, of course, Chris's. They all escaped with their lives, though the short duration of their stay and Chris's story are certainly concerning."

"That's it?" Mara asked. "Only one family left Blackwood intact?"

"That's it." Neil massaged Mara's shoulders, trying to ease the tension from them. "That's why I'd like you to leave. I understand you don't want to feel obligated to anyone, but if there's any sort of help I can offer that you'd feel okay with, consider it given. I just want you safe."

"Give me a moment to think." Mara chewed at her thumb, but her mind was filled with a rush of hectic, frightening pictures and ideas. She groaned. "No, I need caffeine first. Would you mind making us some tea?"

Neil glanced at the door then gave her a sheepish smile. "Would you come with me?"

They held hands as they went to the kitchen. Neil's eyes were constantly moving, scanning Blackwood's shadows as though a monster could leap at them at any second. As they passed the banister, a pale patch in the wood caught Mara's eye. *It almost looks worn away. Possibly by a rope.* She hurried past it and tried to put it out of her mind as they entered the kitchen and put the kettle on.

Mara perched on the kitchen counter and crossed her ankles. Neil leaned on the counter opposite and was polite enough not to stare at her as she let her thoughts consume her.

When I moved into Blackwood, I decided that a violent history was no reason to reject a house. Does it make a difference if there was one murder or twenty?

I suppose that depends on how much impact they have on Blackwood in the present. Five out of eight families were entirely wiped out inside this house, and another two lost multiple family members. Does that mean I'm in danger, like Neil clearly thinks I am? Or can I believe it's pure bad luck? Statistically, there are going to be houses with far more than an average number of deaths—in the same way that there will be hundred-year-old buildings with no deaths. You can assume an average number of deaths occur in every old home, but there will be outliers in both directions. Is Blackwood nothing but a statistical anomaly? If so, I could almost argue that I'm safer here than at other houses. Each death beyond the average makes it increasingly unlikely that there will be further murders.

But that's assuming the deaths are based on nothing but happenstance. Blackwood could be a statistical anomaly, but it would have to be a very, very uncommon one. I need to explore other options. I've checked EMFs and gas, but they're worth checking again, as well as doing a mold inspection and getting a botanist to see if there are any

insanity-causing plants in the forest around here. It'd be expensive,
but it's either that or moving.

The kettle finished boiling. Neil crossed to it and opened his
box of tea leaves. "You said you wanted caffeine, but I also have
chamomile if you'd prefer it."

"Yeah, let's go with that."

Neil wants me to move. I can see it in every fiber of his being. I
don't know what he believes caused the deaths, but he's clearly fright-
ened I'll suffer the same fate. Poor Neil. He's a fixer, and he can see
a problem, but he's not allowed to solve it. That must be killing him.

He handed Mara her mug with a smile that was a little too
tight to appear genuine. She sidled closer to him. "C'mere. I want
a hug."

That earned her a genuine grin. They stood with their backs
against the counter as Neil wrapped his arm around Mara's
shoulder and pulled her close.

If I did leave Blackwood, *what would that mean for me? I don't*
want to stay in Neil's house. I can't afford a hotel. I'm past the
buyer's-remorse grace period for Blackwood, so I can't reverse the sale.
If I ever wanted to see even part of my money again, I'd need to sell
this house. And it's been on the market for twenty years without any
interest besides my own.

Mara raised her eyes to the walls and the ceiling. The aged,
dark-gray wood had never looked so beautiful. *I love this place.*
Even if I could, I wouldn't want to sell it. Despite a couple of weird
nights, and despite a repeat intruder, I've never felt as comfortable
as I do here.

"Neil?" Mara nuzzled against his side. "You're not going to like this."

"Oh boy."

"I want to stay. No, don't try to argue; just listen. I recognize that there may be a cause behind Blackwood's repeated deaths. Don't think I'm ignoring that. But I'm going to hire inspectors and experts until I either find the source or I'm certain that Blackwood is safe." Mara placed her cup on the counter and wrapped herself around Neil. His heartbeat was quick. She rubbed his chest in an effort to comfort him. "This is a good house for me. I don't want to lose it because of some gnarly history."

Neil didn't speak for a moment, then he chuckled. "*Gnarly*. That's a word I haven't heard in the last decade."

"Oh, shut up."

His arms circled around Mara as he dipped his head to kiss hers. "Damn it, Mara. I'd give anything to get you out of this place."

"Yeah, I know." Mara inhaled his scent and smiled. "But I'm staying."

An attic floorboard creaked.

CHAPTER 25
TAPES

BOTH OF THEIR HEADS turned upward so quickly that Mara was amazed they didn't get whiplash. They held still, coiled in their embrace, as they listened to the house. It was quiet for a moment, then the creak repeated, moving across the ceiling.

Mara swore, and Neil's arms tightened around her. She squirmed out of his grip and darted toward the staircase.

"Slow down!" Neil hissed as he followed.

"Shh!" Mara raced up the stairs, keeping to their edges and fighting to make her footfalls as quiet as possible. Her heart raced, but it was an excited, exhilarated emotion, reminiscent of the bravado she'd felt on the first night. She had Neil with her. She had her surveillance camera. This time, the intruder was the disadvantaged party.

She made it to the top of the stairs without much noise, but Neil had to follow at a slower, more careful pace. He was nearly twice her weight, and the steps complained under his feet. Mara waited on the landing with mingled impatience and fierce anticipation. The attic's creaks were following their familiar pattern: the stranger moved through the building with even, slow strides, passing over their heads, turning at the end of the house, and retracing the path. The last two nights, they'd only paced for a handful of minutes. *That'll be enough for us, though.*

Neil appeared at her side. Mara grabbed his hand and pulled him into their bedroom and toward the laptop. She glanced at the alarm clock as she passed it. *Quarter past eleven. That's the same time as before, too.*

Mara nudged the mouse to wake the laptop up, and the pair of them huddled close to the screen.

The familiar, night-vision-tinted image was just as confusing as before. The shapes blended together into a twisted mosaic of light and shadow. Mara scanned the image for signs of movement and held her breath as she listening for the footfalls.

A board not far above their heads creaked, and Neil prodded at the screen. "There!"

"What is that…?" Static bloomed over the lower half of the screen. "Did you see them?"

"I saw *something*." Neil shook his head. "I…I dunno…"

The static flared further as something behind it moved, and Mara smacked the laptop. "Piece of crap webcam. I should've bought one of the billion-dollar monsters like you wanted me to."

"It shouldn't be distorting like that. I don't understand why it's—"

Another creak, another hint of motion quickly hidden behind a flare of digital noise. Mara swore. "We can't see anything like this. One of us needs to go into the attic."

Neil's expression made Mara feel like she'd suggested they hug a grizzly bear.

"Relax; I'll go," she said, patting his chest without taking her eyes off the laptop. "You stay here and watch the screen. I'll be able to hear you through the floor; call out instructions, okay?"

"No. Cripes, Mara, no! I'll let you live in the damn house, but I'm not letting you go into the attic alone. I'll do it."

"Jeez, all right, take the fun job if you really must." *Damn* was about as close as Neil ever got to a legitimate swearword, so Mara guessed the situation had to be serious. "Take a knife and your bug zapper; I'll watch the creep."

Mara bent low over the screen. Two pairs of footsteps competed for her attention: the intruder's, which were cycling close to the place above her head, and Neil's, which moved down the hallway and toward the attic stairs.

"Stupid camera," Mara growled. All she wanted was to see her intruder's face. *Is it a man or a woman? Young or old?* But static buzzed about the figure with every step and never quite faded enough for Mara to make out any details before they moved again.

"There's something tied onto the trapdoor," Neil called. "Like…a white cloth?"

"Yeah, that was me. Cut it." *That's strange; how did they get into the attic without going through the house? I couldn't see anything that could be used to climb the walls when I was outside yesterday…*

"Is it safe to open the door?" Neil called.

Mara's heart ached at the stress in his voice. If it had been up to him, they would both be twenty miles from Blackwood and still moving. She bent slightly closer to the screen as the static spread outward to swallow the image. "The distortion's gotten worse, but last I saw, they were about halfway through the room. I think they're by the hole in the wall. Hang on, the static's fading—"

Mara frowned. The distortion had disappeared. In its place was nothing but furniture and pooled white cloths. She studied the image, but she couldn't see any signs of movement.

The attic was still for all of a second before the trapdoor swung open and Neil's torso appeared on the screen. He turned toward the hole in the wall then began creeping into the room. "Where are they?"

"G-gone." Mara cleared her throat and called a little louder. "They were standing by the hole, but then the static got really bad, and when it cleared I couldn't see them anymore. Be careful."

Neil slunk through the room. Mara could hear his footsteps above her head. They were slightly deeper and quieter than the mystery intruder's. She kept her eyes roving over the screen, searching for any signs of motion so that she could warn him against a potential sneak attack. He cycled through the attic, hunting behind furniture, then faced the camera and shrugged.

"Can you see anything outside the hole?" Mara called. She was starting to feel frustrated. The static had resolved itself a moment too late for her to see the uninvited guest. Now that Neil was in the attic, the picture was clear.

Neil moved to the hole and extended his head and shoulders through it. She could see his body twist as he looked over the ground, the walls, and the roof. Then he pulled back inside. "Nothing."

"Hang on; I'm coming." Mara jogged down the hallway and climbed the stairs. Neil came to meet her and pulled her through the trapdoor.

It felt surreal to see the actual attic after watching the screen. The furniture, although shrouded in darkness, was at least identifiable. Mara scanned the room, but it was clear they were alone.

"This guy is really starting to bug me." She patted Neil's arm. "Thanks for coming up here, by the way. I know you'd rather be literally anywhere else."

"I want to be exactly where you are." He took her hand and squeezed. "Though I'd be lying if I said I was glad you're *here*."

Mara turned in a slow circle, skimming her light over the crowded storage area. "I don't get it, though. Where'd they go?"

"Want me to search through the furniture again? There might be something we missed before."

"Yeah, thanks." Mara went to the hole in the ceiling, leaned as far out as she dared, and pointed her flashlight toward the ground. She could barely make out the indent in the grass, which didn't seem to have been disturbed since the night before. Then she turned her flashlight across the roof in case the stranger had managed to climb on top of it. It was empty. *Of course it is; we would have heard them otherwise.*

"Hey, Mara, do you have a minute?" Neil was crouched next

to the collapsing box of videotapes Mara recognized from their first trip to the attic.

She went to him. "What's up?"

"I think these might be from the second-to-last family that lived here. Remember how I told you the husband was interested in the paranormal?"

Mara's skin prickled. "Yeah?"

"The police found his diaries, but what if he filmed things as well?" Neil ran his finger over the fading, aged stickers. "There aren't any titles on these, just dates."

He was right. Each tape had two dates written on it, presumably to mark the start and the finish of the recording. Some covered spans of several days, but others had been completed in one day. The only tape that didn't match was the last one, which was jammed awkwardly into the box's corner. It had a start date, but where the end date should have been was a dark smear.

Neil hissed as Mara plucked the tape out. "I know that day. That was when the family was killed."

Mara poked at the stain on the tape's label. "Really? Huh. Maybe this isn't a juice spill after all."

"Put it back." Neil stood and dusted his hands on his jeans as though trying to purge himself of the attic's taint. He looked uneasy.

Mara tapped on the tape's side. "It's been up here a while. I wonder if it still works." She squinted at Neil, who maintained a stony silence. "There's a television downstairs. Do you think it has a VCR?"

Neil sighed and crossed his arms. "Probably."

"Then let's get it hooked up to the generator and see what's on this thing."

"I don't like this."

Mara sidled up to her partner and gave him a searching look. "I know you. You're not going to be able to sleep tonight if you don't see what's on this tape. And neither will I. So let's stop being stupid and just watch the damn thing. It probably doesn't have anything on it anyway."

Neil grimaced. "My friends say you're a bad influence. I'm starting to think they're right."

"Psh. It'll be fine." Mara wove her way toward the trapdoor. "Pretend it's a spooky Halloween movie or something. I think we even have some marshmallows left."

CHAPTER 26
KEITH

THE TELEVISION *DID* HAVE a VCR, but it was so dusty that Mara was worried it might not work. She followed Neil as he ran cables from the recreation room to the generator outside, and helped him hook the system up to power. The VCR's lights blinked into life, and Mara turned the television on. It whined and flickered, and suddenly the screen was filled with thick, dancing static. The image jerked Mara's thoughts back to the webcam's distortion, and she hurried to press the tape into its slot.

For a moment, it looked as if it might not work. Then the VCR ground into action and began whirring as the tape played.

"Score," Mara hissed and pressed a button on the TV to switch it to VCR mode. She and Neil sat on the floor in front of the television, wrapped in blankets they'd retrieved from their bedroom and with the bag of marshmallows propped between them. Mara was hyperaware of the red handprints marring the wall not far away and wished she'd thought to wash them off while she'd still had daylight.

The television showed nothing but black for a moment, then a room came into focus. It took Mara a moment to recognize it as their dining area. The camera was set up in the back corner to cover most of the room and the opening leading into the foyer. The video had the inherent graininess and muted colors of eighties' camcorder recordings but was surprisingly sharp for its time, making her think the equipment must have been expensive. It was night. Two lamps sat at either end of the table, and a glow coming through the archway suggested there were other lamps spaced about the house.

The image was so still that Mara began to worry it might have frozen, but then a man's voice said, "If there are any spirits here, I ask that you make yourselves known."

Shudders ran through Mara, and she dropped her marshmallow back into the bag. The words transported her back to when she was ten and hid in the corner as her parents held hands and spoke to their invisible guests. *I should have expected this. He was a ghost hunter, after all.*

Neil pulled her closer and stroked her hair. "Do you want to stop?"

"No, it's fine."

A sheen of sweat developed over her back as the silence stretched out. Then the voice repeated, "I ask that you speak with me." A man paced into the camera's view. He was tall and wiry and had deep crevices across his face as though he'd lost a lot of weight over a short amount of time. "What do you want? Why are you here? Give me a sign if you can hear me."

"That must be Keith, the husband," Neil murmured to Mara. She didn't trust herself to speak, but she nodded.

The man suddenly turned toward the kitchen, which was outside the camera's view. Mara stared at Keith's face, searching for any expression that might indicate whether he'd seen something. He took a step toward the kitchen then stopped. "Hello? Who's there?"

Motion in the back of the foyer made Neil grip Mara's arm so tightly that it was almost painful.

"Relax," she hissed. "It's just a child—look."

A girl, no older than eight and dressed in a nightgown, paced silently toward the dining room. Her hair was tied back in a loose braid, but strands had come free and fell over her pale, sullen face.

Keith hadn't seen her, but took another step toward the kitchen. The girl watched her father for a moment then turned toward the camera. She began sobbing.

"Penny!" Keith's voice was wound tight. He pressed a hand to his heart as he stared at his daughter then stumbled toward her. "What're you doing up, honey? Did you have a bad dream?"

"I want to leave." Penny continued to stare at the camera as fat tears rolled down her cheeks. "A bad man's coming."

"No one's coming, sweetheart." Keith scooped his daughter up and began rocking her. "We're safe here. Don't be afraid."

"Don't lie. People died here. Lots of people."

Keith fell still. "Who told you? Did your mummy say that?"

"Lots of people," Penny repeated. "Peter and Maria and Ethel and Anthony and Reece and Mara—"

"What?" Neil blurted.

"Shh, shh," Keith said, rocking his daughter again. "It was just a dream, sweetheart. C'mon; I'll put you back into bed and tell you a story. How about that?"

"Did she say *Mara?*" Neil looked faintly nauseated.

Mara shook her head. "No, the audio's not clear. I think she said Nala."

"Hang on." Neil shed his blanket and crawled to the VCR player. He rewound the tape then pressed play.

"Lots of people. Peter and Maria and Ethel and Anthony and Reece and Mara—"

"She said Nala," Mara insisted. "The audio's murky—that's all."

Neil groaned and rubbed a hand over his face as he settled beside her. "I don't like this."

Keith, still holding Penny, returned to the camera. He disappeared behind it. Then there was a scraping, crackling sound, and the image turned to black.

The recording resumed in a new location. Mara thought it was one of the upstairs bedrooms, but she couldn't tell which one. The decorations were simple but tidy. Paintings hung on the back wall, and a half-visible shelf was stacked full of recording equipment and binders. Mara thought it might be Keith's hobby room.

Keith himself sat in front of the camera, rubbing one hand

over his stubbly, craggy lower jaw. He was scowling and didn't speak for several long minutes. When he finally inhaled and began talking, it was in a monotonous rush as though he'd said the words hundreds of times in the past. "Keith Spiegleman, twentieth of March, 1984. It is"—he checked his watch—"11:49 at night. And this house is driving me crazy."

He turned his palms outward and shrugged. "I don't know what to do. In every other haunted house I've been in, the spirits all wanted something. Justice. Company. Sympathy. Reassurance that it's safe to pass on to the next life. But here"—he licked his lips—"here, I'm starting to think there's only *one* thing they want: more deaths."

He stood and began pacing across the cramped room, gesticulating aimlessly as he did. "I don't understand why. Usually spirits are focused on having *their* needs met. They don't care about what happens to their human companions—though you will, occasionally, find a ghost that wants to protect a living relative or similar. But a soul that's so malevolent, so evil, that all it wants is to perpetuate suffering…how can you even *begin* to remove that? I've already tried the usual—burning sage, séances, holy water. But this energy is far, far too deeply engrained in Blackwood. It's going to take someone with abilities much greater than my own to purge it."

He stopped walking and let his arms flop to his sides. "I'm about ready to call it quits and leave this mess to someone more capable. My wife cries all the time. Penny hardly sleeps. We're— it's a mess, and I—I'm tired—" He broke off abruptly and turned toward the door. It took Mara a moment to realize why. The camera's audio equipment was barely able to pick up the faint creaking of the downstairs rocking chair.

Keith swore and snatched up the camera. The screen turned to a jumble of indistinct shapes as he ran down the hallway and stairs, then the blur resolved into a fuzzy image of the rocking chair rolling on its struts. Keith adjusted the lens to focus it on the scene. "Mary, is that you?"

The chair continued to move. Mara had to tap Neil's hand to tell him to relax his grip on her shoulder.

"Mary, I want to help," Keith repeated. "I know what you did. But it's okay. I'd like to help you move on to the next life if you can. Your husband and baby boy are already there. Wouldn't you like to see them again?"

The rocking chair slowed then stopped. Keith took a step toward it. "Mary, are you still with me?" The camera swung back toward the foyer, and Keith swore again. "What was that?"

He moved to the foot of the stairs and panned the camera up their length and across the landing. Then he turned back to the living room. "Mary?"

The rocking chair remained still. Keith's breathing was raspy as he edged through the room and toward the library beyond. The shelves were filled with a jumble of books—many with titles that hinted at paranormal subject matter.

Keith slunk into the room. The camera shook as he focused on the walls and then the doorway into the recreation room. There was only one lamp inside, and it filled the area with just as much shadow as light. Mara felt a jolt of discomfort at the sight of the same television they were watching. She half expected to see herself and Neil huddled on the ground, but the area was empty.

"Hello?" Keith called. Everything was still for a moment, then a quiet thud made him swing toward the library. "Hello? I—"

Keith broke off with a horrified choke. The image turned into a blur of shapes as the camera tumbled to the ground. When it settled, Mara was able to make out four of the library's shelves and the entrance to the living room.

"Sal," Keith choked. "Sal, what—are you bleeding? What happened?"

There was no reply, but Mara heard a soft footstep. A low, heavy scraping accompanied it, and Keith's voice rose in terror.

"Good God—where's Penny? What have you done? *What have you done?* Sal—"

A dull *thwack*. Keith's words deteriorated into a scream. Another *thwack*. The screams cut out. A drop of something dark hit the lens and dribbled down the glass. A final *thwack*, then a beat of silence followed by the resumption of the scraping, grating noise.

A barefoot woman appeared in the camera's view, walking toward the living room. One bloodstained hand gripped the handle of a large, vicious-looking ax, which she dragged along the floor to produce the grating sound. Her white nightdress was splashed with red. She paused inside the living room and turned toward the camera.

Mara remembered how Chris had referred to her brother's eyes as dead. *Like the person inside had been sucked out and left nothing but a human husk.* At the time of Chris's story, she'd passed it off as a fanciful embellishment. But staring at the long-faced woman, Mara thought she had never heard such an apt description. Sal's eyes were dead.

The woman knelt on the wooden floor and placed the ax ahead of her. She seemed to be arranging it carefully with the wooden handle pointing toward herself and the sharp blade aimed at the ceiling. Once she was satisfied, Sal rose to her feet and disappeared from view. When she returned, she was carrying a wicker chair, which she placed a few feet behind the ax.

Sal then climbed onto the chair. She stood tall, head held high, and began to tilt forward.

Mara realized what Sal had planned, but was incapable of looking away. The woman fell in a smooth arc toward the waiting ax's blade. A millisecond before impact, the screen cut to static.

CHAPTER 27
BARGAINING

NEIL INHALED SHARPLY AND jerked away from the television. He looked sick.

Mara's mind was blank. The television's crackling static felt like a parasite trying to eat into her head, so she crawled to the box and unplugged both the television and the VCR.

Silence fell over the room. Mara found herself, against her will, turning toward the entryway to the library. She could picture the exact spot where the ax had been laid and how carefully the chair had been arranged before it.

"I guess your friends are right. I am a bad influence." She'd hoped the joke would break the spell that seemed to hover in the air, but it occurred to her a second after it left her lips that it was in bad taste. Neil didn't speak. She turned to see him on his knees, eyes still fixed on the empty television screen, with one badly shaking hand pressed over his mouth. She reached toward him then hesitated, afraid that he might no longer want anything to do with her. But when he turned his blue eyes on her, there was none of the dreaded hatred or revulsion—only grief and shock. He took Mara's hand and pulled her against himself. They clung to each other as they waited for the immediate shock to pass.

"I'm so sorry," she whispered. "I had no idea—"

"No, of course not. That wasn't your fault." Neil held her so tightly that she felt almost crushed, but Mara liked it. She needed the safety he provided. She pressed her ear to the place over his heart and listened as his pulse gradually slowed.

"It wasn't a murder after all." His fingers still shook, but he had enough control to be gentle as he stroked her hair. "Or, I suppose it was—but not by a stranger like the police assumed."

"Who would have expected her to fall on her own ax?"

Neil was silent for several minutes then said, in barely more than a whisper, "How'd that tape get from the recorder to the box in the attic?"

Shudders clawed their way up Mara's back.

He sighed and kissed her forehead. "I think our tea's well and truly cold, but I need it anyway."

Mara nodded and slipped off his lap so that he could stand. They went back to the kitchen, where they'd left their mugs when the footsteps had begun. Neil put the kettle back on the stove then gulped his cold tea. Mara picked her mug up but couldn't bring herself to drink it.

"Ready to leave this place?" He placed both hands on the counter and stared at the kettle. "We can go right now if you want."

She closed her eyes. *Please, not now. I don't want to fight this battle again.* "I still intend to stay in Blackwood."

Neil dropped his head. He looked ghastly. "I was afraid you might."

"That video was horrible, but it doesn't change anything." She didn't know why she felt compelled to explain herself, but she couldn't keep her mouth shut. "We already knew Keith and his family had been killed here. And my leaving won't bring them back."

Neil exhaled. "I don't want to fight. I just wish I knew what was the right thing to do."

Mara blinked at the tears stinging her eyes. She moved to him and wrapped her hands around his forearm. It felt cold; she rubbed at the skin to bring some heat back into it. "What do you mean?"

"Maybe you're right. Maybe you'll be fine here." The kettle had started whistling, and Neil moved it off the stove with a motion that looked more automatic than conscious. "But there's the chance that you're wrong."

He turned to look at her, and Mara lost her breath at the intensity of the fear and fierceness in his blue eyes.

"If I knew for certain you were in danger, I would drag you out of here by force." His voice was low and thick. "There is nothing I wouldn't do for you, Mara. I would even survive your hating me for it afterward. As long as I could make sure you were safe."

"Shh, calm down." She ran her fingers through his hair. He

sighed and leaned into the touch. "Who says you need to look after me? I'm strong. And remember, starting tomorrow, I'm going to hire a bunch of people to test this place. By the time they're done, we'll know for certain that Blackwood is okay."

"EMF inspectors, mold inspectors, botanists, gas inspectors…"

"And anyone else I think might help." Mara lowered her hand to brush it over the stubble developing on his chin. "I'll err on the side of caution; don't worry."

Neil gave her a quick, searching look and wet his lips. "Would you do something for me?"

"Of course."

"Would you hire a priest?"

Mara felt as though someone had plunged her heart into a bucket of ice. She withdrew her hand. "Why would I do that?"

"You want to be thorough." Neil was speaking carefully and didn't meet her gaze directly but watched her out of the corner of his eye. "And I know you don't believe in ghosts. But, just in case—"

"Just in case my house is haunted?" Mara hated herself for the patronizing tone she'd used. "Is that what you think?"

Neil cleared his throat, poured the freshly boiled water into their cups, and opened his box to find tea bags.

Mara took a deep breath and purposefully lowered her voice. "I'm going to be cautious. But I'm not going to be stupid. I don't need a priest."

"Chamomile?"

"No, give me the red one. I'm sick of chamomile."

He dropped their tea bags into the mugs and watched as they tinted the water. "You have a logical answer for everything that happens. And I've tried to believe them. But there's still too much stuff I can't understand."

The cold in Mara's chest was like a vicious vice. "Tell me."

"The mysterious footsteps in the attic that can come and go in a heartbeat. The static distortion from a brand-new webcam and reliable laptop. And you said those handprints on the wall were yours, but they're too small. They belong to children, Mara. I was prepared to think maybe some kids had broken in while you were trapped in the basement, but..." He shook his head. "Chris said her family threw out most of the junk from the attic, but if you look through it, some of that stuff might have been there since Blackwood's earliest owners. Surely someone, at some point in the house's history, would have thrown it out."

Mara shrugged. "People are lazy."

"I would feel more comfortable if we could talk to a priest."

"Well, I hate to break it to you, but I don't give a crap about your comfort."

Neil flinched, and Mara could have slapped herself. "I'm sorry." The ache in her chest had wound so tightly that she could barely breathe. She moved closer to him, hands outstretched, but didn't dare touch him. "Crap, Neil, that was a horrible thing to say. I'm so sorry. I didn't mean it—I—" *No, stop it! Don't you dare cry.* "Neil—"

"It's okay. Shh, Mara, it's okay." His arms were around her. His lips pressed against her forehead and her wet cheeks. His arms moved over her back as she hiccupped. "Shh, sweetheart. It's all right. We're going to be fine."

"Stop being so damn sweet," was all she could manage. Neil rocked her gently as she buried her face in his shirt. The sensation of safety enveloped her, and Mara gradually regained control and fought the tears back. "I'm sorry," she repeated once she was certain her voice was steady. "Sorry for saying those things. And sorry for making you deal with my crap."

"I love your crap." Neil cringed. "The metaphorical stuff. I didn't mean literally."

Mara laughed, and the giggles shook her whole body. Neil joined in, kissing the top of her head as he did. When they sobered, he said, "Can I ask something?"

"Go ahead, and I'll try not to bite your head off this time."

"Don't take this as criticism, because it's not, but why are you so determined to stay in Blackwood? You just watched a video of a family being butchered two rooms away, and you won't even leave for the night."

Mara frowned. "I...I'm not completely sure. I think, um—" She cleared her throat. "Buying Blackwood is the first big thing I've done by myself. And I don't want to be wrong about it."

Neil's hands continued to stroke her hair. The soft, tender motion was unlocking some of the ache inside Mara's chest, and she continued before she could lose her courage. "And I'm so attached to Blackwood. I really, really love this place. When people tell me it's no good, it feels like they're saying that about *me*."

"Ah, Mara; I'm sorry."

"Nah, not your fault," she mumbled. Fresh tears pricked at her eyes, but she blinked them back. "Anyway, most of all, I just don't want them to be right."

"Who's 'them'?"

"My parents." She shrugged awkwardly. "Their friends. All those shams who filed through our house. If I leave Blackwood, or if I call a priest, they win."

Neil kissed her neck then picked her up as though she weighed nothing. He carried her into the foyer and up the stairs, into the bedroom then placed her onto the sleeping bag. When he pulled back, she was surprised by the tight resolve carved into his face. "We won't call a priest. And we won't leave Blackwood tonight. But can we compromise? If all of the other tests come back negative and weird stuff is still happening, can we reconsider leaving?"

Mara wiped the tear tracks off her cheeks and smiled. "Yeah, that's fair."

He gave her chin a gentle knock. "I'll be back soon."

Neil was only gone for a few minutes. When he returned, he'd brought their cups of tea and a box of food. Mara, who had skipped her dinner, happily worked her way through a bag of dried-apple slices. Neil sat close to her, and they talked aimlessly for more than an hour, discussing movies they wanted to see, the snobby waitress at Neil's favorite café, his mother—anything that wasn't connected to Blackwood. She felt herself relax in a way she hadn't over the previous two days, and she laughed freely. When exhaustion began to grind her down, Neil collected his Taser, pepper spray, and knife, laid them beside his bed, and turned the flashlight off.

Mara fell into an uneasy sleep. She woke twice through the night, and each time, Neil stroked her hair until she fell asleep again.

CHAPTER 28
HOT CHOCOLATE

MARA LEANED ON THE window frame and watched dappled sunlight flicker over the vegetable garden in Blackwood's yard.

But I don't have a garden. This is another dream, isn't it?

She turned back to the room and found she wasn't alone. A man was pacing its length, one hand pressed to his lips and the other clutching a black top hat against his chest. He was dressed in formal clothes from what Mara guessed was the early twentieth century, and he didn't seem to care that his heavy sweat would soak into them.

Mara looked around and saw they were in a child's bedroom. A toy box sat at the foot of the neatly made bed, and bright paintings were hung on the wall. The room was a little too orderly and clean for Mara to feel comfortable in it.

"Are you in here, my love?" A woman appeared in the doorway. She looked drawn and pale but smiled when her husband turned toward her. "Did the funeral upset you so much? I thought it was beautiful."

A funeral and a room that's been scrupulously cleaned. They lost their child, didn't they?

The man held his hand out to his wife, and she went to him and embraced him. There was a flash of deep, violent grief in the woman's face, but she quickly smoothed it over. "We must be strong, my love," she murmured so quietly that Mara almost couldn't hear. "If not for ourselves, for the other children. They are struggling."

"They say they see spirits in the night." The man's voice was raw and frightened. "Anne believes the man who once lived here has not fully left. She says he killed Timothy. That he still believes he owns this house. He's angry that we're living in it."

The woman cupped her husband's face and said slowly and firmly, "Put that out of your mind. He's long gone, and we paid good money for Blackwood. This is our house now."

"This is our house now," he echoed.

"That's it exactly, my love."

The scene flickered before Mara's eyes. The peaceful spring sun was replaced by cold winter light. The man, still standing by the wall, looked at least a decade older, and his face was gaunt. And something was smeared over the walls—

Mara's dream shifted back to the spring, just in time to hear the wife say a final time, "This is our house." Then it was back to winter, and the husband was running his fingers across the wall, smearing the red words onto the wood. "THIS IS OUR HOUSE THIS IS OUR HOUSE THIS IS OUR HOUSE."

He bent toward the shape at his feet, and Mara felt nausea pool in her stomach as she saw they weren't just cloths, as she had first assumed, but the wife—older, paler, her chest torn open and dead eyes staring toward the heavens. The man dipped his fingers into the gore between her breasts then rose to finish his message.

The wall was almost entirely covered. He completed the final word, which filled in the last empty gap, and dropped his hand. Then, without so much as a glance at his dead wife, he turned and left the room. Mara stared at the woman's corpse while she listened to the husband's footsteps lead him not to the main staircase, as she'd expected, but toward the opposite end of the house and up the creaking stairs to the attic.

Mara started awake. It took her a moment to remember where she was, but when she rolled over, she saw Neil sitting by the window. He looked haggard but happy. "Check it out. We didn't get murdered in the middle of the night after all."

She snorted and clambered out of her sleeping bag. "Were you awake the whole night?"

"Yeah." He stretched. "But it wasn't as dramatic as it sounds. We stayed up so late that you were only asleep for a few hours. Want some breakfast?"

"Heck yes."

Mara changed and brushed her teeth while Neil started cooking downstairs. By the time she joined him, he'd fried up plates of eggs, mushrooms, and tomatoes. She pecked his cheek then helped carry their plates to the dining table, where she attacked her breakfast eagerly.

"I'm going to call in sick to work today." He passed a spare egg onto Mara's plate.

"Don't do that," she objected through a mouthful of food. "Your business isn't going to run itself. And I don't need babysitting."

"Ha! No, it's not because of you. I'm being entirely selfish this morning. After last night, I'm dead tired, and I wanted to have a sleep at home. I was thinking, though—why don't you borrow my car?"

"Yeah?"

"Yeah. Drop me home and go out for a while—see a movie or something. You need a break from Blackwood. Then pick me up in the afternoon, and we can come back here together."

He doesn't want me staying in Blackwood alone. Mara felt her eyes wandering toward the corner where the camera had been during the first half of the tape they'd watched, and made herself look away. *I probably should get out for a bit. I've been saturated in Blackwood for the last four days, and it would be good to clear my head. Plus, I could recharge my phone at a café.* "That sounds like a plan."

"Great." Neil grinned as he pushed a second egg onto her plate.

They left quickly after washing up. Neil drove them to his family's property, a tidy two-story house in one of the quieter suburbs. As they turned in to the driveway, Mara caught sight of the short, pastel-dressed Pam watering the front garden.

"She's looking a bit better," Mara said as they pulled up outside the garage.

"Yeah, I think it's actually helped her to have some extra

independence these last few days. She cooked dinner for the first time last night."

Mara got out and greeted Pam briefly then kissed Neil goodbye. "What time do you want me back?"

"How's around three sound?"

"Good for me." As she returned to the car, she watched him pick up a spare watering can to help his mother. Part of her wanted to linger in the pretty suburban yard, but she'd already absorbed the bulk of Neil's attention over the previous few days and didn't want to intrude any further, so she reversed out of the driveway and drove toward the town center. Her smile faded before she'd traveled farther than a block.

Neil believes in ghosts. The idea made her feel sick. She knew it shouldn't be a big deal. She'd learned to be comfortable with his religious leanings, after all. But his acceptance of the supernatural—in particular, supernatural at her home—felt tantamount to betrayal.

He's mistaken, not stupid, she reminded herself as the suburbs gave way to clusters of shops. *Once this settles down—once I've had Blackwood checked out—once I've lived in it for a few months without anything bad happening—he'll have to realize he was wrong. Right?*

"Drop it," she told herself as she took a corner too fast. *I need something to distract me, and I've got nearly six hours to fill. What's not too expensive?*

She stopped by a budget movie theater, but the only film screening within the following hour was a haunted-house flick, and Mara figured she'd had enough of that already. Next she stopped at a museum, hoping for some quiet, but a gaggle of schoolchildren came in shortly after her, and she ducked out before the chatter could drive her crazy. Across the street was a small coffee shop that seemed to cater to the hippie population. The name, It's Bean a While, made her smile. *They should have outlets, right?*

She fetched her dead phone and its charger from Neil's car then crossed the street. The drinks were overpriced, but the heavily tattooed barista was friendly, so Mara ordered a hot chocolate, found a small corner seat near a wall socket, and settled in. She had a good view of the large windows looking onto the street, and Mara leaned against the wall as she counted the pedestrians and tried to guess where they were going.

A young couple. Probably on their second or third date, based on how carefully they're dressed. An older, suited man. Might be taking an early lunch break from his work. Ha! One of the schoolkids managed to sneak out of the museum. He's going to be in trouble when they find out.

Then a middle-aged couple stopped outside the coffee shop to read the menu posted in the window. Mara choked on her chocolate.

No, no, no way, no how...

The man, stately and with deep-gray hair, tapped the menu and said something to his wife. She smiled and nodded. Her long hair, once a rich brown, was developing gray streaks at the temple.

They can't come in here. They can't see me. Mara snatched her phone and charger off the wall and abandoned the hot chocolate. She strode toward the door in what she hoped was a casual, brisk pace. *If I keep my head down and move quickly, I might make it out of here before they notice me. Please, please, please…*

The door pulled away from her hand just as she reached for it. Mara jolted backward and, against her better judgement, raised her eyes to the middle-aged couple entering the coffee shop.

Elaine had always been a beautiful woman. Even with the soft wrinkles her forty-four years had given her, she was stunning. Her husband, George, had put on weight since Mara had last seen him but not enough to hide his strong jaw. To a stranger's eyes, they could have been a power couple—high-flying attorneys or professors at a respected college. Only their clothes gave any hint that they deviated from the mainstream. George still wore his skull talisman, barely hidden under his shirt, and Elaine's skirt was too full and colorful for her to fit in with the Stepford wives.

There was no avoiding their notice. Mara made eye contact and found herself unable to look away.

"Mara," Elaine gasped, eyes wide. She stretched a hand forward as though she didn't completely believe what she was seeing.

"Excuse me," Mara blurted and pushed between them. *She still wears the same perfume*, she thought as she dashed across the street, heedless of the car horns and screeches of brakes around her, and fumbled Neil's car keys out of her pocket.

"Mara, wait!" Elaine yelled. She'd snatched up her skirt and was running across the street, but her shock had given Mara a head start.

Mara dove into the driver's seat, slammed the door, pushed the keys into the ignition, and managed to turn them despite her trembling hands. She pressed on the accelerator, narrowly avoided colliding with another car, and sharply veered down the road.

She tried her hardest to pretend she couldn't hear her mother's grief-filled cries. *What are they doing here? It's nearly an hour away from their home! Unless they moved… Crap, they'll know I'm local now. Do they have any way to find where I live? Did they get the license plate number? No—it's okay—it's Neil's car, and he knows not to give out my address.*

Once she was certain she'd put enough distance between herself and her parents, Mara pulled into a sheltered side street. She slumped against the wheel, half gagging as she drew air through her tightened throat. Her clothes stuck to her sweat-slicked skin, and her chest ached.

You're okay. It's fine. You'll just need to stay out of town for a while. Or—or shop at the next town over or something. They won't be able to find you again. It's fine.

"Crap." Mara propped herself upright, blinked the panicked haze out of her eyes, and tried to figure out where she was. *I can't stay around town any longer. I could wake Neil up. He wouldn't mind—no, he didn't sleep last night; he needs the rest. I'll go back to Blackwood. It's quiet and safe. And that's exactly what I need right now.*

This time, Mara had enough control to get back onto the street without a single honk from the cars around her. She drove carefully, keeping below the speed limit as though that would atone for her earlier recklessness, as she circled back to Blackwood.

Hints of uneasiness began to prickle over her back as soon as she turned into the long, potholed driveway, but she dismissed them as leftover anxiety from her encounter with Elaine and George. It wasn't until she reached the clearing and saw a black van parked in front of Blackwood that she suspected anything was seriously wrong.

CHAPTER 29
A SPIRITED ENCOUNTER

THE LARGE BLACK VAN was unfamiliar, and it didn't seem occupied. Mara parked near the edge of the clearing so that her engine's rumble wouldn't attract the notice of whoever was visiting.

The prickles running down her spine became stronger as she got out of the car. Strangers were inside her home—and Mara hated it. *This is my house,* she thought, echoing the sentiment scrawled across the wall upstairs. *This is my house; this is my house; this is my house.*

She rounded the black van and caught sight of the sticker on its side: *Spirited Encounters,* written in swirling cursive, sat next to a cartoon ghost.

"Hell no," she mouthed, backing away from it. The prickles turned into a buzz.

A light glowed in Blackwood's windows. Strains of esoteric music floated to her as she climbed the porch stairs. She twisted the handle of the front door with meticulous care to keep the metal from whining. She felt as though a dozen tiny threads were wrapped around her, barely holding her together, and they could snap at any second.

She looked left, into the dining room, and frowned. The large wooden table was gone, and six of its eight chairs were neatly arranged by the wall. Mara walked into the sitting room.

The rocking chair had been pulled away from its corner and sat in its usual place under the windowsill. Feeling numb, Mara turned toward the library—the source of both the music and the golden light—and stopped in the doorway to absorb the scene.

The dining table had been brought to the library and placed in the center of the room. Three candles were arranged along its length. Interspersed among them were various trinkets: jewels, animal and bird skulls, leather-bound books, and talismans. A man and a woman sat on either side of the table. They were both young—midtwenties at most—and elaborately dressed. The woman wore a high-necked Victorian-style blouse with frills cascading down its front and clustered at the cuffs. She'd wrapped her long, sandy hair on top of her head in a style she must have thought made her look more mature and had multiple necklaces slung about her throat.

The man had his dark hair slicked back. He was dressed entirely in black and wore a heavy coat. He was chanting words Mara didn't recognize while his female companion hummed. They held hands, with the third candle placed between them, and had their eyes closed.

And leaning against the bookshelves at the back of the room, arms crossed, stood Neil.

"What the hell is this?" Mara was shaking too badly to move further into the room. Her voice wavered but didn't break.

Neil jolted away from the wall. His eyes widened, and his mouth opened a fraction, but no sound came out. The horrified guilt on his face removed any faint hope Mara had held that she'd misunderstood the scene.

The couple at the table started at Mara's voice and broke their chants. They stared at her for a second; then the woman, who was closer, stood and took a step forward. A hesitant smile lit up her face. "Are you the owner of this house?" Her voice was breathy, almost reverent. "My goodness…you're absolutely saturated in energy. No wonder the spirits are becoming frantic."

"Get out of my house." The phrase escaped Mara as a whisper.

The other woman didn't seem to hear. Her smile widened as she took another step closer. "Do you have training? No—this is natural ability, I think. Probably from a relative who was highly in tune with the other realm. A parent? A grandparent, maybe?"

"*Get out of my house.*" Darkness edged in at the corners of Mara's vision as the tension inside her built like a typhoon and threatened to break the flimsy threads that held her together.

The woman's smile faltered. Neil stepped forward and reached toward Mara. "Sweetheart, don't be angry at Evereca or Damascus. I called them; this is my fault."

Mara held her hand palm-out to halt Neil. Her voice was a deadly whisper. "I'll deal with you in a moment." She turned back to the woman and her frowning companion. "Get out of my damn house."

"It's all right." The woman's bright smile had returned. "I know this sort of thing can seem strange or confusing at first, but we're here to help purge your house. We're attempting to communicate with the spirits in order to—"

The threads snapped. "*Get out! Get out! Get out!*"

"Mara, no!" Neil grabbed her around the waist and dragged her back before she could claw at Evereca's face. Mara screamed and elbowed him in the stomach. He grunted and dropped her, and she turned on the table as she unleashed her fury.

"Get out!" She sent the candles clattering to the floor, where their flames fizzled and died. "Out!" The antique books were thrown at Evereca, who ducked just in time. "I said *out!*" She placed her hands under the table and lifted. Fury gave her strength, and the table flipped over with a deafening crash.

"Let's go." Damascus snatched up an armful of their equipment and grabbed his companion's wrist. Evereca seemed to be trying to speak, but Mara didn't—*couldn't*—listen. She lifted one of the chairs and hurled it after the mediums as Damascus physically pulled his companion out of the room. The chair smashed into the wall and tumbled to the ground, a fracture running down the wooden back.

Mara kept her feet, listening to the van door slam and the wheels screech as the spirit mediums sped off the property, then she staggered. Neil appeared at her side, and his arms moved across her back to support her, but she smacked him away.

"All right." Neil stepped back and raised his hands in peace. "I know you're angry, and you have every right to be."

"Honestly?" Breathing made her chest ache, and her vision was nearly blotted out. She stumbled to a wall to hold herself up. "It would hurt less if I'd found you entwined with a hooker."

Neil flinched.

"How could you?" Burning tears bled into the black patches at the edges of her vision, and Mara didn't try to check them. "You bastard."

Neil swallowed thickly. His lips were twitching, but he kept his voice soft. "This place is sick, and I can't watch you live here any longer. Yesterday morning—the morning I skipped work and found you locked in the basement—I was woken by my phone ringing. You know the first thing I thought? That it would be the police calling to tell me my girl was dead." He blinked furiously. "I'm frightened for you all the time. I can't lose you, Mara."

"You bastard," she repeated. Her voice had dropped to a whisper, and malice coagulated in it. "You know how I feel about people like that. And you invited them into *my home.*"

"That's why I called them while you were out." He took a half step toward her, and Mara bared her teeth at him. "I thought—if they could get rid of whatever presence was here—and you wouldn't have to know—"

"*There's nothing wrong with Blackwood!*" She took a long, shaking breath and pressed a hand over her aching chest before continuing in a lower voice. "There's no such thing as ghosts. I had the first eighteen years of my life to saturate in those toxic

lies. And y-you knew how much I hate mediums. And you...
invite th-them into my home. Not yours! *My* home!" She moved
her hands to her head, where a stress headache was blooming
over the temples. "You're scum, Neil. Lying, manipulative, back-
stabbing scum."

He didn't speak, but his eyes were red. Mara thought he might
be trembling, but it was hard to tell with her own vision so erratic.
She was too drained to yell, so she said, as clearly as she could
manage, "Get out, and don't ever contact me again."

Neil broke his cardinal rule and swore. "Mara, I wasn't trying
to hurt you. I only wanted to help."

"It wasn't wanted, and it wasn't needed." The ache in her chest
burned almost more than she could endure. "This was unforgivable."

He took a deep breath and stepped closer. "Let's talk about
this. I'll make you a cup of tea, and we can—"

"No. I'm done talking. I hate you, Neil. I hate you so much."
Hot tears ran down her cheeks as hysterical laughter mixed into
her words. "I think I might even hate you more than I hate my
parents. We're over. Stay away from my house, and stay away
from me."

Every time she said *hate*, Neil flinched. The hurt in his face
would have crushed her the day before, but at that point, all she
felt was relief. Then his beautiful blue eyes narrowed as anger
rose to mingle with the pain. "You're horrible," he said at last.
"You think you're so superior to your parents, but you're twice
as deluded as they could ever be. You've been given so many
signs—so many clues—so many warnings—but you do nothing

except close your eyes and block your ears. There are evil spirits in Blackwood, living in plain sight, and you're willfully oblivious."

"Shut up!" Mara threw herself at him. She beat against his chest and kicked at his legs, doing everything in her power to cause him pain. He hissed and shoved her, sending her reeling backward. "I hate you!" Mara screamed. "Bastard! Get out!"

"With pleasure!" He kicked at the chair that lay by the door, sending it skittering across the room. "*Don't date crazy*, people told me. Now I know why."

Neil disappeared through the living room, through the foyer, and out the front door, slamming it in his wake.

CHAPTER 30
BROKEN

MARA, FEELING NUMB AND cold, followed Neil's path into the foyer and stared at the closed door. His car's engine roared then faded into the distance.

She stood there for far longer than she should have. A cold, cutting realization slowly wormed its way through the shock. *Neil's gone.* She hated him, but when she tried to untangle the anger from her heart, she found that another emotion still survived underneath. Despite the cutting betrayal, the cruel words, and the screams, she loved him desperately. *He's gone, and he's not coming back.*

"Nngh." Mara crumpled to the floor and wrapped her arms around her torso. Everything hurt. Her head pounded. The black had faded from her vision, but her eyes were blurred by tears she couldn't stop. Hate and love danced a violent tango inside of her. She wished he were dead. She wanted to see him smile again. She craved his suffering. She wanted him to hold her and kiss her and tell her everything was all right.

All gone. Mara bawled unashamedly. She slumped to her side and rested her cheek on the dusty floor as she painted the wood with her tears. She'd thought she'd known pain before, when she'd walked into the library and seen the séance Neil had arranged, but it was nothing compared to what she was experiencing afterward. She'd lost her companion, the one person she'd learned to trust above all others, the one person who had been her ally against the world, and the kindest man she'd ever known. She felt as though she were being torn apart.

Time blurred. One moment, it was early afternoon; when she next looked out the window, twilight painted the sky a violent red. Mara rolled onto her back, gasping and groaning. Blackwood seemed to exhale around her as the aged wood relaxed in the cooling air.

"It's just us now," she whispered to the building. Her throat was raw, and the throbbing in her skull told her she was dehydrated. She made it to her knees then got to her feet. She was unsteady and dizzy but navigated her way through the near-empty dining room and into the kitchen. "I don't hate you," she said as though soothing the building could ease her own pain. "I think you're beautiful. Did you see how I defended you against them? There's nothing wrong with you. Anyone who says otherwise is a liar."

She turned the tap. Red water poured out.

Mara watched the crimson water gush into the sink but felt

too hollow inside to muster any reaction. She waited until it cleared then filled her glass and drank.

"You're a good house." She placed the emptied glass back onto the counter. "We're really quite a lot alike." Goose bumps spread over the back of her neck as a deep, slow creak came from the living room. Mara licked her lips. "You've got some quirks; that's all."

She turned, compelled more by habit than curiosity, and followed the pathway back to the foyer. "No one else understands you the way I do." She stopped in the living room's archway as a sickening, cold dread bloomed over the ache in her chest.

The rocking chair rolled on its struts. A red liquid dripped from the wooden back and onto the seat.

"Did they do this to you?" Mara's voice was a tight whisper as she crept toward the chair. "Is this one of the mediums' tricks?"

She touched the red substance. It felt warm and tacky under her fingers. The chair continued to roll despite Mara not feeling any sort of breeze. She began to back away from it then startled as a child's cry came from the chimney.

"Just the wind. That's all…"

The cry broke into a hiccup then resumed. Mara turned to escape back to the foyer and saw the blood-encrusted cross-stitch on the wall. *Their Hearts Are in My Home.*

Her palms were sweaty, and she rubbed them on her jeans. "It was the mediums. They did this—cruel jokes—"

A slow, painful noise came from the foyer. It sounded like straining rope. Mara turned, shivering, to look through the opening.

Robert Kant hung below the stairs, his dead eyes staring blindly as he twisted on his noose.

Mara felt as though she'd been fused to the ground. She couldn't control her shaking as the symphony of the dead—the rocking chair, the crying child, and the straining rope—filled her and suffocated her. Robert's body continued to twist as though he'd only recently leaped from the banister. He looked human but was made of a strangely fluid smoky substance. It reminded Mara of ink dropped into a glass of water; the body kept its shape even as it swirled. His eyes—a madman's eyes, sunk deep into the haggard face—flicked toward Mara. She clasped her hands over her ears and screamed.

When her voice died out, the house had returned to silence. Mara carefully lowered her trembling hands and opened her eyes. The space under the stairs was empty. The rocking chair lay still. The chimney was silent.

"It's not real." Her mouth formed the words, but she couldn't say them. "There's no such thing as ghosts."

The basement door slammed. Mara gasped and began running, tearing up the stairs, tripping over her feet and crawling the last few steps until she could press her back to the hallway's wall.

"*The axman is coming. Run, run, run.*"

"No." Mara turned toward the master bedroom door as it creaked open. She caught a swirl of motion through the opening.

"Run, run, run." The figure slipped into view, its eyes bulging with insane fear as it paced, white gown and tendrils of pale smoke fluttering in its wake.

"No." Mara, bent double, began edging down the hallway toward the safety of her own room.

The figure reappeared in the doorway, her pale face frantic as her crazed eyes fixed onto Mara. "*The axman is coming.*"

"No!" Mara fled past the specter. Bloodied fingernails stretched through the opening and scratched at her arm, leaving stinging scores in their wake. Mara dove into her room and slammed the door. Panicked sobs shook her. *What's wrong with me? Have I gone insane?*

She pressed a hand to the place where the nails had grazed her. Blood welled at the site. She was able to touch it, feel its viscosity, and smear it away. *This cut is real. The pain is real. It's not a dream. It's not a delusion. And I don't think I'm insane—not quite yet.*

A crackle made her turn toward the bureau, where Neil's laptop stood open. The screen flickered into life, showing the attic's jumble of indistinct shapes…

…and a man.

He stood in the center of the room, almost directly above her head, and stared at the camera. The figure was slightly hazy as though it had been constructed out of congealed mist. Long-dried opaque blood streaked the remainder of his face; the left half of his head was crushed.

"Sweet mercy…" Mara pressed her hands over her mouth.

The man swayed, turned, and began pacing. Static buzzed over him with every step. The distortion obscured him but not as wholly as it had the previous night.

"This can't be real." Mara fell forward to kneel on the ground as the footsteps echoed over her head. A small trail of dust spilled from one of the disturbed floorboards.

All those years, all those séances, all those sham mediums… I can't have been wrong.

The footsteps reached the end of the house, turned, and began their slow return journey down the length of the attic.

They were fakes and liars. I know that with complete certainty. But then…what's this?

The steps groaned above her head. A new, different sort of pain was growing in her chest. She watched the screen, which showed the static-shrouded man stopping beside the hole in the wall. He pressed his head and shoulders through it then began creeping forward, shifting onto the roof inch by inch until the feet disappeared from view.

Mara turned toward the window just in time to see the white figure plunge past.

"I was wrong. Ghosts are real." Mara, overwhelmed by the aches and the shock, keeled over. Hysterical, uncontrollable laughter rose inside of her, but she didn't try to fight it. If she didn't laugh, she would have to scream.

Even as she crouched on the bedroom floor and held her aching chest as though it would fall apart if she released it, Mara's mind still tried to find a way to justify what she'd seen. *The mediums planted tricks—*

"No. They weren't clever enough to put together something like this."

It's a hallucination brought on by stress—

"Am I hallucinating the cuts on my arm, too?"

Insanity…?

"Not as far as I can tell."

Mara tried not to throw up.

Ghosts are real. What does this mean? Were my parents right? All of those tricks—all of those shams—did they hold any truth?

Blackwood House is something wholly different. There aren't any tinkling bells or flickering candles here. The spirits inside these walls are tortured. They're visible. And they're constantly reliving their deaths.

"Sweet mercy," Mara whispered. Simply admitting she'd been wrong felt inhumanly difficult. Having to face the ramifications was a hundred times worse. *I don't want to do this alone. I can't do it alone. If I had Neil—*

The thought of Neil set the ache flaring again. He'd been right about Blackwood. More, he'd taken a risk and tried to save her, and Mara has screamed insults at him in repayment. "Crap, crap, crap!"

She remembered his words from the night before, when he'd pleaded with her to call a priest. *There is nothing I wouldn't do for you, Mara. I would even survive your hating me for it afterward. As long as I could make sure you were safe.*

Mara shook her head as she paced around the sleeping bags Neil had bought for her. *Was he planning the séance as early as that? He knew it was risky—he knew he would lose me if I found out—*

I'd give anything to have him back.

Mara pulled her phone out of her pocket and gasped in relief as it turned on. She hadn't spent long in the coffee shop before seeing her parents, but it had been enough to give her battery a little bit of charge.

He might not want to talk to me. The things I said were brutal. But maybe...

She dialed Neil's number and raised the phone to her ear. The call ended without any way to leave a message. *Crap. He's turned his phone off.*

Mara passed her hands over her face. *Where does that leave me? I'm stuck at Blackwood until it's light enough to walk to town. Whatever's happening in this house is magnifying. And the night's still very, very young.*

Mara tried to remember the séances and meetings her parents had participated in when she was a child. She'd deliberately tried to repress those memories in the hope that they would eventually be forgotten, and returning to them was like reopening scabbed wounds.

She saw the scores of faces, many weathered with age, of the mediums who had been invited into their home. She saw the candlelight wavering over a small collection of trinkets from lost loved ones as she, her family, and a collection of strangers and acquaintances had held hands and participated in a séance. She saw Miss Horowitz, the spirit medium her mother had wanted her to train under, bellowing a garbled message as thunder cracked outside the room.

But none of that was helpful. George, Elaine, and the spiritualists they were friendly with all sought contact with the dead, never the opposite. Mara knew a half dozen ways to begin a séance but not a single method for exorcising an unwanted ghost.

She looked back at her phone. The battery was almost dead. She tried calling Neil a second time but with the same result. *There's no one else I can call.*

Mara prided herself on her independence. She'd lived a nearly entirely solitary life. The only exception—the only chink in her armor—had been Neil. She'd never been so close or so comfortable with another person. But without him, she felt wholly, completely alone. She didn't have friends. She'd even kept her old co-workers at arm's length.

For half a second, she considered calling her parents—but they would be incapable of helping, even if she knew their number.

Then an idea occurred to her, and she cringed. *I'm out of options. It's them or nothing.* She took a deep breath, clutched her nearly dead phone to her chest, and poked her head out of her room.

The rocking chair continued to groan. Now that she could no longer excuse it as a breeze, the sound sent chills through her. She kept as much distance between herself and the master bedroom as possible as she crept along the hallway. The door remained closed. The space below the stairs was empty. Only the rocking chair remained active. Mara, her heart in her throat, hurried to the ground floor.

She didn't want to pass through the living room, so she took the longer route around the dining room and kitchen. Mara kept her eyes moving, scanning the walls and furniture and glancing behind herself frequently, but saw nothing to disturb her until she reached the recreation room.

The red handprints had spread across all four walls. They stained the wood and seemed to scrabble up the basement door. The hairs on Mara's arms rose as she moved through the room in the straightest line she could manage. She couldn't tell if the sensation of eyes on her back was her imagination or not.

The library was a mess. She felt a rush of shame at the sight of the overturned table and broken chair. *In a twisted way, though, my anger might just be my salvation.*

She knelt behind the table and began picking up the scattered talismans and herbs. Damascus, the medium, had grabbed his music player and the more expensive equipment, but he'd been so eager to escape Mara's wrath that he'd abandoned the smaller trinkets. Mara went through them carefully, turning them over and examining them, then gave a small cheer as she found what she'd been searching for. On the inside flap of a small, cheap Bible was the inscription, *Spirited Encounters: Evereca and Damascus, verified spirit mediums*, followed by a phone number and post office box address.

"Verified by who?" Mara snorted then bowed her head. *You're in no position to mock them. They're your last chance.*

Mara dialed the number. Her phone rang twice before it was answered. "H-hello." She hadn't planned anything to say, and her mind went blank. "Uh—this is Mara. You were at my house a little earlier—hello? Hello?"

They hung up on me. Of course they would. Honestly, I'd hang up on me as well.

Tears built, but she brushed them away. Then she looked at her phone and saw, to her horror, she hadn't been hung up on after all. Her battery had died.

CHAPTER 31
COMPANY

MARA SAT ON BLACKWOOD'S porch. Night had thoroughly descended, and she was left with nothing but a flashlight to light the trees surrounding her. Animal calls bounced through the night air. The wind was cooling, but Mara was reluctant to return to the house while the rocking chair continued to groan.

Everything hurt. Her head throbbed from crying, her pride was shredded, and her heart felt as though it had been through a meat grinder. Every time she tried to come up with a plan, she ended up circling through the same unanswerable questions. *Where will I live? What will happen to Blackwood? Is there any chance Neil will forgive me?*

A faint rumble floated through the cold air, and Mara started upright. She strained to hear more and was rewarded as a vehicle's engine became clear.

The headlights were the only discernible part of the van as it rounded the bend in the driveway. Mara grinned and shook her head as it slowed and eventually came to a halt near the other side of the clearing. *They actually came back. These people are either really desperate for the money or way more idealistic than they have any right to be. Probably both.*

The woman bounded out of the van and approached Mara. Her companion followed at a slower, more cautious pace.

"Hey!" Evereca stopped a little outside Mara's reach. "You, um, called?"

Mara couldn't fight the wonky smile that was forming. "You have no idea how glad I am that you came back. And, jeez, I'm sorry about…all of what happened this afternoon. I really messed up. But my house is haunted, and I don't want to be alone tonight, and if you could maybe get rid of the ghosts that would be pretty cool, too."

Evereca's grin scrunched her whole face up. She moved forward, arms extended, and pulled Mara into a fierce hug. "I knew it. Of course we'll help. We're verified mediums, you know."

"A-ha, yeah." Mara awkwardly patted the woman's back. "That's—that's what I need, I guess."

Evereca drew back and gave her a quick, searching look. "We kinda got off to a rough start today, huh? How about we try again. I'm Evereca."

"That's the stupidest name I've ever heard," Mara said cheerfully, shaking the woman's hand. "I'm so glad you're here." It was hard to see in the dark, but she thought the other woman's face turned pink.

"Uh, well, my name's actually Erica. Evereca is my spirit-medium name. It sounds more impressive."

Mara let her breath out in a rush. "No, it sounds like something you'd find in a Mary Sue fan-fiction contest. Erica's way better." She turned toward the man and gave him the warmest smile she could manage. "Do you have a sensible name, too, or am I going to have to call you Damascus?"

"Damian." A slow, faint grin was curling his lips. "Where's Neil?"

"I chased him off because I'm a horrible person." Mara kept her voice bright despite the pain that cut through her at the sound of Neil's name. "But at least I didn't murder him. So, y'know, I'm doing better than the average."

The joke had been a last-ditch effort to maintain her cheerful façade. As soon as the words left her mouth, the horror of her situation washed over her, and she doubled over. She pressed her palms into her eyes until stars shot across the back of her eyelids. For a second, it was a toss-up between being sick and collapsing, but then Erica's arm threaded around her shoulders and pushed her toward Blackwood.

"Let's get you inside, yeah? We'll have a séance set up and your house cleared in no time."

"Nuh-uh." Mara tried to pull back. "Shouldn't go back in. It's not safe."

"Naw, it'll be fine. You've got *us* with you now." The glee in Erica's voice was unmistakable. Mara dropped her hands from her stinging eyes to see the other woman staring up at

Blackwood with unabashed delight. "This place is incredible. It's…it's like it's buzzing. Did you feel the attraction as soon as you saw it?"

"Uh…" Mara remembered her first day at Blackwood, when the supposedly locked door had opened without objection and the vast building had enthralled her.

"It attracts people like you," Erica continued, oblivious to Mara's discomfort as she ushered her through the front door. "People with the gift. Yours is really strong, so you probably feel the house's pull really strongly, too. Now, where'll we go? The library again? It's got awesome atmosphere."

Mara had no energy left to object. She let Erica lead her through the house while Damian trailed behind. She shot a look at the rocking chair as they passed it, but the blood had disappeared, and it sat dormant. *It's almost like having company dulls the haunting effect.*

As they entered the library, Mara grimaced at the sight of the scattered equipment. "Sorry about that, by the way."

Erica patted Mara's shoulder. "It's cool. Dame?"

Damian took one end of the table while Mara and Erica lifted the other. It was heavier than Mara had expected, but they managed to correct it. She propped her flashlight upright on the surface to diffuse its light, and Erica cheerfully forced the candles back into their holders and lit their tips. Damian left while the women collected the trinkets, then he reappeared with two extra seats from the dining room. They sat down, Mara on one side of the table and the mediums on the other.

Mara sighed, breaking the silence. "Okay. I want to apologize—again—for this afternoon. I was raised in a spiritualistic household. It wasn't a great experience for me, and I've spent the last four years avoiding any mention of ghosts. So, um, I sort of overreacted when I found out my boyfriend had set up a séance."

"Don't worry about it." Erica leaned forward as excitement lit up her face. "Honestly, I'm pretty excited to be back here. I've never seen a house like Blackwood before. Did you know a renowned spiritualist called Victor Barlow built it? He was really quite brilliant—"

Damian caught the sour look on Mara's face and tapped his companion's arm. Erica obediently fell silent.

Mara inhaled and held the air for a beat before saying, "Yeah. He's my great-great-grandfather."

"A-*ha*." Erica's eyes shined in the candlelight as she shuffled her chair closer. "I knew you had to have some sort of gifted history. Did you know about Victor before you bought Blackwood, or did it call you to it?"

A headache was growing at the back of Mara's skull. She massaged her temples as she tried to find a peaceful way to express herself. "Look, today's been a really, really bad day. I don't understand half the things you're saying. I'm having to confront the idea that I've been *wrong* about something pretty damn substantial for most of my life, and it feels somewhat like having surgery without an anesthetic."

"That's quite all right." Erica had been slowly leaning closer and was nearly out of her chair by that point. "I'll be glad to guide you through this period of discovery—"

"Stop." Mara held up a finger to halt Erica's progress. "I believe in ghosts. But I don't believe in you. Not yet anyway. You symbolize everything I've hated for the majority of my life. But I'm willing to give you a chance because—well, I'm sort of out of options right now. Can we make a deal? I'll do my best to trust you and follow your instructions. But in return, I want you to cut the BS. No tricks. No smoke and mirrors. No stupid fancy stage names, props, or attempts to look cool. You can impress me by dealing with Blackwood's ghosts. All right?"

The two mediums looked at each other then nodded. "That's a deal," Erica said.

"Great." Mara tilted her head toward the jumble of trinkets she'd collected off the ground. "Do we need all of these?"

Erica hesitated, and Damian spoke in her place. "No. They're almost all for show."

"Really? You don't even use the Bible?"

He shrugged. "It's more for demonic spirits, which we don't deal with."

"Those things are nasty," Erica agreed.

"Neil mentioned he was Christian when he called us, so we bought the Bible on the way to pick him up. We figured it might get us in his good books."

Mara sucked on her teeth as she nodded. "Was the chanting also for show?"

"Not entirely. It creates atmosphere, but we also use it as a meditation to help Erica center in on what beings are in the house so she can figure out how to handle them. But it doesn't do anything for the ghosts per se."

"C'mon, you're giving away all our trade secrets," Erica hissed. Damian gave her a patient smile.

Mara swallowed and traced a pattern over the wooden table. "So you can…what? See spirits?"

"I can't," Damian said, "but Erica can sense their presence and get a feel for what they looked like, how they're feeling, and when they died. She's basically really good at picking up on spiritual energy."

Mara grimaced. "Yeah, that sounds made up."

"Don't worry; it's not." Damian's mouth twitched. "Everyone and everything that's alive is sustained by energy. It's what separates, say, a plant from a rock. When we die, our energy can sometimes be left behind—like a residue. With a strong enough energetic imprint, you get a ghost."

Mara glanced toward the doorway to the foyer. "I'm guessing violent deaths leave more energy than peaceful ones."

"Bingo. Murders, betrayals, insanity, that sort of thing. If the victim is full of very strong emotions when they pass, it can leave a residue."

"Or if they feel maligned," Erica interjected. "Super strong resentment or regret can make ghosts, too."

Mara thought through all of the spirits she knew of in Blackwood. *The mother cradling her dead child after killing her husband. The man who broke a hole in the attic's roof and threw himself to his death after losing his family. Robert Kant, a tortured soul. The insane wife, butchered by her husband as she tried to claw her way out of her room. Yeah, they all count.*

"Normally, residues will fade," Damian continued. "It can take many hundreds of years, but eventually they stop being strong enough to be felt. They can also be released by someone with spiritual aptitude."

"Is that what you're going to do?"

"We'll give it a try."

Mara placed her elbows on the table, laced her fingers, and rested her chin on them. "How much experience do you have?"

"Heaps," Erica said instantly. Mara narrowed her eyes and let the silence stretch until Erica cleared her throat and dropped her gaze to the table. "I've been practicing heaps, at least."

Great. They're rookies. "The van looks new," Mara observed.

Damian gave a nonchalant shrug. "We officially opened our business last week. You're the second house we've visited."

"Have much luck with the first?"

They shared another glance. "Th-there were some complications—" Erica started.

"We botched it," Damian finished.

"Well." Mara tried to keep her voice cheerful. "There's plenty to practice on here."

"You bet." Erica's mood was instantly restored. "Like I said, this house is absolutely buzzing. It's got to be built on a massive spiritual hot spot."

"Explain that."

"Well, it's sort of like…" She cast around for a moment then snapped her fingers. "Like acupuncture. Have you ever had that?"

"Nope."

"Oh, it's great. I had this crick in my neck that just wasn't going away and—"

"Focus," Damian murmured.

"Right. So the idea behind acupuncture is that you have all of these energy points around your body. Sometimes they become blocked, and that causes problems. Now, imagine the earth is like a really big body. It has all of these energy points scattered around. They're locations where spiritual energy naturally collects. The Bermuda Triangle includes a cluster of several large patches, and a lot of famous haunted locations are built on these spots."

"And Blackwood is one of them," Mara said.

"Exactly. My skin's tingling from the power. I'm guessing Victor Barlow could sense it, too, which is why he built Blackwood here in the first place. He was really into experimenting with spiritual connections and getting closer to communicating with the afterlife, and he probably thought being on a hot spot would help. Except, of course, it backfired."

"Robert Kant stumbled on it."

"Robert Kant was *drawn* to it." Erica's voice was rising with her increasing excitement. "He would have had some basic spiritual aptitude; I'm sure of it. Everyone who's come to Blackwood has. It repels normal people. They either get a bad vibe from being here or find something about the house they don't like. But people like you and me—people who have the gift—are attracted to it. You love Blackwood, don't you?"

Mara opened her mouth, but she couldn't disagree. She knew that, after everything that had happened, the building should repulse her. But there was something almost magnetic about it that made it hard to hate. It was like being in a relationship with an abusive partner.

"Exactly." Erica looked far smugger than Mara thought she had any right to. "Blackwood called you just like it called Victor Barlow, and just like it called Robert Kant, and just like it called every other poor soul who lost their life here. It craves people like you."

Mara had a sudden flashback to her childhood: Miss Horowitz, caught in the throes of a séance, bellowing, "Beware the home that craves!" She shook her head. "You're saying it wasn't a coincidence that I bought the house my great-great-grandfather built?"

"Not at all. You inherited his gift and were naturally drawn to the same place that attracted him. You're—how can I put this? You're like a battery that never runs out. You're constantly leaking a low amount of spiritual energy. When you're frightened or stressed, you produce more. When you're calm, less. The house, and the spirits in it, consume your energy to become stronger. That means the house's activity will become more severe with each day you spend in it."

Mara frowned. Erica's theory was consistent with what she'd experienced. "Why did Victor Barlow build his house on a hot spot if he knew it was dangerous?"

"Well, it wouldn't have been dangerous at all when he found it. Spiritual hot spots aren't inherently bad—it's just what happens on them that dictates their state. If Victor had died a peaceful death, this would probably be a really pleasant place to live. You might have a few extra dreams or have an easier time communicating with the dead, but that's it."

"But because of Robert Kant—"

"Everything went to hell, yeah. A murder on a spiritual hot spot is a sure way to taint it. I didn't get time to research this place—Neil kinda insisted on a rush job—but would you happen to know any of its history?"

Mara quickly filled her companions in on Robert's multiple victims, his suicide, and as much as she could remember of the subsequent families. Partway through her story, the rocking chair began to creak again. They all pretended not to notice.

Damian's face darkened as he listened. When Mara had finished, he turned to Erica and whispered something in her ear.

"Stop worrying; we'll be fine," Erica laughed.

That's the sort of thing I'd say to Neil. Fresh pain cut through Mara. *What's he doing right now? Would he be having dinner with his mother and trying to pretend like nothing happened? How much does he hate me?* She shuffled forward and tried to bring her mind back to more immediate matters even as her heart felt as if it were being crushed. "What's the plan? Do we need to deal with the ghosts one at a time?"

"Probably not," Erica said. "To keep with the acupuncture analogy, the house's energy has been blocked by a violent death.

Probably either Victor's or Robert's though it could be one of the children, too. Following that, every other death at Blackwood has increased the energy level. There's been a lot of bloodshed in this place. It's built up to the point where it's ready to explode. All it needs is an acupuncture needle to unblock the cause, and all the other spirits will dissipate with it."

"And the acupuncture needle is…?"

"Me!" Erica looked thrilled at the idea. "I wish I could get some cameras in here. It's going to be pretty amazing."

Mara thought of the camera that had captured Keith and Sal's last moments and shivered. "Stick with a low-key approach. Do you need to do anything special to unblock the energy, or does it sort of just…happen?"

"The easiest way is to hold something that belonged to the spirit and concentrate really hard on releasing it. Before we do that, though, we've got to find out who the main ghost actually is. I'll need to do some meditating to work that out." Erica glanced at the trinkets, and a guilty smile flickered over her mouth. "They're only for show, but d'you mind if I…?"

"Go ahead." Mara found she cared far less than she would have expected as she watched Erica distribute her talismans across the table. Damian moved around to take Mara's seat, placed one of the candles in front of him, then took Erica's hands to begin the session.

CHAPTER 32
FOCUS

"THIS MIGHT TAKE A while," Damian said as his companion closed her eyes. "Make yourself a cup of tea or something. You look pale."

Mara was feeling queasy but didn't want to miss any of the meditation process. She leaned against the wall, imitating the pose she'd caught Neil in that afternoon, as she watched the mediums. Whereas the afternoon session had included chanting, this time the couple hummed. As far as she could see, they were keeping their promise of cutting out the theatrics.

Time stretched on. Erica's face was completely blank at the session's start but gradually darkened. Perspiration stood out on her forehead and began running down her cheeks. Damian remained calm but occasionally opened his eyes to check on Erica.

Mara shifted uneasily as the footsteps in the attic joined the rocking chair. Neither Damian nor Erica flinched when a door slammed.

At the ten-minute mark, Mara began pacing. At fifteen minutes, she sat on the ground and pulled her legs up under her chin. The wait seemed painfully, inordinately long, and despite having company barely five feet away, she was starting to feel isolated. Erica and Damian were wholly focused on each other; Mara doubted they would notice if she spontaneously combusted. She ached for a companion of her own. *Neil.*

She was nearly at the point of getting the suggested cup of tea when Erica opened her eyes and sucked in a lungful of air. She was shaking, but a smile spread over her face. "Oh, wow; this place is intense."

Damian rubbed Erica's hands as Mara quickly pulled up the third seat. "What did you see?"

"There are a bunch of spirits here—mostly women and children—but the dominant one is a man. He's tall and thin and carries an ax. That ax is super important; it's almost like a part of himself."

"Robert Kant," Mara supplied. "The ax was his signature weapon—so much so that the media called him The Chopper."

"That'll be our ghost, then." Erica looked elated but exhausted. "If we can get rid of Robert, the rest of the ghosts should flow out easily. Just like unblocking a drain."

"Most of the other murders in Blackwood were also committed with an ax," Mara said. "Is that normal?"

"It means Robert was possessing or influencing the perpetrators," Damian said. "Which isn't surprising. It would be extremely unusual to see so much violent death in one house if there wasn't a powerful spirit orchestrating it."

"Why?" Mara asked. "What does he get out of this?"

Erica shrugged. "He's probably just a sick puppy. Deranged and violent in life, deranged and violent in death."

The footsteps above them finally fell silent. Mara imagined the smokelike man plunging to his death for what could have been the thousandth time.

"Now we just need something connected to Robert," Erica said. "Preferably something he was emotionally close to and frequently carried, but I could probably make do with an object he'd held a few times if it came to it."

Mara raised her eyebrows. "What, are you expecting me to magically produce one of Kant's favorite keepsakes? I don't want to disappoint, but...*no*."

"There's got to be something," Erica pressed. "Did he use the cutlery here? It'd be a weak connection, but I bet I could make it work."

"Sorry, the cutlery belonged to the last people to own this house. Six families have lived here since Robert. I really don't know how much would be left over from his time." Mara gazed about the room. "Could you use the house itself...?"

"You mean like touching the walls? Not really, unless you can identify a specific part of the wood that he was in frequent contact with. And it's got to be more than just leaning on it—I need skin contact."

"Jeez; you're fussy," Mara muttered. Damian snickered. "Uh...

he hung himself from the banister. I've seen his ghost there a couple of times."

Erica almost burst out of her seat. "Really? You've actually…? Wow—it usually takes years of practice to *see* ghosts. Not even I—though I guess the energy hot spot is helping a lot. Still… have you ever considered a career as a spirit medium?"

Mara cringed.

"Focus." Damian tapped Erica's arm, and she settled back into her seat.

"Oh, yeah, right. Knowing where his ghost hangs out will help us if we want to communicate with him, but it's no good to dispel him. I've got to *touch* something."

"Ugh." Mara rubbed at her face. "Sorry, but I've only lived here for, like, five days. I have no idea if anything would have come from Robert's time, let alone which items he was fond of."

"We could ask one of the spirits," Damian suggested.

Erica's face lit up. "Yeah, great idea. Let's do that."

"What, it's really as simple as that?" Mara glanced toward the now-still rocking chair. "We just say, 'Hey there, Mrs. Ghost, got any gossip you want to spill?'"

Damian grinned again, but Erica crossed her arms and puffed her cheeks out. "Of course it's not that simple. As the lead ghost, Robert will probably still be quite intelligent. But the others might be nothing except a bundle of impulses—the last emotions and motives they experienced as humans, replayed every night. Still, there's a chance they can lead us to something, or give us a hint, if they have much awareness about them. We'll have to go about it carefully, though."

"All right, all right." Mara took a slow breath to calm herself. "Which ghost would you like to try first?"

"Got any suggestions? Not Robert—he probably doesn't want to be dispelled and is just as likely to attack as help. Otherwise, the more active, the better—and they'll be more likely to cooperate if they still had their wits at the point of death."

The lady killed in the master bedroom was clinically insane for a year before she was killed. The woman in the rocking chair didn't have a diagnosis, but if my dream can be trusted, she was also unhinged. That leaves…

"The spirit in the attic. He paces up and down its length before throwing himself through a gap in the roof. I can't guarantee he was sane—it was a grief-prompted suicide—"

"Let's try him." Damian rose from his chair. "Do you know of anything that can summon him? Does he follow a pattern?"

"He's already gone through his routine twice tonight, but the last few nights, he appeared between eleven and eleven thirty. He only stays for a couple of minutes, though."

Damian checked his watch. "It's ten to eleven now. Let's get up there."

Mara led them to the attic. The familiar jumble of furniture, shed cloths, and clotted shadows greeted her. She scanned the area, but it was still and quiet. Mara waited for her companions to join her then shifted her light from the furniture to the hole. "He usually completes a couple of laps before crawling through there."

"Have you seen him?" Damian asked.

"Yeah, earlier tonight, actually, on a webcam we set up."

"Did he seem angry or aggressive?"

Mara strained to remember. She'd been almost hysterical at the time of the encounter, and the images were faint. "No, I don't think so. He seemed sort of blank, like he'd been driven to the point of exhaustion. The police report said he took his own life after his last child died and his wife killed herself, so my guess is he was probably in grief."

"That's okay," Damian said. Mara thought he'd relaxed slightly.

"Is it important?"

"Eh..." He shrugged. "Normally a spirit's emotional state isn't an issue, but in a house as charged as this—well, if a ghost is angry or resentful, it might lash out at any interference—even a human one."

Mara frowned, and her hand rose to scratch the spot on her arm where the woman in the master bedroom had grasped at her. "Ghosts can hurt us, can't they?"

"They can if they have enough energy. And you've been feeding them your excess energy since you arrived." Damian dusted off a discarded cushion and offered it to Erica, who still looked tired after the meditation. "That's why the supernatural events become stronger each night. The spirits gain power the longer you stay here."

"Damn," Mara muttered. "Is there any way I can...maybe... *not* do that?"

"You could learn to control your energy with some practice.

But, for tonight, I'd recommend you try to remain calm. The more frightened or anxious you become, the faster you'll radiate energy."

That explains why my worst nights were when I was alone. I felt safe when Neil was around.

Damian checked his watch. "Shouldn't be long now. How're you doing, Erica?"

"Nearly there."

Mara started and turned to see the other woman crouched in a patch of floor she'd cleared. Erica had produced a stick of chalk and was scribbling strange shapes and runes on the wood. Mara took a half step away. "What's this for?"

"It helps focus her energy." Damian indicated some of the shapes. "These attempt to wear down the barrier between the human world and the spiritual realm so that she can mediate between them." He pointed to another group. "Those are supposed to act as protection. And those"—he gestured toward the last group—"will enhance her power."

Erica finished by drawing a circle around the odd collection of shapes then knelt on the cushion in its center. "Do we have everything? I'm not—ugh, the sage!"

"Do you think you'll need it?" Damian checked his watch. "It's two minutes past eleven. I could run down and get it…"

For the first time, Erica looked anxious. "No, I want you here. We'll make do without it tonight."

"I could get it," Mara said, and Erica swung toward her.

"Would you—? Thanks heaps. It should be on the table."

"Be back in a minute." Mara turned to the trapdoor. She slid down the stairs, ran along the length of the hallway, and took the steps to the ground floor two at a time. Her skin was prickling. Something big was coming, and it wouldn't wait for long.

CHAPTER 33
SAGE AND ROPE

MARA KEPT HER FOOTSTEPS light as she moved through the foyer and the living room and into the library. She didn't know how important sage was to the ritual Erica had cooked up, but if it could offer even a little protection, she wanted to grow a garden of it. Or at least learn what it looked like.

I never expected this to be one of the downsides to kitchen ignorance. I bet Neil would recognize sage. Damn it—put him out of your head, Mara. Get through tonight so you have the chance to apologize tomorrow.

The three candles still burning on the table cast flickering shadows about the room. The rocking chair began groaning again, but Mara ignored it as she sifted through the trinkets. Half-hidden under a cat skull was a bunch of small, soft leaves. Mara raised the herb to her nose and inhaled. *This better be the sage.*

She pushed the bunch into her pocket and turned to run

through the living room but snapped back when she reached the doorway. The rocking chair, groaning softly on its struts, was occupied. The large, red-haired woman faced the window as she kicked her toes against the floor.

Crap, crap, crap. Mara's stress spiked. She knew she was supposed to stay calm, but her heart felt as though it was trying to leap out of her throat as she pressed her back to the wall. *This is fine. You've got sage, remember? And—and that's probably useful—somehow—*

The woman didn't seem to be aware of having company. She was faced away from Mara, hiding her expression, but the pose was relaxed and the rocking gentle. She wasn't completely solid but made up of the same swirling mist as the spirit in the attic. Mara began to slink around the edge of the room.

Faint snatches of the foreign lullaby floated through the air, but it seemed somehow wrong, as though the woman was no longer able to hit all of the notes.

Mara was nearly at the foyer's doorway when she hit a creaky floorboard. She flinched, clenching her teeth, as the wood groaned.

The woman's feet fell still, stopping the rocking chair's motion. She turned slowly, and Mara pressed a hand over her mouth to smother her cry.

It hadn't been immediately noticeable behind the thick hair and dress, but the woman was severely decayed. Clumps of translucent flesh had sunk around her eye sockets and sloughed free of her cheeks. She seemed to be grinning, but it was hard to tell without any lips to frame the teeth.

Mara squeezed her eyes closed and stumbled backward until her shoulder hit the corner of the doorway. When she opened her eyes again, the woman was gone. The rocking chair shifted, as though it had been recently vacated, then came to a halt.

Cold sweat built over Mara. She backed through the doorway, reluctant to take her eyes off the chair and prepared to run at the slightest sign of motion. Sickness rose in her stomach, but she swallowed it.

Two stories above, someone began pacing through the attic. The steps were too even and too familiar to belong to either of the mediums. "Damn it."

Mara turned to run for the stairs, but before she could take a step, something dropped in front of her eyes and snagged around her throat, tugging her back. She grunted and tried to shake the object off, but it was heavy and scratched her skin. Her blood chilled as a deep, cracked voice whispered into her ear, "Surprise, sweetheart."

The weight around her throat was suddenly much, much tighter as bony hands tugged against it. Mara struggled to pull free, clawing at what she now realized was a coarse rope, but it was already cinched. She opened her mouth to scream, but a sharp jolt pulled her toward the stairs and her feet left the ground.

No! Her throat was forced closed. She kicked, but her legs only touched air. *Make noise! Call for help!* She opened her mouth, but the only thing that escaped was a stifled gurgle. She couldn't breathe, let alone speak. She stretched a hand out. Her fingers grazed the wall, but it was too far away to beat against.

A heavy, slow footstep reverberated behind her as Robert Kant circled his prey. She couldn't see him, but she felt his icy hands brushing against her back as he toyed with her. "Why don't you scream, sweetheart?" he purred.

Mara scrabbled at the rope, but it was too tight to get her fingers under it to reduce the pressure. Her lungs burned. A high-pitched ringing echoed through her head, and darkness bled into the edges of her vision.

Do something! Think of something!

A voice seemed to be trying to break through the ringing sound, but she couldn't make out the words. She couldn't see, and her fingers felt numb as they scratched at the rope with increasing sluggishness.

Then an arm wrapped around her waist and lifted her. The pressure across her throat slackened enough for her to suck a thin gasp of oxygen into her starved lungs. The voice was speaking to her, but the words seemed garbled.

A blade pressed against her throat. Mara impulsively twitched back, but the knife didn't cut her. Instead, it wormed between her skin and the rope and began sawing at the fibers.

"Hold still, Mara. Don't struggle. I'll have you out in a moment."

I know that voice. I know these arms. He came back.

"Neil," she croaked.

"Shh, shh, hang on—"

Her hands, too oxygen starved to hover around the rope any longer, dropped to his shoulders. She could feel the muscles, taut under his shirt, as he fought to hold her weight and cut the rope at the same time. Every rub of the blade against the noose increased the pressure around her throat, but there was just enough slack in the cord for Mara to breathe around it. Then the last strand broke with a quiet snap, and Mara tumbled forward.

She didn't have the strength to raise her hands to brace herself against a fall, but it wasn't needed. She came to a halt, wrapped in the thick, strong arms she loved so much. Neil's calloused fingers massaged at her throat as he murmured, "Breathe, sweetheart. You're okay. Just breathe."

Air had never tasted so sweet. Mara forced her eyes open and found Neil hovering over her, his face sheet white and eyes wide with fear. She tried to smile but wasn't entirely certain what expression her face made. "You came back."

"Shh, don't try to talk."

His fingers trembled as they massaged her aching throat then moved higher to brush strands of hair out of her face. Mara tried to stroke his chest, but it turned into more of a weak pat. "Why'd you come back?"

He shook his head, but his eyes never left her face. "I know— you don't want me here—you can yell at me as much as you want later, I promise—just relax—"

"Don't you dare leave me ever again." Mara's face cracked into a wonky grin. The relief and gratitude and fear boiled together, and before she realized what was happening, she was crying. She couldn't stop it; the tears came hot and fast, and all she could do was clutch Neil and hope he didn't think she was completely deranged.

The arm behind her head and shoulders raised her a little and pulled her close. His other hand alternated between rubbing her back and wiping tears off her cheeks when he could reach them. "It's okay," he whispered into her hair. "You're safe now. I won't let anyone hurt you."

"We can hire that priest you wanted," Mara managed between gulps and hiccups. "We can hire the whole Vatican. Install the pope in the spare bedroom."

Neil's body shook as he laughed. His hands were all over her—in her hair, stroking her cheeks, and caressing her arms. "Mara, Mara, Mara," was all he seemed able to manage. "I'm so sorry."

"Don't be." Mara wiped the wetness off her cheeks. "I'm a billion times more sorry than you could ever hope to be, so don't even try to compete. I was horrible to you."

"I went behind your back. I broke your trust. You had every right to be angry."

"Yeah, but you were right." Her lungs still ached, but the dizziness had faded, and her energy was coming back. Neil didn't seem to want to let her go, though, and Mara was more than happy to stay pressed close to him. "Oh my gosh; I was such an idiot."

Neil tilted his head to see her expression. He looked cautious. Mara cursed herself for making him feel the need to be wary around her.

"Yes, don't worry; I'm not being stupid anymore. I called the mediums back. They're up in the attic right now."

Neil's face darkened as he glanced away. "They shouldn't have left you down here alone."

Mara followed his gaze toward the sawn rope still hanging from the banister. She shuddered then ran her fingers over Neil's cheek to bring his attention back to herself. "Hey, don't be angry with them. I went to get some stupid herb they needed. It wasn't like they threw me to the house or anything."

"Regardless." Neil's arms tightened around her. "I almost lost you. Jeez, Mara. If I hadn't come back—"

He kissed her. It was a painfully sweet expression of so many emotions: fear, desire, remorse, relief, love. It sent thrills racing down Mara's back. She wrapped her arms around him and tugged him closer despite her growing dizziness.

"Sorry," he said, pulling back. "You need to breathe. Here—"

"I'm fine," Mara objected as Neil pushed her into a sitting position. She rubbed at her aching eyes, relieved that the tears had stopped. "Thanks, by the way. For coming back. Saving me. Not being a jerk about it. All of that."

Neil chuckled. He shifted so that he could sit next to her with his arm at her back to keep her steady. "Are we okay?"

"I want us to be okay."

"Me too."

Mara leaned her head against his shoulder and rejoiced in his warmth and solidity. She knew they couldn't stay there for long. The footsteps in the attic had ceased, which meant the ghost must have completed its fated march. Any moment, Damian and Erica would be coming downstairs to see why she hadn't returned with the sage.

"Neil? Why'd you come back?"

He kissed the top of her head. "You're not the only one in this relationship who can be obnoxiously stubborn, you know."

"Me, stubborn? Perish the thought." She sought out his hand and squeezed it. "Truthfully, though. Why?"

"It was a couple of reasons. Partly because I hated the things I'd said to you. I didn't mean them, and they're not true."

"About me being delusional and crazy? I think they were at least somewhat true at the time."

Another kiss. "No, they weren't. And that was the other reason I came back. I'd been incredibly angry. And I mean much, much angrier than I should have been even for an argument. I dunno—this probably sounds weird—but it was almost like the house was manipulating me."

"No, it's not weird at all." Mara thought of all of the spontaneous, violent murders that had occurred within Blackwood's walls—husband against wife, wife against husband—and was deeply grateful that Neil had had enough restraint to walk out of the room. Mara remembered beating her fists against his chest, desperate to hurt him, and wondered what she might have been capable of if she'd had access to a knife. The idea wasn't pleasant. She pushed it out of her mind.

"But the main reason was I didn't want us to end like that," Neil continued. "Especially not with you still inside Blackwood. I was going to come back and see if I could convince you to let me stay the night. If not, I figured I could wait in my car at the head of the driveway in case you needed a getaway vehicle."

"Seriously? I said some brutal stuff—none of which I stand

behind, by the way. How could you come back after that? Are you sure you weren't just planning to collect your laptop and leave again?"

Neil laughed. "I *do* want that back, by the way."

As she glanced up at his profile, Mara was amazed at the change in his expression. He still looked pale, but he'd lost the tightness about his lips, and his smile was genuine. He seemed far more relaxed than he had during the previous two days. *I can't believe I put him through that much stress.*

Then she thought of someone else who had suffered from her poor decisions and felt her mouth turn dry. *Be honest with him. He deserves it.* "Can I tell you something personal?"

"Of course."

She inhaled and held it for a beat. "I bumped into my parents today. I ran off before they could say anything."

"Ah, Mara." His arm tightened around her. "That's why you came home early, huh? I'm sorry."

"I've been horrible to them, Neil. And I'm starting to think they didn't deserve it. I never told you, but I looked them up online a few months ago. I don't even know why. I think I was hoping they'd been arrested or something. Well, they used to be prominent members in a bunch of spiritualism forums and on the council of a local association. But I discovered they'd resigned from all of them. I can't find any trace of them communicating with other spiritualists since four months after I left home."

"Do you think you prompted that?"

"I have no idea." Mara's voice cracked, and she cleared her

throat. "Maybe they grew some sense. Or maybe they thought I'd come back if they weren't affiliated with those groups. Whatever the cause, it wasn't enough to make me forgive them for believing what they did while I was growing up. But now…" Mara waved a hand toward the house then let it flop back into her lap. "Were they very wrong?"

Neil's cheek was warm on her forehead. He was silent for a moment then said, "Does it negate what they did to you?"

Don't cry. Mara swallowed the emotion as well as she could, but she was ashamed to feel it creep into her voice. "They weren't bad parents. They did some stuff that hurt me. But not deliberately. Like the rabbit they killed—do you remember me telling you about that?"

Neil nodded.

"It was sick anyway. Dad asked for spiritual guidance and said he was told it was suffering. We couldn't afford a vet, so he drowned it. I loved that rabbit. At the time, I felt like he was a murderer. But he wasn't trying to be cruel. He never was."

"They kept you from having friends." Neil's voice was gentle, but there was a hint of bite at the back of it. *Does he actually resent my parents for that?* The thought simultaneously warmed Mara and made the guilt swell. She dropped her head.

"That wasn't their fault. They tried to organize play dates, but the other parents wouldn't let their kids visit." *Don't cry. Don't you dare.* "Mum threw me a birthday party once. She invited every kid in the suburb. Not a single one came. B-but she still t-tried to make it fun. Just Mum, Dad, and me. We played all the games and—balloons everywhere—and—had cake—" Mara pressed her palms to her eyelids. The effort of holding her tears in was constricting her throat. "Y-you should have heard the way Mum cried when I left home. And I cut them off for four years because I was a narrow-minded, self-righteous, arrogant little—"

"Stop that." Neil pulled her close. He cradled her against his chest and stroked her hair until she calmed. Once her breathing had steadied, he said, "Maybe they're not monsters. They're probably not blameless, either. Mistakes make us human; don't torture yourself over a choice you made four years ago. If you think you were wrong, make a plan to change what you can. Action is good. Choices are good. But guilt on its own never fixed anyone's problem."

"You're wasted as a carpenter," Mara mumbled into his shirt. "You need to get yourself a motivational show like Oprah. Fix the world's problems."

The attic's trapdoor slammed. Mara twitched, and Neil tightened his grip on her. "That'll be the mediums, right?"

"Yeah." She wiped her eyes with her sleeve. She hoped they weren't too red. "Where'd you find them, by the way?"

Neil got to his feet and carefully pulled her up with him. "I called my pastor, actually. He said he couldn't help, but he suggested Spirited Encounters. Though I'm starting to suspect he just did an internet search for 'mediums for hire.' I got the feeling haunted houses aren't something he has to deal with often...or at all."

Two figures appeared at the top of the stairs. Mara was

relieved to see that both Damian and Erica seemed calm. The sage couldn't have been necessary after all. "Oh, hey, Neil!" Erica clattered down the stairs. "When'd you get here?"

"A few minutes ago." The serious note had returned to his voice. "And I found my girl hanging from the stairs. Where were you both? She could have died."

Erica shoved past him, oblivious to his disapproval. "Wait, back up. What happened?"

Mara felt herself turning red. "It looks like you were right—Robert Kant doesn't want to be dispelled. He, uh, tried to hang me."

Damian moved closer to Neil. He spoke too quietly for Mara to hear. Before she could join the conversation, Erica clasped her shoulders, eyes wide and voice breathless. "That's so cool. Did he say anything? What did he look like?"

"Erica, have some tact," Damian said before turning back to Neil.

"Sorry." Erica didn't sound like she meant it. "Did he give you any clues? The ghost in the attic was a bust."

"He just said 'surprise, sweetheart' then told me to scream. Which I couldn't." Mara rubbed her neck, which she suspected would be bruised the following morning. "I didn't see him. What do you mean about the attic ghost? I heard his footsteps. Didn't he know anything?"

"I couldn't even talk to him." Erica deflated like a balloon. "I could hear the footsteps—even see the boards move and little puffs of dust come up—but I couldn't see anyone. I asked questions, but he either didn't hear or didn't answer. We waited for ages after the footsteps stopped, but he didn't come back. So, we're back to square one."

Mara glanced at the rope, which still hung from the banister. *What're the chances that's the same rope Robert hung himself with? Neil cut it easily, which means it's probably old. I bet that would have amazing spiritual energy.* She cringed. *Crap, I'm even starting to think like them. Goodbye, self-respect.* "Would the rope be any good?"

"Huh." Erica approached the dangling cord, circled it, then brushed her finger over the noose section. She closed her eyes then pulled back with a shiver. "Yeah, this has a man's energy all over it. I'm pretty sure it's the right time period, too. Good work, Mara!"

Mara rubbed her neck again. "Thanks...I guess?" She turned back to Neil and Damian, but they were deep in discussion. Their faces were both stern, and Neil kept shooting looks at her. Damian had his arms crossed and was working his index finger over his thumbnail in what looked like an anxious habit. Mara wished she could hear what they were saying.

"You ready for some ghost busting?" Erica was turning in a circle as she surveyed the room. "It's a good space for it, too. Nice and airy—" She broke off as Damian, finally finished talking to Neil, approached her and nudged her arm.

"A word?" he asked his partner.

CHAPTER 34
DISSENT

DAMIAN DREW ERICA AWAY and began talking to her in tones that were a little too quiet to hear. Mara turned back to Neil, who had moved to stand next to her. He looked tense.

"How are you feeling?" Neil asked.

"I'm fine. Erica thinks she can use the rope to summon… unsummon…extract…whatever she plans to do to Robert."

Neil tugged on her hand to draw her away from the others so they could speak in privacy. "I was just talking to Damascus—"

"His real name's Damian."

Neil gave her a tight smile. "Trust you to get the truth out of them. Well, I was talking to Damian. He wants to call it off."

From across the room, Erica half gasped, half yelled, *"What? No!"* Damian said something quickly, and Erica lowered her voice. They began a hushed but heated debate.

Mara turned back to Neil. "How come?"

"He thinks it's too dangerous. He said he's happy to work on passive spirits but the energy here is too high to risk playing with malevolent ones."

"And Robert's definitely malevolent." Mara sucked on her teeth. She tried to repress the panicky sensation that was chewing up her stomach. *I have everything invested in Blackwood. I can't sell it, but I can't live in it, either.*

Neil's hands brushed up the sides of her arms, and Mara relaxed into the touch. "I told him how important Blackwood is to you." Neil's voice was gentle and warm. Mara stepped closer to absorb more of it. The tangles in her stomach unraveled when he spoke like that. "He's sympathetic, but he doesn't think it's worth the risk. He said maybe if you took a few years away from it and let the energy subside, it might be safe to try again."

A few years! Mara pressed her eyes closed. *No, don't act like a mule. Be grateful for what you have.* "I'll need a place to stay. I dunno if your offer is still open, or…"

"You're always welcome in my home." Neil spoke gently. "I'll talk to Mum. Maybe we can put the religious stuff into storage…"

"Thanks." Mara had been creeping closer to him and was near enough to lean her forehead against his chest. His heart—a steady, even tempo—was soothing. He wrapped his arms around her back and rocked her gently.

"I'm sorry. I know how much this house meant to you."

"I'm not dead," she said, partly to remind herself. "I've got an amazing boyfriend who, against all odds, doesn't hate me. I have a house to stay in even if it's not my first choice." She inhaled his scent and smiled. "And money's just paper you exchange for stuff. I can get more of it."

"I love you, Mara," Neil whispered into her hair.

"Shut up!" Erica shrieked from across the room. Mara turned toward the commotion. Evidently, the mediums' discussion hadn't gone as smoothly as hers. "You are such a jerk, Dame. This is a once-in-a-lifetime chance!"

Damian bent low to murmur something then drew back with a hiss as Erica stomped on his foot.

"Years? I'm not waiting years! *Mara!*"

Mara impulsively leaned away from the fuming woman. "… hi?"

Erica stormed forward, grabbed Mara's wrist, and attempted to drag her away from Neil. "Looks like it's just you and me tonight. Ready to do this thing?"

"Slow down!" Neil attempted to pry Erica's hand off Mara's. "You'll hurt her!"

"Erica." Damian, coat whipping behind him, rushed in to block his companion's path. "You can't do this alone."

"I'm not alone," she spat. "I have my best friend, Mara, who, incidentally, is way cooler than you."

"…best friend?" Mara blinked and shook her head. "Lady, I wouldn't even call you an acquaintance."

"Shut up, I'm trying to do you a solid here." Erica glowered at Damian. "This is private property, and I've been hired to do a séance, so you can either stick around and help or buzz off."

Damian's eyebrows rose, but he didn't speak.

The grip on Mara's wrist was hard enough to hurt. She tried to worm her hand free. "Calm down, Erica. If it's dangerous—"

"Nothing important was ever achieved by playing it safe," Erica said. Mara opened her mouth to question that logic but found herself fixated by Erica's gaze. The woman's eyes were wide. "C'mon, I *need* Blackwood. Its energy is so high that I'm sure I'd have no trouble dispelling Kant." She turned back to Damian. "You said I needed real-world practice. This is the best I'm going to get! And after the last place—I don't want to be zero-for-two. Please."

He sighed and dropped his head. When he spoke, the tone was low and cautious. "Mara, how important is this building to you?"

Mara turned her eyes toward the ceiling. She felt such a complicated mix of emotions that she couldn't easily untangle them. There was a sting of betrayal; the house she'd trusted—the house she'd loved—had turned against her. But there was also fondness. She'd repaired its walls. She'd scrubbed its floors. She'd fallen in love with the building, and saying goodbye would feel like ripping a vital part out of her chest.

Then she looked at Neil. His brow was creased, and his beautiful blue eyes anxious. She took a deep breath. "I really, really, really like the house. But I don't want anything to do with it if it's going to put the people I love in danger."

She felt as though she could survive a year on a desert island with nothing except the smile Neil gave her.

"No, come on," Erica whined. "You're meant to be on my side!"

Damian looked relieved. "She's the boss. Come on; let's pack up."

"Hang on." To Mara's surprise, Neil stepped forward, a hand held up. "Damian, how dangerous would an attempt be?"

Damian glanced at Mara before returning his gaze to Neil. "Mara's the biggest wild card. If she becomes panicked, the burst of energy could push a malevolent spirit into doing some truly horrific things."

"Could she leave the house?"

"Ironically, it would help to have her present. A gentle, sustained radiation of her energy would fuel Erica's work."

"Okay." Neil crossed his arms and looked the room over. "If she stayed calm, could we try it?"

Damian let his breath out in a rush but didn't answer.

"I'll pay extra," Neil added, but the other man shook his head.

"Don't worry about the money. If she can stay calm—and if we take precautions—and if you understand there are no guarantees—"

Neil took Mara's hand. "Do you think you could stay calm? If I was with you the whole time?"

"Yes." Mara had never known safety like being close to Neil.

"Yes?" Erica, who had been following the exchange as though she were a starving woman and their words were food, edged closer to Damian. "Yes?"

He sighed. "All right; let's do it. But—" He held up a hand to quiet Erica's cheer. "*But* we're not taking any risks. If things start to fall apart, or if I judge the situation is becoming too risky, we bail immediately. Deal?"

"Deal." Erica raced toward the living room. "I'll get my stuff!"

"Hey, don't split up!" Damian barked as he ran after her.

Mara watched them go then turned back to Neil. "Do you really want to do this?"

"I want you to be happy." He wrapped a hand around the back of her head and kissed her before she knew what was happening. Mara's heart did a happy little flop in her chest. "And this house is important to you, so I want you to have it if that's possible. I think that's worth a little risk."

Mara stretched up on her toes to reach Neil's lips again. He was so tall that he still needed to duck to meet her halfway. She poured all of the love and warmth she felt into that kiss and felt giddy as he shuddered. When she pulled back, she was breathing quickly. "I don't need this house." She ran her thumb along Neil's jaw. "But I do need you. We don't have to go through with this if—"

"Gangway!" Erica yelled as she barreled between them, arms full of equipment.

Be calm, Mara told herself as Neil chuckled. She squeezed her eyes closed, took a deep breath, then stretched and turned toward Erica with renewed enthusiasm. "All right. What're we doing here? Is it a séance, or…?"

"Think of it like a séance with a twist." Erica dropped her collection of trinkets into the center of the foyer. "We're going to attempt to summon Robert Kant's ghost and then dissipate him. Remember, he's nothing but energy. So, we're going to set stuff up to attract that energy, untether it from the house, and disperse it. If he's no longer concentrated in one form in one place, he'll literally cease to exist. Hey, Dame, could you grab that rope?"

Neil passed his pocketknife to Damian, who climbed the stairs to cut the noose free from the banister.

Erica opened a packet of chalk, took a fresh stick out, and began scrawling symbols onto the floor. "The muk for protection. The aejis to call Robert to us. The vesp to enhance my power. And, most importantly, the quinet to disperse Robert." She drew each symbol multiple times except for the last, which she created only once, larger than the others and directly ahead of herself. She then drew a circle around the marks. "The muk and vesp will be active constantly," she said in answer to Mara's silent question. "We'll activate the aejis by concentrating on Robert's rope. The quinet, our ace, will only be used once we have him close and contained."

"How important is it that the shapes are correct?" Mara asked, glancing between two muks, one of which was slightly distorted.

"Not really at all." Erica turned pink. "Technically, I should be able to do all of this with just my mind. But I'm, uh, still getting used to real-world application, and the symbols give me something to focus on."

Still getting used to real-world application. That's a pretty way of saying you need practice. Mara bit back the comment as Damian laid the rope on top of the quinet symbol.

"Got the sage?" Erica asked, and he held up a bunch of the herb and a lighter.

Mara could still feel her own bundle of leaves in her jeans pocket. "What's it for?"

"Burning sage is traditionally used to dispel spirits. It's not going to be enough to completely purge one as strong as Robert, but it should weaken him if things start getting hairy." Erica began laying new items around the border of the circle: a locket, the cat's skull, a black-and-white photograph, an aged, folded letter, and a cracked teacup.

"Mara, sit just outside the circle." Damian directed her to a space beside Erica. "Neil, stay close to her."

Mara settled into her indicated place, being careful not to touch the chalk outline. Neil knelt beside her, and she leaned against him. An anxious, jittery sensation was growing in her stomach, and it was proving hard to dampen. "Do you ever do these sorts of rituals yourself?" she asked Damian.

He grinned and shook his head. "No, I'm about as spiritually talented as a rock. I keep an eye on Erica, make sure she's not in danger, and read all of the books she refuses to because they're, and I quote, dead boring."

Mara nodded. "Do I need to do anything—?"

"Not at all. Sit there, stay calm, and Erica will use your energy as she needs it. Remember"—he looked at Erica pointedly—"this is the equivalent of trying to fight fire by pouring a barrel of fuel on it. It could go wrong very quickly. If I give the word, we're all bolting for the door. I don't need any heroic 'I can handle it' moments tonight. Agreed?"

"Agreed," they all chimed.

Damian nodded. "All right. When you're ready, Erica. Take it slow."

CHAPTER 35
PRESENCES

ERICA CLOSED HER EYES and picked the rope up. She turned it over in her hands several times, squeezing the fibers, and began swaying. Damian leaned against the nearest wall, arms folded and eyes darting about the room. The door above them slammed.

"Come on." Erica spoke so quietly that Mara almost couldn't hear her. "Come on."

Damian shifted forward. "What's wrong?"

"Ugh…" Sweat beaded over Erica's forehead. "It's really weird. He's harder to find than I would have expected. Almost like he's hiding."

"He won't want to go. Be careful."

Erica bent lower over the rope, and her knuckles bulged white as she strained.

Motion drew Mara's attention to the wall under the stairs. A shadow flickered over the wood. She caught the impression of twitching feet, suspended above the floor, then it was gone again. She shifted backward, and Neil slid his arm around her shoulders.

"Don't be afraid," he whispered into her ear, and Mara nodded as she tried to swallow the fear.

It felt different from the previous days, when her armor of certainty that the spiritual realm didn't exist had protected her. Without that security, she felt vulnerable. The only thing keeping her grounded was Neil's arm. She focused on his warmth and on his steady heartbeat.

"Got him," Erica hissed. She had her fingers pinched in the air, and drew them closer to herself, almost as though she were pulling an invisible thread. Anxiety prickled over Mara's arms and scalp.

Behind them, the rocking chair began groaning. Mara didn't dare turn to look at it. She could still picture the woman, flesh sliding off her face, rolling her feet to move the chair as she watched them.

"Stay calm, Mara." Damian's voice cut through the cloud of fear that was building. Mara nodded and refocused on Neil. She carefully relaxed each tight muscle and forced her breathing to become slow and even. Only her heart, which fluttered like a frightened bird, wouldn't obey her.

Erica began humming as she swayed. She held her pinched fingers carefully and gave quick, short tugs. With each tug, the air seemed to grow thicker and the prickles on Mara's skin increased. She could sense something big coming.

"Can you feel that?" Mara whispered to Neil.

"Feel what?"

She shook her head.

Then a man exhaled. It was a deep, crackling, rough noise that reminded Mara of dead tree branches scraping together. There was something deeply *wrong* about the sound. Mara tightened her grip on Neil's hand. He squeezed back.

"Come on, Robert," Erica muttered. She was shivering, and sweat stuck her bangs to her forehead. She kept twitching the pinched fingers toward herself then relaxing them. Mara found herself intensely curious about what the other woman was seeing and feeling. She stared at the fingers, trying to imagine what they might be touching, and an image flashed through her mind.

She didn't *see* it so much as see an impression of it, as though her mind created the picture and laid it on top of reality in the same way that an animator paints onto a transparent sheet of paper then places it on top of the background to create a complete image. They were separate but created a whole.

A dozen black threads ran between Erica's pinched fingers. The threads were airy and thin, like spiderwebs. They were attached to the rope coiled in front of Erica and stretched across the room before disappearing into the wall under the stairwell. When the medium twitched her hand, the threads were pulled taut. When she relaxed, they slackened and floated freely.

Mara looked away and felt panic swell as she realized the room was *full* of threads. They drifted about her, weaving through walls and floors, bunching in some areas while loose ends drifted

276

fluidly in others. Several of them slid against Neil's face. Mara raised her hand to brush them away from him but couldn't feel anything except his warm skin.

"What is it?" Neil's voice was low and careful. He looked worried for her. "Sweetheart, why are you shaking?"

Mara blinked, and the image was gone. Her lungs burned, and she realized she'd been holding her breath. "I'm okay," she whispered back. "Just—thought I saw something—"

She didn't dare look at him, but she could feel Damian's dark eyes watching her.

Erica's breathing was ragged, but a hint of a smile flickered around her mouth. "Come on. Come on."

Mara turned back to the wall below the stairs, where she'd seen the threads disappear. A wisp of something dark and smoky leaked through the wood. It was the same viscous, unreal substance the woman in the chair had been made of. As Mara watched, Erica twitched her hand again, and more inky smoke billowed through the wall. It was beginning to form a familiar figure.

"He's here," Erica breathed. Her eyes were closed, but triumph bloomed in her sweaty face. She pressed her left hand to the muk, the symbol that was supposed to protect them, and tugged on the threads again.

Robert stepped into the room, passing through the wall as though it didn't exist. His eyes were wide and furious, and he half crouched like a predator. He was clearer than the previous ghosts, but his outline was still smudged and smoky. The noose, made of the same swirling clouds, hung about his neck.

His eyes passed over Mara then fixed on Erica. He began pacing forward, no longer fighting the thread's pulls, as he stretched his knobbly, hooked fingers toward the woman who had called him.

Mara shrank back as Robert moved closer. Neil's arm tightened around her. "Stay calm, Mara. You're safe." She heard his words but couldn't absorb their meaning. Cold terror washed through her. She wanted to run, but her body felt like lead. The chair in the living room was swinging frantically, its harsh tempo like a saw on her nerves. Footsteps paced the attic floor. The child in the chimney began to wail.

"Get her calm," Damian barked. "She's waking them up."

"Don't yell at her," Neil hissed. He ran his hand along Mara's cheek, turning her face away from Robert and toward himself. "You're going to be fine, Mara. Don't be frightened. I'm right here."

He smiled, and Mara let herself fall into his beautiful blue eyes. His arms encircled her, the muscles pressing against her back and calloused hands stroking her arm. He radiated strength and warmth and safety, and she let herself soak it in.

The chills still ran along her skin, but now she was able to feel them as nothing but an interesting sensation. She could hear Robert's feet scraping along the wooden foyer floor and the dry rasp of air being dragged through a damaged throat, but it no longer made her feel sick. The sounds held no more danger for her than a monster in a horror film.

"Almost," Erica hissed. "Just a little more—" Her breathing was thin and quick. Mara was amazed at her enthusiasm for the session; it seemed exhausting, bordering on painful. Erica switched her hand from the protective muk to the dispelling quinet.

Robert Kant was almost on top of her, his madman's eyes bulging as he reached toward the medium's face. He scraped his long, jagged nails across her cheek. They didn't score the skin, but Erica shuddered as though she could feel them. With her left hand still pressed to the quinet, she dropped the threads from her right hand and plunged it into Robert's chest.

The quinet began to glow. It seemed to be sucking light out of the room. Mara blinked and looked again. *No, not light... but something* like *light.* The foyer was still dim, lit only by three candles and two flashlights, but another sort of glow permeated the area. It was so subtle that she hadn't even noticed it until she saw it shifting toward the quinet.

Mara looked down at her hands and saw that the light was being drawn from her, too. *It's the energy they keep talking about. Of course.*

The glow was sucked into the quinet then ran up Erica's arm in twisting, rushing spirals. It burst down her outstretched arm and poured into Robert's chest. He screamed.

Mara clamped her hands over her ears. The raw, furious, pained bellow was deafening. But, just as with the light and the threads, it seemed to exist slightly apart from reality. Covering her ears couldn't dim it. She shot a glance at Neil and Damian. Neither reacted to the noise though Damian's eyes were intense as he watched Erica. He seemed ready to drag her away at the slightest sign of trouble.

Robert doubled over as the light was funneled directly into him. His black form swirled, like ink in water being agitated by a spoon, as he thrashed and screamed. The glow cracked through him like lightning through storm clouds. He twisted, his limbs seeming to burst apart and reconnect in the same motion, then straightened.

Erica's jaw fell open as she withdrew her hand. She looked terrified. "It didn't work."

"What?" Mara asked at the same time as Damian dove forward.

"Get out," he yelled to Neil and Mara. He seized Erica around her waist and began to pull her back. She didn't respond but continued to stare at Robert, her eyes wide and lips shaking.

"It didn't work," she repeated. "It's like…he's stuck…"

Then Robert lunged. He swiped Damian aside with a crack of his hand, sending the medium flying. Damian hit the wall and slumped to the ground, gasping.

Erica stared blindly as though too shocked to move. Robert bared his teeth in a feral grin as he picked the rope off the ground.

"Watch out!" Mara yelled, but Erica didn't react in time. Robert dropped the noose about her neck and cinched it tight.

Mara threw herself toward the spirit, desperate to free Erica from the rope. She punched both fists into Robert and smothered a scream at the sensation. He was cold—cold enough to be made of ice—and had one of the strangest textures Mara had ever felt. He wasn't solid, but wasn't quite liquid, either. The smoke felt somehow slimy under her fingers, but left no residue.

Robert turned toward her and hissed. His hand fixed around her throat and squeezed.

"Mara!" Neil was at her side. He was trying to free her, but he couldn't see Robert or know where to direct his swipes. The hand tightened, and Mara gagged.

Damian had scrambled to Erica's side. She'd slumped to the ground and stared dumbly at the ceiling as Damian fought to undo the rope. Her lips were turning blue.

"No!" Mara screamed again, struggling against Robert. She kicked and clawed, trying to hurt him, but her hands were no more effective than trying to slap sunlight. Noise surrounded her as the house's restless dead roared into action. The rocking chair, the sobbing, screaming child, the footsteps—no longer pacing but running above her head—and a multitude of pleading voices surrounded her as every door in the building swung open and slammed closed.

Then Robert hit her. The sensation, just like the light, seemed to belong to a different dimension. It hurt, but the pain came from somewhere other than her skin. She fell to the floor, gasping and trying not to cry out, as her vision swam to black. Footsteps moved past her. Neil yelled, then his voice was cut off. There was another grunting, pained cry, and then the room fell still and quiet.

CHAPTER 36
THE BASEMENT

MARA RAISED HER HEAD. Everything was dark; the three candles and two flashlights had all been extinguished. She felt in her pocket for the USB light Neil had given her and clicked it on. "Neil?" she whispered.

The light was too weak to illuminate more than a few feet ahead of her, but it caught the glint of silver near her side. She crawled to it, picked the flashlight up, and was relieved when it flickered back to life. She turned it over the room and felt her blood run cold.

The carefully constructed chalk circle had been blown outward as though someone had swept hands through it. Erica lay half in it, the rope still tight about her neck. Mara scrambled toward her as she continued to pan the room. "Neil?"

She caught sight of him standing near the back of the room. His face was impassive as he watched her, but he didn't seem hurt. She sucked in a relieved breath. "Neil, see if you can find Damian."

Mara dropped the flashlight as she knelt at Erica's side and began to worm the noose free. Erica was white as a sheet and didn't move. Mara managed to pull enough of the rope through its knot to slip it over the other woman's head then pressed her fingers to her neck. There was a pulse. *Thank mercy.* Mara then raised her fingers to Erica's mouth and felt the gentle flow of air.

"Neil, did you find Damian?" She turned back to her partner with a flutter of anxiety. He hadn't moved but continued to watch her with unnatural calmness. *Is he in shock? Did Robert hurt him?* "Neil? What's wrong?"

He turned and began walking. Mara snatched her flashlight off the ground and ran to follow him. He didn't seem to notice her presence as he stalked through the dining room and into the recreation room.

Mara hesitated in the dining room's doorway, shaking and gasping in thin breaths. She turned back to the foyer and turned the light over the room. Erica lay still, her chest rising and falling, but Damian was still nowhere in sight.

Crap, crap, crap.

A door creaked open. *The basement.* Mara turned back to the recreation room, where Neil had disappeared, and shuddered. "Neil?"

The deep thud of footsteps on stone told her that Neil was taking the staircase to the house's lowest level.

You need to get out of here, the logical part of her mind insisted.

There's something very wrong with Neil, and you don't want to mess with that. Grab Erica and run.

No, her heart replied. *I can't leave him at the house's mercy. He came back when I needed him; now he needs me.*

A loud cracking came from somewhere below Mara's feet. She couldn't hesitate any longer. Her mind threw up a hundred horrific ideas about what might be happening to Neil, and completely shut down the part that was campaigning for self-preservation.

She ran through the dining room and into the recreation room. The door to the basement stood wide open. Mara held her flashlight high and angled it to shine down the stairs, but it wasn't able to illuminate more than a dozen steps. She took a deep, aching breath and began the descent.

The difference in temperature was immediately noticeable. Her parents had often talked about cold spots when she was a child. They were supposed to indicate places where spirits resided though Mara had eventually pegged them all as drafty parts of their house. *If the whole basement is cold, what sort of ghost lives there? Or is it multiple ghosts? How many spirits can this house hold?*

The chill tickled Mara's nose. She pressed her spare arm over it to muffle the sound of her breathing. There was no way to keep her footfalls quiet, though; they echoed around her, bouncing off the stone walls and ringing in her ears.

The stairs opened into the basement, and Mara hurried to put her back to a wall as she turned her flashlight over the area. She couldn't see Neil, but a dark patch at the back of the room caught her attention.

There was a hole in the opposite wall. Someone had broken through the stones, leaving them littered across the floor in clumps and dusty fragments. Mara's nerves were wound tight, keeping her ready to jump back at the first sign of motion, as she crept closer. The gap wasn't wide but was tall enough for a person to step through without trouble. Mara crouched and tried to see through the clouds of disturbed dust as she drew closer.

The area beyond the wall was much larger than the basement she'd known. The stone walls stretched away for at least twenty meters. Hundreds of sheaths of parchment, colored with ink and crumbling from age, were stuck to them. Tables and shelves collected along one wall, their contents all desiccated. And near the back of the room stood Neil, facing the wall, hands clasped behind his back as though he were admiring a painting in a gallery.

"Neil?" The echo made Mara's voice sound far louder than she'd intended.

Neil didn't turn but inclined his head a little to indicate he'd heard. "Come and have a look at this, Mara."

Oh, hell no. I don't care what he's found; we're not going into the creepy room. No way.

"Neil, come back. Erica's hurt. We've got to go."

He showed no sign of hearing her. The prickling warnings crept over Mara's arms, and she switched the flashlight to her left hand so she could wipe her sweaty palm on her jeans. She tried to keep her voice steady as she called, "I'm serious; get out, or I swear I'll ditch your sad ass down here."

Still no answer. Despite her bravado, there was no way on earth she was leaving Blackwood without Neil. Panicked tears pricked at her eyes as she struggled to breathe deeply enough to keep her limbs supplied with oxygen.

Don't go in, her logical side pleaded. She knew she should listen to it. Nothing good could come from stepping through the hole in the wall.

But Neil wasn't moving, and she knew he wouldn't move unless she went to him. And every minute they spent in the basement felt like it increased the risk exponentially. *This is a bad choice. But I would make a thousand bad choices as long as they kept him safe.*

Mara climbed through the hole.

CHAPTER 37
SUPPLANTED

BROKEN ROCKS CRUNCHED UNDER Mara's feet as she sidestepped through the hole. When she'd first discovered the basement, she'd been bothered by how small it was. There was nothing to disappoint about the extended room, however. It would easily stretch the length of Blackwood, possibly farther. *I wonder when it was bricked up? The paper looks ancient, so it must have been around the time the first couple of families came here. But why?*

Mara glanced at some of the sheets pinned to the walls. They held diagrams, scribbled drawings of dark figures, and cursive that was too intricate for her to easily read. She didn't stop to examine them. All she wanted was to get Neil out of the basement and into his car.

He continued to face the wall and showed no sign of awareness as Mara drew closer. She hoped he was in shock. There weren't many other explanations for his behavior that didn't carry horrible implications.

"Neil." She kept her voice low and gentle. Only a few paces separated them, but he still hadn't turned. "Take a moment to think. You said the house can affect you. If you're feeling…uh, angry, or negative, or like you want to do something bad…" She cleared her throat. "Remember that it's just the building. Come outside with me. I love you, Neil. I want you to be okay."

"Love." There was a strange lilting tone to Neil's voice, like an accent she couldn't place. He finally turned to face Mara, and his smile turned her blood cold. "Do you think love can save you? Do you think it will grant you any more mercy than my other guests?"

This isn't Neil.

It was the same angular, handsome face she adored. The same sky-blue eyes. The lips she'd loved to taste, the strong nose she'd run her finger down, the eyebrows that held more good humor than mood. But the expression wasn't Neil's, and it arranged his beautiful, good face into something horrible—arrogant, self-satisfied, and malicious.

He picked an object off the ground, and Mara's anxious prickles turned into a buzz as she began backing away. When she tried to speak, the words came out as a hoarse whimper. She swallowed and tried again. "Why are you doing this, Robert? What's keeping you from moving on?"

"Ha!" There was no humor in the laugh. Neil—or the creature that had taken over Neil's body—began to pace toward her, eating up the distance she'd put between them. "You're entirely unaware of your own ignorance, child. Don't struggle. I'll make this quick."

Neil raised the ax. It was a huge, aged, wicked-looking implement. The handle was dark wood and the silver blade was sharp. It wasn't a small implement, but Neil's muscles carried it easily. He swung it toward her in an easy, practiced motion.

Mara leaped backward. A gust of air brushed her arms as the blade barely missed her. It made a deep, whistling noise as it moved. Neil stopped the swing and brought it back around far more quickly than Mara had expected.

She ducked and felt it snag her hair. *I can't fight him. I've got to get away—put some distance between us—get back to Erica and hope she's woken up and knows what to do. Because there has to be a way to reverse what's happened to Neil. There has to be.*

Mara turned and scrambled toward the hole in the wall. A second's rumble was the only warning she had before a huge slab of rock tumbled away from the wall and collapsed in front of the gap, blocking it. The impact of the slab hitting the floor shook Mara so badly that she lost her feet and collapsed to the floor. Dust clouds exploded around her, and she choked on the taste. She flipped over and shined her flashlight through the smog-like particles. She made out Neil's silhouette pacing closer, ax held at the ready.

Neil would be strong enough to move the stone slab, but Mara had no hope of budging it herself. There wasn't another exit. The two of them were trapped in a deadly dance—and she couldn't envision an end that didn't result in death.

Neil came within swinging distance, and Mara staggered to

one side. Her shaking flashlight's beam highlighted a sheen of sweat on his face. The sight of the perspiration gave Mara pause.

The ax is heavy, but two swings shouldn't be enough to tire him. No way.

"Neil." Mara fought to keep her voice even as she circled away from the slowly pacing man. "Are you still in there? Can you hear me? I need you to fight, baby. Remember how much I love you."

Neil flinched. A drip of sweat ran down his cheek, but he didn't stop moving. The human reaction gave Mara a flash of hope, but with it came a heavy dread. *If Robert wins—if he kills me—it will destroy Neil. I can't do that to him.*

She bumped against a wall and felt something press into her thigh through her pocket. Mara drew a sharp breath. It was a small hope—a stupid, desperate endeavor—but she seized it. Mara dug the bunch of sage out of her pocket.

Her moment of inattention was the opening Neil had been waiting for. He pitched forward, moving far faster than she'd expected him to, and this time Mara wasn't able to avoid the blade. It cut her arm just below the shoulder. The blow was glancing and not deep enough to disable her, but the pain was unbearable. Mara screamed and dropped the flashlight. She fell back as Neil raised the ax for the killing blow.

There was no time to think. Mara stuffed the herb into her mouth. Damian had said its smoke was supposed to weaken and dispel spirits, but Mara had no way to light the plant. Instead, she chewed furiously as she threw herself toward Neil.

Being close to him was risky, but at least he couldn't bring the ax down on her. Mara got as near him as she could, pressing herself against his chest, and glimpsed the fury and malice in his eyes as she spat the herb at him.

Neil roared and staggered backward. He wiped a hand across his face, trying to smear the crushed plant fragments away, then collapsed to the ground.

Mara backed against the wall. The roaring pain from the cut made her vision swim, and she could feel hot blood running down her arm and dribbling off the elbow. She knew she should apply pressure to stop the flow but was frightened that touching it would make her pass out.

The flashlight had fallen in such a way that it threw its light across the left half of the room. She could see Neil crouched on the ground, shaking his head. Brief glimpses of his face showed two sides: the furious, cruel face of Robert but also her Neil—frantic, desperate, and struggling with everything he had.

"Neil, fight him." Mara's voice was cracked, but the words made Neil's shoulders shake. "Don't let Robert win."

"Not—" Neil gasped then threw himself backward, his face contorted in agony. He spat the phrase through gritted teeth. "Not—Robert—"

Not Robert? Mara's mind—dulled by pain, fear, and shock—struggled with the words. *Is he saying he's not going to let Robert win? No—wait—*

Neil's hand fluttered to his jacket pocket, then he contorted again, straining as though he'd been run through with a knife. A pained cry escaped him, then he fell limp.

Mara pressed herself against the wall, barely daring to breathe, as she watched Neil's still form. He lay motionless for so long that Mara began to fear he was dead, but then his hands twitched, and he drew himself into a crouch.

"Neil?" she whispered.

He pulled himself to his feet before turning to look at her. It wasn't Neil.

And it wasn't Robert Kant, either.

The clues fell into place as Mara stared at the face that was simultaneously so dear and so repulsive. Robert Kant wasn't Blackwood's dominant ghost as they'd thought. He was only a pawn for the house's true master. That was why Erica hadn't been able to dispel him.

When she'd sensed the spirit that had held control over Blackwood, Erica had described a tall, gaunt man who carried an ax. Mara had simply assumed that it was Robert, who'd favored the ax as his primary weapon. *But the ax hadn't been his choice, had it? Instead, it was imposed on him by the entity that used him as a puppet.*

The truth was so obvious that Mara wanted to hit herself for not seeing it sooner. Blackwood's true master was its original owner, the renowned spiritualist and Mara's ancestor: Victor Barlow.

Victor had been obsessed with bridging the gap between the mortal world and the spiritual. Judging by the vast swaths of paper and tools in the basement, he had done significant work toward that goal. He'd chosen Blackwood's location carefully and built a house that was far larger than what a single man would need, in anticipation of the families that were destined to live in it. Once he was ready, he'd taken the most drastic and dangerous step in his plan: he'd drawn Robert Kant to his house and allowed his own murder.

From then, Robert had been Victor's puppet to pull additional lives into Blackwood. Robert had killed five children before he had slipped up and let one escape—possibly even deliberately, Mara thought, to put an end to his miserable existence. Then, instead of fleeing Blackwood, he'd hung himself from the banister. He'd served Victor in life, and would continue to serve him in death.

Every other family to live in Blackwood had fallen to Robert's will. He'd influenced them to use the ax, a tool he was deeply familiar with thanks to a lifetime working as a woodcutter. Each death had increased Blackwood's energy. To what end, Mara wasn't sure—though she knew it couldn't be an altruistic goal. Victor gained energy with every murder. And Mara, charged with years of bottled-up spiritual energy, would be an ideal victim.

She felt sick. The blood loss was taking its toll, and the adrenaline, having carried her through most of the evening, was failing. And as long as he inhabited Neil's body, Victor was both stronger and faster than Mara could hope to be.

But knowing the spirit's identity gave her a desperate plan. Neil no longer held his ax and was off balance, but Mara knew he wouldn't take long to collect himself. She ran at the man, praying that she'd guessed correctly.

CHAPTER 38
IMPROVISED

NEIL HAD FUMBLED FOR his jacket pocket when he'd broken through Victor's hold to speak to Mara. She also had a faint memory of Neil promising to remove Victor Barlow's photo after it had fallen out of the hacked-up bed. *Please let me be right.*

Victor hadn't expected her lunge, and she caught him unprepared. He staggered two steps backward when she slammed into him, but he didn't fall. *Damn it, Neil, why do you have to be so solid?*

Mara forced her hand into his pocket. She touched something papery and latched onto it as Neil's hand gripped her neck and squeezed, sending a flare of pain through her already bruised throat.

"Neil!" she squeaked around the pressure. There was a tiny flash of familiarity in the cold eyes, and the hand loosened a fraction. That was the opening Mara needed. She raised her foot and kicked him in the stomach, using the impact to throw them apart. Mara hit the ground and screamed as the stones scraped her cut shoulder.

Victor hissed his fury as he straightened Neil's back.

Hurry, hurry, hurry! Mara slapped the picture onto the tiles. She had no chalk, but Erica had said the symbols didn't need to be exact. Mara hoped that meant the art materials were open to interpretation, too, and scraped blood from her arm. She used the crimson liquid to draw as much of the quinet as she could remember.

A scraping noise warned Mara that Victor had retrieved his ax. She knew she only had seconds until he reached her.

Mara had almost no idea what she was doing. All she had to go on was the knowledge that she was charged full of energy, and the memory of what Erica had done in the foyer. She placed both hands on Victor's picture and focused as hard as she could, searching for the black threads she'd seen floating through the upstairs room.

For a second, nothing happened. Victor took a heavy step closer and raised the ax. Then something clicked for Mara, and she saw the threads—dozens of them, thin and floating gracefully—rising from the picture. She pinched a bundle of them between her fingers and tugged.

It was a bizarre sensation. Half of her knew she was touching nothing but air. The other half could feel the threads. They sent tingles through her fingers as though they were filled with a very low electrical charge. She was aware of how fragile they were and innately understood that if she pulled too hard, they would break. *Gentle tugs. Draw him out slowly.*

She gave a soft pull and felt the tension run through the threads. Neil, ax raised above her exposed back, shook, and took a staggering step backward. Mara risked another tug. A wisp of ink-like smoke floated out of Neil's chest. The cold malevolence on his face distorted into shock, then horror. She pulled a third time and slowly, carefully drew the ghost out of Neil.

They split like oil and water dividing. Neil fell backward while Victor's smoky spirit form was dragged forward. Mara saw her partner collapse but couldn't risk diverting her attention from Victor to see if he was hurt. He didn't move, and that frightened her. The thought that it might be possible to kill a human by forcefully splitting a spirit crossed her mind, but she repressed it.

Focus. You're so close. Victor stood before her. He was both clearer and more cultured than Robert Kant. While the serial killer had been scruffy and low class, Victor radiated intelligence and confidence, from his sideburns to his expensive clothing. Anger flared across his face as he reached for Mara. *Now, hurry!* She dropped the threads, pressed her left hand to the quinet, and threw her right hand into the spirit's slimy, unnatural, swirling form.

She pictured light rising from the quinet just as she'd seen it in the foyer. On command, energy rose through her, burning up her arms and stinging the cut. It was powerful, hot, and overwhelming. She felt as though she'd stepped off a ledge and was in a free fall; her stomach flipped, her heart stopped, and she couldn't have drawn breath even if she'd wanted to. The power roared through her—out of her core, out of the room, out of Blackwood—and flooded Victor. The black form swelled, and Mara felt a cut of doubt. But she couldn't have stopped even if she'd tried to. The energy moved through her like an electric tornado, pouring into Victor, causing his inky self to billow out as he tried to contain the power. She caught a glimpse of his eyes, filled with uncontrollable fury, then he exploded.

That was the only way Mara could describe the sensation: an explosion. Victor burst outward, his black-smoke form sizzling into nothing as the golden light surged through Blackwood. Mara felt pressure on her skin though it didn't even ruffle her hair. It stole her breath and sent blood rushing to her head.

In that moment, she saw Blackwood as it truly existed: a matrix of black threads—the spiritual form of memories and emotional connections—crisscrossed the room and shrouded the walls like cobwebs. They disintegrated, shriveling like spun-sugar threads under heat, as the energy wave blasted through them.

The energy hit the walls and ceiling then washed back, running down the building in rivulets. It coursed toward the ground, pouring along invisible paths on the wooden beams, and disappeared through cracks in the stone floor.

More light followed in the wake of the explosion. It dripped through the ceiling, slipping through every crack and pinprick hole. Mara felt it slither under her hands, which she'd rested on the floor. To her horror, there were emotions in it—grief, fear, anger—and she snatched her hands away as the golden light passed. *It's the other spirits. They're flowing out of Blackwood now that Victor's gone. How did Erica put it? That's right—like unblocking a drain.*

The last of the energy slithered down the walls and through the floor. As its glow faded, Mara was left with nothing but the flashlight. The man-made light seemed woefully inadequate in comparison to the previous glow, and Mara blinked against the pressing darkness as she turned toward Neil.

No, I don't think I can blame the darkness on the flashlight. Mara's dizziness rose. She didn't like to think about how much blood she'd lost. She stretched a hand toward Neil's still form, but even that effort was too great. The ground tumbled up to catch her.

CHAPTER 39
CLEAN SLATES

FOR THE FIRST TIME since moving to Blackwood, Mara's sleep wasn't troubled by dreams. She wished she could enjoy more of it, but her surroundings conspired to drag her toward consciousness.

The biggest annoyance was her arm. Put simply, it hurt like hell. The sharpness of the fresh cut had faded, but a dull, spreading ache took its place.

Light pushed against her closed eyelids. She thought it was probably still night, which meant she would have to yell at whoever had turned the lights on. *Doesn't anyone respect bedtime anymore?*

Then there was the voice. It wouldn't shut up. Shortly after leaving her parents' house, Mara had moved into a flat with two Russian students. They'd woken up at four every morning to go to the gym. They would use the blender, slam doors as they got their gym clothes, and chatter incessantly in their heavy accents. The experience had been enough to convince Mara that she never wanted to room with someone she met on the internet again. And yet, the Russians might have actually been less annoying than the voice that was bothering her at that moment.

"Mara, please, wake up. Can you hear me? You've got to wake up, sweetheart."

Why's Gregory calling me sweetheart? And what happened to his accent? And why's he so upset?

Mara forced her eyes to open a crack. A headache roared through her skull, and she squeezed them closed again.

"Mara, thank goodness." A rough hand ran over her cheek, and memories began to flit back into her mind. The séance—the basement—Victor—*Neil*.

"Neil!" She tried to call the word, but it came out as a croak.

The hand ran over her hair, smoothing it back from her forehead. "It's all right, sweetheart. You're safe. You're going to be fine."

Mara blinked her eyes open again. Neil's face swam into view. His skin was white, and a blot of dirt was smeared over his cheek, but she was relieved to see his eyes were bright and alert as they scanned her face.

They were back in the foyer, based on the corner of the banister visible over Neil's shoulder. She was being cradled like a child, and a blanket had been wrapped around her. Only her upper arm had been left exposed, where the blood had congealed in its cut.

"You okay?" Mara mumbled.

"Yeah, I'm fine." A shaky smile rose over Neil's face then dissolved. "I'm sorry, Mara. I—I couldn't stop him— I'm so, so, so sorry—"

"Uh-huh." Neil's safety assured, Mara let herself sink back into the exhausted daze. "It's cool. Get me some of those cookies your mum makes, and we'll call it even."

Neil shook as he half chuckled, half sobbed, then he pressed a kiss to Mara's forehead.

"How's she doing?" The voice was familiar, but it took Mara a minute to recognize it. *Damian. Wow, did I really invite mediums into my home? Just how crazy did I get over the last twenty-four hours?*

"She's awake," Neil said. "Were you able to call an ambulance?"

"No, I can't get any reception. Did you hear that, Mara? Your house sucks."

Mara grimaced and opened her eyes. "*You* suck. Call yourself a spirit medium? You totally botched this whole thing. Don't think I'm going to pay you."

Damian crouched beside Neil. A red-tinted bruise rose over his cheek and forehead, and his eye was swelling closed, but he still grinned at her. "Sounds like you're going to be just fine. I'll clean out that cut, then we'll let you rest until we can get you an ambulance and a blood transfusion."

Mara pressed her head closer to Neil's shoulder as Damian poured a bottle of water onto a cloth. "Is Erica okay?"

"She'll be fine. I put her on your couch to sleep it off. She's mad that you got rid of the spirit when she couldn't, though."

"Not her fault," Mara mumbled. "It wasn't Robert; it was Victor."

301

"Really? Huh—that makes a lot of sense." Damian moved the cloth toward her arm. "Hold still. This will sting."

Out of respect for his preferences, Mara normally tried not to swear around Neil. But all self-restraint left her as the damp cloth touched the cut. She screamed every bad word she knew and invented a few new phrases in the process. Neil bore it well.

The following hour was a blurry haze. Damian bandaged the cut despite Mara's stream of threats. She slipped back into unconsciousness shortly after. When she woke again, she was in the upstairs bedroom, wrapped in the sleeping bag. The heater was on, and she had what she thought was every blanket in the house draped over her, but she still felt cold.

"Hey, you awake?" Neil's voice was soft. Mara mumbled some sort of reply, and Neil slipped his hand under her head to lift it. "Here, drink this."

It was one of his herbal teas. Mara realized she was parched and drank deeply. When she finished, she tried to sit up, but Neil nudged her back down. She was annoyed at how little resistance she could put up.

"Stay still, sweetheart. You lost a lot of blood. Damian's driving to get an ambulance."

"No, I'm good," Mara grumbled. "Tell him not to bother. I'll get up in a moment."

"Not a chance." Neil stroked her cheek tenderly. "You need rest."

She peeked up at him. He'd regained some of his color, but anxious lines still creased his eyes. She raised her uninjured hand to tug at his sleeve. "C'mere. I want a hug."

Neil obediently lay down beside her. He shuffled close and wrapped an arm around her waist. Mara nuzzled her head into the space below his chin and inhaled his scent. "Are you okay?"

"Ha. Yes, I got out of it without a scratch." He spoke lightly, but she could hear a crushing grief lingering in his words. She slipped her hand up to his neck and ran her fingers over his skin. He felt warm and soft and good.

"It was all Victor," she said. "Don't you dare hold on to any of what happened in that basement. It wasn't your fault."

"I wasn't strong enough to stop him—I tried, but—"

"Shh, I know." She hated hearing the pain in his voice. "It was my stupid house and my stupid great-whatever-grandfather. You got roped into this mess. I'm just grateful you stuck with me." She hesitated. Failed séances, possession, and attempted murder were all things an average relationship wasn't expected to endure. *Don't presume. What if he can't move past this? Tonight could have permanently changed the way he feels about you.* She licked her lips and shifted slightly closer. "*Are* you sticking with me?"

"Like glue." Neil's arms tightened around her, and Mara heard a note of relief in his voice. He'd been worrying over the same thing about her. She couldn't stop her grin.

"Love you, Neil."

"Love you more."

She closed her eyes and let her consciousness focus in on Neil's steady breathing and his heartbeat. He ran his hands over her hair and her back, soothing and comforting.

"You were right, by the way." Neil's words startled Mara out of her sleepy haze. "When you first found Victor's photo, you said he was twisted. And he really, really was."

Mara frowned. "Did you see stuff when he was in control?"

"Sort of. I could hear his thoughts—his plans—and see snapshots of what had happened."

"Jeez." Mara wished there was something more she could say. If Neil had experienced Victor's memories of the murders committed at Blackwood, she wondered if he would ever sleep again.

"Hah, don't worry. It was all sort of hazy. I suppose even a ghost's memories fade over time."

"What did you see? Do you know what his goal was?"

Mara felt Neil smile into her hair. "Yes, but you'll laugh."

"Well, now you've *got* to tell me." She poked his chest as emphasis, and Neil's smile cracked into a chuckle.

"He had a theory that if a spirit could absorb enough energy, it could create a physical, tangible form for itself. One that was no longer limited by human conditions such as hunger, pain, or death."

Mara raised her eyebrows. "Are you seriously telling me he was trying to become immortal?"

"Bingo."

"Oh my gosh." She buried her face in Neil's chest and cackled. "That's like something out of a cheesy sci-fi novel."

"Stop it." Neil wasn't quite able to keep his voice stern. "Don't demean his supervillain goal, okay? He was actually really close to having enough energy."

A floorboard creaked below them, and Mara started upright. Dizziness crashed over her, and Neil had to catch her before she collapsed. "Wha—" she started then cleared her throat. "What was that?"

"Shh." Neil carefully lowered her back into the bed. "It's just Erica. Don't worry—Damian says the ghosts are gone."

"Ugh. Are we sure we trust him?" Mara grimaced as her head swam.

"He says he's certain. You cleared Blackwood, sweetheart. It's safe to live in now."

Mara opened her eyes. Neil was right. It was such a subtle change that she hadn't noticed it before, but the ponderous, heavy atmosphere had cleared. Blackwood felt like any other house.

She peeked at Neil. "Does that mean you're okay with me staying here?"

He grinned and shifted forward to kiss the tip of her nose. "It's your house. You can do whatever you like with it. And this time, I won't complain."

"C'mere." Mara snagged his collar before he could retreat and brought his lips to hers.

CHAPTER 40
NEW PLANS

Three Months Later

EVEN WITH A WI-FI amplifier, Blackwood's reception remained terrible. Mara turned her phone over in her hands as she sat at the dining room table. Morning was shifting into afternoon, and thick sunlight poured bright rectangles over the floor. The rocking chair groaned in the living room and, far above her, footsteps paced through the attic.

In the days following Mara's slapdash spirit clearing, there had been a tangible lack of energy in Blackwood. Even Mara, who had the most primitive understanding of spiritual energy, found it unnatural. But the energy spot under the house hadn't let it stay dormant for long.

Blackwood was gradually building its charge back. If she concentrated, Mara could feel it thrumming around her and sometimes even see the floating black threads. It was far more moderate than during Victor's reign, though. He'd charged the house until it was close to bursting.

Mara turned her phone over and checked its reception. Zero bars.

The footsteps above her head paused then moved toward the trapdoor. Mara listened to them travel down the second-floor hallway, then she leaned back in her chair to see through the dining room's arch to the landing at the top of the stairs. Damian appeared and paused at the railing. "We've got another request. A couple bought a house last month and say they can't sleep because of strange noises. They want us to check it out tonight. You in?"

"It's probably raccoons," Mara called back. "But sure, I'll come."

Damian nodded and returned to the attic.

Eighteen years spent in a spiritualistic household. Four years of freedom. Now I'm working as a medium. I feel like a walking joke.

Erica had been the first to broach the idea of renting a room at Blackwood. She needed somewhere with a lot of energy to practice, she claimed, and Damian didn't like repeatedly breaking into abandoned buildings. *What the hell; it's good money*, Mara had thought. *It's not like I need to interact with them.* But, before she knew what was happening, she was being invited on their ghost-hunting jobs…and actually *enjoying* it.

The commissions weren't amazing, but it was enough that Mara could be comfortable without looking for a second job.

And though she hated to admit it, the excitement was becoming addictive.

Damian and Erica worked in the attic most afternoons, but they weren't the only people moving through Blackwood. The day after the last of the holes had been patched, Neil and Pam had moved in.

The amalgamation had gone far more smoothly than Mara had been prepared for. Pam was overly considerate almost to the point of being humorous. Mara couldn't count the number of times she'd reassured the older woman that she didn't have to hide her Bible.

Pam had made the house feel like a home. She'd decorated the rooms deftly, cooked Mara's meals, and was responsible for the steady creaks of the rocking chair. They'd thrown out the original chair, of course, and Pam had replaced it with her own. She liked to sit by the window in the afternoons and work through the cartons of secondhand books she'd bought at charity events. Mara had been surprised and delighted to discover the older woman was a voracious romance reader.

A door slammed, and a minute later, Neil appeared in the kitchen doorway. He was sweaty and dirty from working in the garden, but his smile was bright enough to send a thrill through Mara.

"How're you doing?" He swooped in to peck Mara's cheek, but she twisted to catch him by surprise and met his lips. They lingered for a moment before he pulled back with a self-conscious chuckle. "Sorry; I'll have a shower before I get you dirty, too."

"Damian wants me to go on another ghost hunt tonight. You coming?"

"Why do you even bother asking? I wouldn't miss it for the world." Neil caught sight of the phone in her hands and nodded toward it. "Are you thinking of calling them?"

"Yeah." She turned the phone over. Three bars. That was about as good as she could hope for. "It's probably going to be horrible."

"Maybe." Neil leaned against the table's edge and took his work gloves off. He tilted his head to one side as he examined her face. "But if it doesn't work out, you don't have to see them again."

"Hmm."

"Hey, Mara?" She met his blue eyes and felt her heart leap at the tender smile he gave her. "Whatever you do, I think you're amazing. Don't forget that."

Heat rose over her face, and she waved him off. "Get out of here, gorgeous. You smell terrible."

He laughed, kissed her cheek, and left for the shower. Mara sat for a moment, listening to the faint sounds of Erica and Damian working in the attic, the gentle creaks of Pam's chair, and the running water as Neil showered. Then she took a breath and dialed a number.

The phone rang four times before a woman's voice answered. "Hello?"

"Hi, Mum." Mara's mouth was dry, but she was able to keep her voice steady.

Elaine drew a sharp breath. Mara caught notes of mingled shock and hope. "Mara?"

She let a cautious smile grow. "Hey. Did you and Dad want to come over for dinner sometime?"

ABOUT THE AUTHOR

Darcy Coates is the *USA Today* bestselling author of *Hunted*, *The Haunting of Ashburn House*, *Craven Manor*, and more than a dozen other horror and suspense titles. She lives on the Central Coast of Australia with her family, cats, and a garden full of herbs and vegetables. Darcy loves forests, especially old-growth forests where the trees dwarf anyone who steps between them. Wherever she lives, she tries to have a mountain range close by.

THE HAUNTING OF ROOKWARD HOUSE

SHE'S ALWAYS WATCHING...

When Guy finds the deed to a house in his mother's attic, it seems like an incredible stroke of luck. Sure, it hasn't been inhabited in years and vines strangle the age-stained walls, but Guy's convinced he can clean the building up and sell it. He'd be crazy to turn down free money. Right?

But there's a reason no one lives in Rookward House, and the dilapidated rooms aren't as empty as they seem. Forty years ago, a deranged woman tormented the family that made Rookward its home. Now her ghost clings to the building like rot. She's bitter, obsessive, and fiercely jealous…and once Guy has moved into her house, she has no intention of letting him go.

THE CARROW HAUNT

THE DEAD ARE RESTLESS HERE...

Remy is a tour guide for the notoriously haunted Carrow House. When she's asked to host guests for a weeklong stay in order to research Carrow's phenomena, she hopes to finally experience some of the sightings that made the house famous.

At first, it's everything they hoped for. Then a storm moves in, cutting off their contact with the outside world, and things quickly take a sinister turn. Doors open on their own. Séances go disastrously wrong. Their spirit medium wanders through the house at night, seemingly in a trance. But it isn't until one of the guests dies under strange circumstances that Remy is forced to consider the possibility that the ghost of the house's original owner—a twisted serial killer—still walks the halls.

And by then it's too late to escape...

For more info about Sourcebooks's books and authors, visit:
sourcebooks.com

CRAVEN MANOR

SOME SECRETS ARE BETTER LEFT FORGOTTEN...

Daniel is desperate for a fresh start. So when a mysterious figure slides a note under his door offering the position of groundskeeper at an ancient estate, he leaps at the chance, even though it seems too good to be true. Alarm bells start ringing when he arrives at Craven Manor. The abandoned mansion's front door hangs open, and leaves and cobwebs coat the marble foyer. It's clear no one has lived here in a long time... but he has nowhere else to go.

Against his better judgment, he moves into the groundskeeper's cottage tucked away behind the old family crypt. But when a candle flickers to life in the abandoned tower window, Daniel realizes he isn't alone after all. Craven Manor is hiding a terrible secret...

One that threatens to bury him with it.